Forever Chrysalis

by

Maija DeRoche

Forever Chrysalis

Cover Art by *Kim Mendoza*

The Wild Rose Press, Inc.
PO Box 708
Adams Basin, NY 14410-0708
Visit us at www.thewildrosepress.com

Publishing History
First Edition, 2022
Trade Paperback ISBN 978-1-5092-4164-4
Digital ISBN 978-1-5092-4165-1

Published in the United States of America

Dedication

This book is dedicated to mothers and daughters everywhere.

Acknowledgements

Not only do I want to acknowledge important people along my journey, I want to extend my warmest gratitude to them for their encouragement and support.

When I moved to a new community a few years ago, I was in search of a new local connection, a fresh interest to enrich my life. A creative writing course at the local community college was the catalyst for renewing my old love: writing. Jon Palzer at the head of the seminar convinced me that my writing had potential. Being a septuagenarian among very young students was also illuminating.

Members of my newly found writers' group have been instrumental in pushing me on in my endeavor.

Forever Chrysalis presented questions beyond my knowledge base. Therefore, I want to thank Catherine Cantwell, MD, Tom Marafioti, Esq., and Dawn Yehl, LRES, for issues medical, legal, and pertaining to real estate, respectively, as well as Barb Warner Deane, who introduced me into the world of publishing.

I want to thank my Beta readers: Kate Collier, Martha Horton, and Diane Jones for their invaluable insight and gentle critique.

I am grateful to my husband, who tolerated my erratic schedule and hours of isolating myself for writing.

Most of all, I am thankful to my editor, Nan Swanson of The Wild Rose Press. She has guided me in a professional yet comfortably friendly manner through the process. Without her, I would still be questioning myself.

"Maybe," said Christine quietly. "I am worried about my mother and her future. Being so far away from her is not easy. Not that I could in any way slow down her dementia, but I somehow feel I am neglecting her." She stared ahead of her, seeing nothing.

"I have the same feeling about my mother, and I'm right here," chimed in Alice, pouring herself another glass of Pinot Noir. "I know the time will come when she has to move out of her house, and I know she'll do anything to avoid it. She already can't function too well. She pretends to be self-sufficient, but if it weren't for me, she'd be in trouble."

"I hate to say this," said Crystal, "but I feel that no matter what you do, your mother is impossible to please. You run yourself ragged, only to get criticism and more demands placed on you."

Alice turned abruptly to face Crystal. "It's easy for you to say! Your mother acts like she's younger than we are, trotting around the world with strange..." Alice stopped in mid-sentence.

Crystal's face fell. She looked at Alice with amazement.

Alice looked lost. "No, I mean...I didn't mean...I am so sorry. I didn't mean it like that. But you have to admit Lola is not a traditional mother figure." Alice realized she had stepped onto thin ice with both feet in heavy boots.

The old grandfather clock ticked audibly.

"Well," Crystal broke the icy silence. "It wasn't fair of me to say what I did about your mother, either. I'm sorry. Isn't it odd that our mothers have such a strong hold on us, as different as they are from each other?"

Praise for Maija DeRoche

"An engaging cast of characters features the members of the Chrysalis Quartet, now middle-aged, who face a variety of conflicts with mothers, daughters, husbands, lovers, careers—and each other. Maija DeRoche sorts out their problems with grace and humor, taking the reader along for a delicious sojourn in the Finger Lakes of New York. Readers will find much to identify with—and to learn from—in this impressive debut novel."

~Martha Horton, author

Chapter 1

Christine Lindqvist Thurston was ill at ease with surprises. In pitch darkness, she was aware of a small but bright light in the bedroom, and she heard a muffled buzz, a gentle tone she had chosen for her new phone. She couldn't see it from behind her long hair, which had let loose from its neat night-time bun, held together these days by a less-than-efficient band. Her hair stylist had advised her against a rubber band and the potential damage to her thick mane. From behind the wild curtain of hair, she located the phone, whose face yelled 4:45 a.m.

"Thurston," she said hesitantly with a slight upward tilt to her voice at the end of the greeting, as if doubting her name.

"Hi, this is Alice. I thought I'd catch you before I have to start my class."

"What's wrong?"

Christine was alarmed. Her high school friend in New York State was not in the habit of calling her on the other side of the country, especially at this hour of the morning.

"Nothing's wrong. Well, nothing unusual except…well, you do know that my dad died, right?"

Christine was not aware of her friend's father's passing and said so without making Alice feel guilty about failing to notify her. She expressed her condolences. Alice apologized for her oversight and continued, "Well, anyway, do you remember how my dad loved to listen to our quartet? My mom wants us to sing at the memorial service next month."

Christine was quiet in her thoughts for a second. "When is it?"

"It's on the twenty-ninth of June, after school gets out. I do hope you can come."

Christine thought about the quartet. She had put it aside for twenty-some years, in the memories of the carefree times, a high school on a hill surrounded by vineyards in New York's beautiful Finger Lakes. She and three of her friends had excelled with their youthful, innocent voices, talented, although not formally trained. The corners of her lips turned upward, and she began to feel warm and nostalgic. She said cautiously into the phone, "You do realize that we haven't sung together in more than twenty years? We would need to practice, minimally a couple of times, choose the music, decide on accompaniment or a capella, et cetera."

"I know," Alice agreed. "Don't worry, my mother has the music all picked out. It would be nice if you could come a few days early. Since Crystal and Lisa still live in town, practice is not a problem. You can stay at my house."

"Thank you. I'll most likely stay near my mother's assisted living residence."

"So it's a 'yes'?" The excitement in Alice's voice was noticeable.

"It's a 'yes.' I will call you back, when I wake up properly. It's only five o'clock in Seattle, you know."

The other end of the line was deadly silent. Then

Alice reacted. "Oh, my God, oh, my God, I am such a ditz! I'm so sorry. I completely forgot the time difference!"

Christine knew that Alice would apologize for her faux pas from now until, in her old age, she could no longer remember the conversation.

Christine got out of bed and opened the wide shade to the city and its fabulous sea of yellow and white lights seventeen stories below. She reaffirmed to herself that it was a good idea to go back and rejuvenate Chrysalis, the quartet with the composite name fashioned after the four members: CHRistine, CrYStal, ALice and (L)ISa.

Memories flooded in of the labor pains for coming up with a suitable name for the high school ensemble. There had been serious contests among the music students for naming the foursome. The school's music department had featured vocal quartets before, but they had always performed nameless, either as "the ensemble" or "the quartet." A few acceptable suggestions had been received; however, the real work was done at Christine's house on a dark October evening while her parents attended her father's office party.

With the aid of Mr. and Mrs. Lindqvist's wine cellar offerings, Chrysalis had been born, influenced by the illegal activity of four teenagers. The girls had been giddy with their wine-induced cleverness. They were not worried about a time when one or two of them would graduate and the composite of the names would no longer hold together with names removed and new names added. Happily, Chrysalis as a name could stand alone as a symbol of a waiting future butterfly, just as the young girls were anxious to develop colorful, light, yet strong wings to fly away.

Christine thought of the sisterhood of the four girls. Lisa, Alice, and Crystal were leading members of the choir and obvious choices for an ensemble. Christine, although a musical and talented senior, had had to choose between two loves: singing in the choir or competing on the record-breaking swim team. Practice times were overlapping, and she had chosen the sport over performing arts. Mrs. Jones, the choir director and catalyst behind the ensemble, appreciated her talent, and with flexible practice times, Christine joined the quartet as the valuable bass.

She was pleased. This allowed her to be competitive in the pool and still join the quartet Lisa belonged to. She wanted to prove to Lisa that she lived up to her level of ability. Lisa was a great pianist; a talent Christine had envied from the time they were pre-teens. Christine felt that with her school and pool records in the butterfly stroke, they were even. Christine and Lisa, the two tall, slender seniors, were the pillars of the group, standing solidly as bookends to the juniors, Alice and Crystal, who looked up to them both physically and mentally.

Christine found the idea of singing with the girls again invigorating—"girls" who were now almost middle-aged women. She wondered if Lisa had married, if Alice was still a scatterbrained girl controlled by her mother, and if Crystal, the sweet, empathetic, caring person of their high school days, had ever found out the identity of her father.

Christine decided it was also time for her to visit her mother, the person who had amazing insight in difficult situations, who was the buffer in all confrontations. She counted, and came to the sad conclusion that she had not visited her mother for six months. She cringed.

Christine had kept in touch with her mother, alone now for the sixth year after her husband's death, but admitted that phone calls and FaceTime were not enough. However, her busy schedule prevented her from sustaining a tighter connection. Whenever Carol called her, Christine experienced a twinge of a slightly negative, guilt-ridden feeling. The feeling did not entirely dissipate with Carol's assurances that she understood the hectic nature of Christine's life and that she was proud of her CEO daughter, who had systematically and resolutely built herself a life at the very top.

Christine's dream in high school had been to become a doctor, the revered woman in a white coat, there to cure diseased people and to comfort those who could not be cured. Her classmate and Chrysalis sister Lisa had been accepted through an early admission to Cornell Medical School at the beginning of their senior year. Christine's feeling of happiness for Lisa was at odds with feeling sorry for herself. Her own grades did not carry her to any medical school, reputable or less so.

She had entered Keuka College on a lake with the same name, with occupational therapy as her major. In addition to choosing a "helping field," her decision was calculated. Statistics showed that baby boomers would experience wear and tear on their bodies, and, in the near future, be in need of various services, occupational therapy among them. Christine excelled in her studies.

She dove into the course work: anatomy and physiology, psychology, human development, physics, kinesiology, sociology. She found the campus on the lake beautiful, away from home yet close enough to stop in for dinner with her parents or her hometown friends.

After graduation, Christine accepted a job at the local hospital. The small clinic gave her a solid base, and after a couple of years, she decided to see the other side of the continent and moved to Seattle, a huge city full of possibilities.

As she dealt with patients with various needs, it quickly became clear that the adaptive equipment required by patients was not always readily available. Christine started a rental business providing strengtheners of all kinds: pulleys, braces, and balance builders. She later designed special braces for hands, ankles, and knees, and eventually established an industry producing them.

She exchanged the therapy setting providing services for sometimes reluctant patients for the board room and a private office, the headquarters for directing the staff and the multitude of issues involved in a large company. Although a bit hesitant at first, she quickly learned the ins and outs of supervision, management, and administration.

Christine looked at her calendar for the end of June. She would need to change the dates of some regularly scheduled meetings, but her calendar was otherwise flexible. She sent an e-mail to her administrative assistant, asking him to work on the needed schedule changes and to book a flight to Rochester, New York, for the fifteenth of June.

She then made a mental note to buy a box of famous West Coast chocolates for her mother: the custom mix of raspberry truffles, marzipan, and black bear paws.

Chapter 2

Carol Lindqvist had lived in the assisted living facility for three years now. After her husband John's death of pancreatic cancer five years ago, she had started to deteriorate mentally. She had, uncharacteristically, written scathing letters to the editor of the local newspaper, politicians being the most frequent target of her ire. With a degree in political science, she sounded perfectly logical; however, the logic was lost in her choice of belligerent words and expressions. Gradually, Carol had morphed into a different woman in her personality and habits, with stereotypical symptoms of burgeoning dementia.

Carol had been a meticulously clean and neat person, sometimes to the annoyance of her family. Her hair was always in a smooth chignon, her makeup flawless, and her wardrobe designed according to the color palette determined by professionals to be best suited for her complexion. Her house was immaculately clean, with furniture arranged to accommodate the flow of everyday life, tasteful in its design and color scheme.

In the kitchen, the pantry cupboards were organized by categories: ingredients for baking (flour, sugar, baking powder and soda, vanilla and almond extract, cinnamon, and nutmeg), ingredients for soups and stews (beef and chicken base, onion and garlic powder, cumin, bay leaves and parsley). One shelf was dedicated to snack foods to be enjoyed with before-dinner cocktails. Outside of the cheeses and patés, which were kept in the refrigerator, she and her husband enjoyed their bourbon with a variety of nuts and cheese-flavored spicy corn chips that left the fingers sticky. This assortment of tidbits was kept in transparent square designer glass dishes in a straight row at eye level, easily accessible. On the bar in the corner of the den was a round tray leaning against the wall. It was a facsimile of a clock face, on which every hour was marked with the number five, a mark for a cocktail hour. The Lindqvists had had a custom of enjoying a cocktail or two before dinner, never three, and never after the evening meal. For the couple who had met in political science classes in college, cocktail time conversations had invariably led to domestic current events and worldwide unrest.

Carol's sense of organization had started to slip. She forgot to replenish her larder. Friends who casually stopped by discovered opened peanut butter and preserve jars left on the kitchen counter, apparently overnight, and a suspicious smell led them to the pantry with packages of gray, putrid ground beef or rotten bananas on the shelves. Visitors often found Carol dressed in a T-shirt and jeans, barefooted, with her hair untidy and out of place. There were moments of forgetfulness with names and events on the calendar, and times when she had lost the car keys only to discover them in the medicine cabinet or under the kitchen sink in a dish side by side with the pot scrubber.

After their father's death and the displays of forgetfulness, Christine and her brother Magnus lived through several months of worry and insecurity about their mother, frequently relying on reports by Carol's friends. They were concerned about her driving, whether she had left the gas stove on after fixing a meal for herself, or whether she even remembered to bathe. Magnus, a metallurgical engineer in Florida, was a brilliant man whose common sense was almost nonexistent. He deferred all practical considerations about their mother to Christine. "You know best. Just let me know. I'll transfer money into the account."

Christine realized that, most of the time, issues with aging parents fell on the daughter, the woman, the nurturer. She had accepted her role, and with monetary help from her brother, arranged for paid household help and assistance with personal care for their mother. But Carol had wanted to continue driving.

"I'm fine driving," Carol had insisted to Christine.

"I beg to differ with you, Mom." Christine saw that the conversation was not going to be easy.

"I've had no accidents. Well, I don't count those little scrapes on the side of the car. They make the parking spots so much narrower these days."

"Well, they were costly little scrapes, Mom."

"I'm not old, you know, and I love my freedom. I like to come and go as I please. My friends and I go out to lunch. I have my church group, and I get my checkups at the doctor's and at the dentist. And my hair. Don't forget my hair."

Well, maybe way back when. Recently, your hair has not gotten much attention.

"So, wouldn't it be nice to be driven around, to have a chauffeur like a society lady?"

"Like in a taxi?"

"No, Mom. Just like you have help with cooking

and cleaning, you would have a helper drive your car wherever you want to go."

"My car?" Carol's face lit up.

"Yes. Your own car. Your car would still be seen in the streets. It would appear like nothing had changed. You could go anywhere you'd like, and Magnus and I can relax knowing you are safe."

"You two worry needlessly, but if it makes you feel better, I'll consider it. I don't want to be a burden to you."

Christine had heard the statement from countless elderly people. A bit of guilt was a small price to pay for peace of mind.

The arrangement worked seamlessly, until, one day, Carol received a call from Karen, an old friend of hers who lived in the next small town about ten miles away. Karen's husband had passed away, and she was inconsolable on the phone. Carol decided that her friend needed her, her hugs, her comforting shoulder. Deliberately ignoring the promise to her children, she took her car keys, drove through the countryside of lakes and vineyards, and arrived in Karen's hometown. She was distracted by street signs, banners on lamp poles, and private mailboxes, all painted purple for solidarity, some with white grapes on them, and she turned onto a one-way street going the wrong way. Despite the warning honks of a truck horn and the desperate yells of concerned pedestrians on the sidewalk, Carol was hit head-on by a garbage truck. She sustained a splintered collarbone, a mangled wrist, and a broken femur. After surgeries and rehabilitation, which she took on with surprising vengeance, Carol became physically whole again.

Christine and Magnus decided their mother would be safer and happier in a place where she had company, activities, and some supervision. Reluctantly, understanding that her independence would be seriously curtailed, Carol agreed to sell her car, and, after sleepless nights and some secret tears, with the help of her real estate friend and Christine, she put her beloved house on the market. She sold it to a busy young couple, similar to her and John in their first years of marriage. The husband was a college professor like John had been. With the money from the sale of the house, Carol had been able to afford the condominium at Long House, a local assisted-living facility with a good reputation.

Chapter 3

Alice texted Crystal and Lisa, "Christine is coming!"

She dropped her cell phone into her purse, a colorful bag woven of cut, folded strips of used coffee bags. She was fond of unique, functional handiwork, especially if it was made of recycled materials. She was anxious to confirm to Crystal and Lisa that her dream of Chrysalis members being together again was going to be a reality, but the bell for the history class was about to ring, and she swallowed her enthusiasm. Alice's mind was racing. She felt it was her obligation to come up with some activities for Chrysalis, outside of practices, for the time they were together. Recognizing the different personalities in the group, she had to be imaginative.

Students started to fill the classroom. Alice wrote on the grease board: "Civil War—What were the causes and the consequences?" and sat at her desk. The students continued to talk incessantly in overlapping conversations, a cacophony that distressed Alice.

"Okay. Calm down! Who wants to be the note taker?" With no volunteers, Alice assigned Beau, a student whose family had moved to New York, in the beginning of the school year, from a small, rural, Southern town at the lower end of the Mississippi.

Beau straightened his lanky body and sauntered to

the front of the classroom.

Alice gave instructions to the class. "Last time, we looked at the geographic parameters of the Civil War. Today we are going to talk about the causes and the consequences. You will see that the geography will make more sense after today." As the students listed numerous reasons for the war, Alice drifted off into the world of planning for Chrysalis. Gradually, she realized that many of the students were snickering. Among the established reasons listed on the board were "shortage of computers," "disagreements regarding football teams," and 'Dolly Parton." Alice looked at the class, whose members were pleased with themselves for having caught their teacher daydreaming. She now paid attention, and the board filled with consequences acceptable to Alice: economic changes, emancipation, loss of lives, international impact.

"Thank you," Alice said to Beau, who put the grease pen on the desk, then quickly took it back into his hand, and walked to the board. He crossed out the words "Civil War" and, with powerful strokes, replaced them with "Northern Aggression." The students looked at each other. There was a collective mumbling, an atmosphere of unease. Some boys stood up from their desks. Alice's heart did an extra beat. She did not want the defensive restlessness to follow the students outside the classroom. Alice told the class that any topic can be seen from differing points of view, depending on a variety of factors. She chided herself for coming up with such a safe platitude. She promised the class they would be discussing each item on the list in detail and with appropriate decorum. She wrote on her private notepad: "Talk to Gavin re: CW." She wanted to touch

14

base with Gavin Koladziejski, the teacher who had previously covered the course work on the Civil War. Whether a Southern point of view was something he had experienced was not clear to Alice. It had not been mentioned in their discussions about the curriculum before Gavin had left teaching to pursue a career as an organic farmer. Alice was shocked to see the term used by such a young man, a term she thought of as a relic among forgotten terms. Alice knew homogeneous small-town student populations did not have the diverse experiences of students in bigger cities, that the past often lived on in a place where time stood reasonably still, and Beau had moved to New York from a very small community.

After school, Alice picked up the dry cleaning and stopped at the pharmacy to fill her mother's prescription. She steered her SUV into the long, birch-tree-lined driveway of her childhood home. Of all possible trees available, the silver birch had been the only acceptable choice for her mother, whose loyalty to Finland, her country of birth, was a large determinant in choosing anything for the forever home of her and her new husband decades ago. The single-trunk birches grew tall and majestic, straight as soldiers dressed in a white-and-black ceremonial uniform. Alice drove over a pothole and hoped that she would remember to tell her husband Tom to fill it. Was that pothole there yesterday? The day before? She could not remember, as for most of her days, she lived her life in a haze of haste, responsibility, and obligation.

Alice knocked on one of the double doors leading from outside into the large foyer. The doors had full-length windows on each side, the glass etched with pine tree branches and cones. Without waiting for an answer, Alice walked in. Should her mother keep her doors locked? she wondered. It was no longer the safe, uncomplicated world of her mother's youth of more than a half century ago, when people in the countryside left for an out-of-town visit for several weeks without locking their doors behind them.

"Mom!" she called. No answer.

"Mother!" she tried again.

Alice thought she heard footsteps upstairs.

"Mom?" She raised her voice.

"I'm coming, I'm coming, wait just a cotton-pickin' minute!"

A cotton-pickin' minute? For a second, Alice was alarmed. Her mother wouldn't use those words. A person who moved to the United States in the early seventies would not necessarily relate to picking cotton, even if it was just a saying. Was this a sign that her mother's Parkinson's disease was already changing her thought patterns?

"Cotton-pickin'?" she said to her mother as soon as Kaisa appeared on the top landing. Her mother smiled.

"Funny, isn't it? I wonder how much cotton one can pick in a minute."

"Maybe as much as a woodchuck could chuck wood," said Alice. Both burst out in laughter. Alice stopped laughing abruptly. "I'm sorry. This is not appropriate." Alice had an image of slaves picking cotton in the hot Deep South. Her classroom experience earlier in the day was influencing her thoughts.

"What do you mean?" Kaisa frowned. "What's not appropriate?"

"I'm sorry," said Alice, "I had a tough moment or

two at school today regarding the Civil War and slavery. Got me thinking."

"I'm sorry. I'm the one who brought it up. How easy it is to speak without thinking of the origins of certain expressions."

Kaisa descended the rest of the steps into the foyer. With her skinny jeans, her fashionable, short hairstyle that emphasized her high cheekbones, and her almost wrinkle-free skin, she looked years younger than a septuagenarian. With her hair almost white, she looked ash blonde, not gray.

"I just went up into the attic to see if I could find pictures of your father as a youngster," Kaisa said.

Alice looked at her mother's empty hands and asked, "Did you find any?" What she was thinking about was not the photographs but the fact that her mother had ventured into the attic alone. Although the steps were closed with a railing on each side, the incline was steep, and a fall possible even for a sure-footed person. "Mom, you could have fallen—"

"Nonsense! I am fine. Besides, you don't know where anything is up there."

"Well, obviously, you don't either. I don't see any pictures."

"I'll just have to go back. I was interrupted when you were yelling for me."

"I wasn't yelling. Why don't you wait for the weekend, and I'll go up there—we'll go together."

Alice pictured herself as the buffer to break her mother's fall down the steps, suffering her own broken bones in place of Kaisa's. Sometimes, old people didn't survive broken hips, she'd heard.

"Okay. Fine," Kaisa surrendered. Alice felt she was

also a buffer to Kaisa's terse mannerisms and speech. There had been numerous times when Alice had felt the need to step into a conversation to prevent hurt feelings of a person conversing with Kaisa.

Alice took her mother's medication into the hall closet. On the shelf, away from the moisture and humidity of the kitchen and the bathrooms, next to a collection of Kaisa's late husband Richard's golfing gloves and caps, appropriately stored medication bottles were lined up with the names of the drugs facing frontward: Richard's blood pressure medication, his proton pump inhibitor, his vitamins.

Alice gathered them in her hands.

"Mom, I can take Dad's pills to the police station's drug disposal container."

"I will take care of that," said Kaisa quickly, with a strong emphasis on the I.

Alice rolled her eyes, knowing that at the time of the next refill for Kaisa, she would find the bottles for her father in the same spot. She obediently put the bottles back on the shelf. She turned around.

"I have to run. Pam has a band practice, and Tom will be late coming home tonight." As a real estate broker covering several counties, Tom was often late. He worked an inordinate number of hours, even on weekends, either on his own sales or those of his staff. "Call me, if you need anything."

"Oh, I almost forgot." Kaisa lifted her index finger for effect. "I do need some natural soap for the sauna. I prefer the pine soap from Finland, so next time you're online, would you get that for me? You are so much better on the computer than I am. No hurry."

"No problem."

Alice said goodbye, and walked out. Leaning her back against the massive door, she let out a deep breath while her body slid downward until she was squatting. She closed her eyes and rested a moment. It appeared that after losing her husband, her mother had grabbed onto her daughter with a stronger hold than usual. Kaisa needed to control her environment, including the people around her. Alice wondered if the Chrysalis reunion was even partially an idea she herself had thought of, or if it was her mother's idea exclusively. She realized her father had thoroughly enjoyed listening to the group, but it was her mother who had internalized her daughter's success and wanted to perpetuate it.

Alice started for her car, listing in her head the items on her to-do list—cook dinner, take out something to thaw for tomorrow's dinner, get Pam to practice, help Bobby with his homework, grade the last test papers from two days ago, call Crystal and Lisa, and, yet another item for the list, order Mom's soap.

Chapter 4

When Richard Weston died suddenly of a heart attack in the middle of a court hearing two months ago, Kaisa, in order to keep her grief in check, launched herself into a planning mode. She decided there was to be a small, private interment, with only the closest family members present, with a festive, public memorial service to follow at a later date. She planned the timeline between the burial and the larger event, the program, the speakers, the music, and the food. She wrote the obituary for the local paper and the publications in the area of her husband's birth and the site of his schooling:

The Honorable Richard James Weston of Haudenosaunee Hills, NY, died unexpectedly on March 30, 2019. He was born in Manlius, NY, on October 24th, 1946. Surviving are his wife, Kaisa Virtanen Weston, his daughter Aliisa Weston Fitzpatrick (Thomas) and his grandchildren Pamela and Robert, all of Haudenosaunee Hills, NY.

He was preceded in death by his parents Amanda and Carl Weston, his brother Carl Weston Jr., and his aunt Pamela Weston.

Judge Weston was a graduate of Fayetteville-Manlius High School of Manlius, NY. He received his undergraduate degree from Syracuse University, where he also earned his law degree.

He worked for the law firm of Jones and Anderson, and became the County Judge in 1989, which position he held at the time of his death.

Judge Weston was highly respected by all, especially his colleagues. The law was his calling. He believed in true justice for all and worked tirelessly to that end. He was an avid reader and an accomplished golfer, encouraging his grandchildren to participate in both activities.

There will be a private interment. A memorial service will be scheduled for a later date. In lieu of flowers, please consider a donation to a charity of your choice.

Kaisa was frustrated. The newspaper had parameters for the length of obituaries. The obituary was boring and did not say what she wanted it to say, but there were rules. She did not like the wording "died unexpectedly." That was sometimes interpreted as suicide. She felt that including the manner of death was unrefined. In her youth in Finland, Kaisa had been used to the matter-of-fact death announcements with a minimum amount of information published, but had grown to like the lengthy, sometimes too verbose obituaries in her new home country. She had desperately wanted to include in the death announcement her husband's many accomplishments, the accolades he had received, and a more comprehensive description of Richard as a person, a husband, a father, and a grandfather. Alice, however, had aptly pointed out that any additional information on his achievements, albeit important to her as his proud wife, would perhaps be seen as ostentatious and pompous. Although disagreeing, Kaisa reluctantly capitulated. She stated to Alice, "I should be able to do what I want, but, at a time like this, I don't want to appear obnoxious."

She did leave in the text Alice's properly spelled name given to her in baptism: Aliisa. Kaisa was proud of her Finnish background and felt strongly about keeping in her family the language, the customs, and the foods of Finland, and making sure that she never forgot her deep roots. Aliisa had been her grandmother's name. In the mouths of English speakers, it had morphed into a name that rhymed with "Melissa." With the Finnish language rule of the major emphasis always on the first syllable, "Alice" sounded more correct and appropriate, but Kaisa preferred Aliisa in the written form for its authenticity and Finnishness.

Kaisa's immersion into planning served to keep her mind busy. Her symptoms of Parkinson's disease had appeared about two years ago. At 72, she did not feel old enough to have any maladies. When the first tremor in her right hand had become visible, she thought of it as a normal consequence of overuse.

She had washed the winter curtains, wrinkled from months of being folded in a box, and put them up in the windows at a most inconvenient and cumbersome height for hanging. Her fingers felt pain from attempting to pinch the pleats together and feed the metal three-pronged clips into their proper channels in the fabric. Alice had made fun of her for using the old-fashioned drape clips, but Kaisa was happy with her choice. After all, she was the one with the home economics degree, even if from decades ago. She could not trust the newfangled gadgetry made for today's youth, who wanted everything easy and effortless, involving no work.

Her fingers were sore. When the twinges of pain subsided, a small tremor remained in her right hand, discernible only when she was resting, with her hands completely free, not holding onto an item, or twiddling with this, that, or the other, as often was her habit. Kaisa was taught from an early age that "the devil finds work for the idle hands."

Kaisa hid her concerns and visited a doctor far enough away from Haudenosaunee Hills to avoid running into a familiar person in a neurologist's waiting room. She was forced to admit her doctor's visits to her husband when Richard started to notice symptoms she was unable to hide from him. Richard had been surprised. He had assumed against all reasonable thinking that Kaisa and he would live healthy and happy till the end of time.

Gradually, other symptoms of her Parkinson's appeared, among them most recently a diminished sense of balance. Kaisa had been proud of her agility in running up and down stairs without holding onto a railing. Her friends, some of them younger than she, struggled with their depth perception and lack of strength, and descended stairways with intended carefulness.

She had only fallen twice so far, both times while hurrying to be on time for a lunch with a friend and miscalculating the depth of a step into the restaurant. She was thankful the falls had not happened on the way out of the restaurant, giving an erroneous impression that she had exited from the bar and not a food establishment. After her falls, Kaisa was careful to use the handicapped entrances whenever possible. She kept the falls as information between herself and her doctor. The rather large purple and yellow bruises had been easy to hide under slacks and long sleeves. Kaisa worried about the summer and New York's sometimes hot and muggy weather calling for lightweight outfits. Soon after the falls, the formal diagnosis of Parkinson's was entered into her medical record.

Kaisa and Richard knew that Parkinson's was a progressive disease, but they relied on the scientific findings that the disease progresses more slowly in older people. Richard delved into an extensive private investigation on the computer and read everything he could find on the topic, spending time at the local library. He also increased the size of his personal library by purchasing pertinent publications on the topic. Kaisa took a frequent peek at the pages Richard had marked with bright green stickies poking out randomly from between the pages. Her neurologist had prescribed a new, promising medication for her, and Kaisa thought it was helping in controlling the tremors. Both she and Richard had felt they were prepared for what was to come.

But Richard's death created a new reality for Kaisa. She knew she needed to be strong. She vacillated between an outwardly steadfast woman in control of her future and a female who tried to hide her insecurities from her family and friends.

Chapter 5

Crystal dug up her ringing phone from under the backpack, blanket roll, and cooking gear. She had just returned from a vacation trip to the Adirondacks, where she and Gavin, her teacher-turned-farmer boyfriend of a few years, had completed a climb of one of the forty-six High Peaks of the Adirondack Mountains. They had now mastered thirty-one of them, some more challenging than others. Crystal was bubbling with enthusiasm.

She had needed this trip into the fresh mountain air, the spring brooks, the majestic views. The trip had been the first real vacation in a couple of years from her job as an obstetrics nurse at the hospital, a job that was mostly rewarding, but, at times, exhausting and, due to bureaucracy, infuriating. Crystal also had a habit of always being the good-hearted colleague who offered to work holidays in order to give her friends, especially those with children, a chance to spend Christmas, Easter, and Thanksgiving with their families. Now she had the rest of the day left to "turn her hat around," to exchange the knitted headband for headgear familiar to all food service workers and labor and operating room personnel, a shower cap-like hair cover, complimentary only to those with a classically beautiful face like Crystal's.

She fumbled too long to catch the call, and decided

she was too tired to talk after all. The phone indicated the caller was Alice.

After a good night's sleep, Crystal decided to walk to work. She was humming, stepping along briskly through the quiet streets of Haudenosaunee Hills. Her condominium was just far enough from the hospital to allow for a healthy walk before starting her shift. On her walk this morning, she rehearsed in her mind lyrics to several different tunes of varying vintages. Chrysalis had performed throwbacks to earlier times encompassing several decades, careful, close harmony in songs that made the audience sway from side to side, mouth the words along with the quartet, and sometimes, annoyingly, snap their fingers to an unusually vibrant tune. Crystal had always been thankful to be accepted as one of the Chrysalis singers. Alice had the most beautiful voice, and Lisa and Christine were probably technically the best. Today, children waiting for the school bus stared at Crystal unabashedly, some giggling, some with furrowed brows. *Who sings in the street alone?* She could see them wondering, and she realized she'd been singing out loud.

Crystal liked children. In her view of the future, she hoped it was not too late to entertain the idea of having children of her own. She stopped to join the younger children of the group in a game of hopscotch. Her small stature and her long, curly hair flying in the air with each hop blended her almost seamlessly into the picture.

Around the corner, behind gigantic red maples, was the hospital, facing the lake. Crystal walked across the parking lot of the red brick building—1920s vintage but well taken care of, with extra departments added through the years. A woman waved to her from her window of the skilled nursing wing. She had done that every morning for a few weeks, same time, same window, every morning of Crystal's day shifts. Every now and then, there were patients in the unit whose only contact with the outside world might be a look out the window. Crystal waved back.

When Crystal arrived on the obstetrics floor, she changed her clothes, engaged in small talk with her peers, and then settled down into a more serious review of the status of the mothers in the labor rooms. As on most Wednesdays, there was a scheduled Caesarean on the list for the day.

Crystal saw Lisa in the hallway. She had stopped in to discuss the Caesarean with the anesthesiologist. While rushing off, she yelled to Crystal over her shoulder, "If you talk to Alice, tell her I'll call her." As a busy obstetrician, Lisa would be the slippery one to rein in for Chrysalis practices.

Crystal's choice to become a labor nurse had been a conscious one from early on. Instead of caring for chronically ill patients or taking care of wounds of victims of accidents or assaults, being a part of the birth experience was rejuvenating, a promise of life's renewal every time.

On the way home, Crystal called Alice.

"Sorry I missed your call yesterday. I did get your text." Crystal added excitedly, "Can't wait to see what we come up with! I haven't sung in quite a while, but I'm looking forward to getting back into it."

"I know it," said Alice. "When Mom suggested it, my first inclination was to tell her she was crazy, but, as you know, you can't say that to my mother. There is a saying, 'You can always tell a Finn, but you can't tell them much.' "

Alice heard Crystal chuckle. "Really? I think that's true of any mother regardless of their nationality. At this moment, I don't even know where my mom is. In my pile of mail, there was a letter from her mailed from Austria and another from Slovenia. And, if you remember, she is roaming around the world without a cell phone, leaving me in complete darkness. For all I know, she's traveling with some painter, or a poet she picked up in Paris! Maybe she's hooked up with my father, whoever he is."

"She still hasn't told you? That's odd."

"That's my mom. Go figure!"

Chapter 6

Loretta Giordano, whose family and close friends called her Lola, had been sending mail to her daughter Crystal from all over the world for years now, old-fashioned postcards and handwritten letters in actual paper envelopes with interesting stamps on them. After leaving her job as a buyer for Lord & Taylor in New York City, she had moved upstate and devoted her time to her then teenage daughter Crystal and to her own hobbies of painting and drawing.

Painting had been her passion in high school and her major in college. She had hoped to use her degree in fine arts as a full-time artist, but soon realized she needed a steadier source of income to support herself. A few years after returning to the Finger Lakes, she had evaluated her life and determined it to be unbelievably boring. She found the small town of Haudenosaunee Hills stifling, insular, and parochial. It was not enough for her to read books about other places and other people and their experiences. She needed to live it all herself.

Finally, after several years, when Crystal was settled in her job, which Lola found boring and mundane, Lola systematically started to visit countries in Europe, Asia, South America, and Africa. She would never stoop to what she named a "Three-Tower Tour— Eiffel, Pisa, and London" and call it having seen

Europe. Instead, she made it her style to find a small, out-of-the-way village where she could get a menial job, be paid under the table, or work for her room and meals. She immersed herself in the lives of fishermen, seamstresses, farmers, florists, at times communicating only with body language and the aid of a ragged dictionary which she kept in her back pocket. She had amassed a large collection of them by now, each language more challenging than the next.

Each time she returned home to her small cottage on the lake, she added a push pin to the world map covering a whole wall in her living room. Holland and Belgium down. Countless more to go. Crystal was glad Lola deliberately stayed away from the corners of the world where wars were raging or where the political situation was balancing on a teeter-totter. She was an adventurer but not a fool.

Other than Crystal, very few people were interested in her travels beyond the usual questions—"How was your trip?" and "Where did you go, again?" Her letters to Crystal served as diaries, written when an experience was fresh—her feeling of fear immediately prior to the running of the bulls in Pamplona, the desperation she felt in a Romanian orphanage, or the anger on a sandy beach in Thailand where she walked among plastic bottles, single-use packets, and cigarette butts.

Today, she was getting ready to drive from Piran, Slovenia, to Northern Italy, from where she would fly home for a bit, but only until her wanderlust got the better of her again.

Aside from her strong emotional connection to Crystal, Lola called herself a free bird. Although her parents of Italian descent had been family oriented, they had always honored Lola's obvious free spirit and her notable discomfort with things usual, everyday, and safe. They had encouraged her creativity and her need to develop her persona as an artistic, adventurous woman.

In her younger years, Lola had an inordinate number of female friends. However, the friends were just a degree above acquaintances, and she liked it that way.

Lola had a few torrid love affairs that left her spent and miserable when they ended. The men she chose were exciting and romantic, yet they never considered her their equal. They either put her on a pedestal or treated her as someone who was subservient to them.

Later, during her travels, she had been in comfortable relationships with interesting men, such as the artist who worked as a tour guide at Eagle's Nest, Hitler's hideaway in Austria, or the South African pool boy, thirty-some years her junior, or the Saudi oil prince who had wanted to marry her.

Lola was sure there was no man extraordinary enough for her, or whom she could tolerate as part of her everyday life. Her requirements included qualities of being gentle yet rough, understanding yet strong in his own opinions, open to the world yet a homebody. She knew no one who would meet her expectations.

In the end, she had only one close friend who shared her thoughts about the world: Margaret Quinton, more than two decades older than she.

Lola was comfortable with herself. She was a whole person who did not need to look for the other half. When anyone questioned her life choices, she quietly stated she was a very happy woman.

Lola stepped into the miniature hatchback, a rental car that had served as a bedroom for her during her trip. She looked at her map, and chose a road to Trieste and then on to Venice.

Chapter 7

After performing the Caeserean section, Lisa walked to the nurses' station. She reviewed necessary paperwork and exchanged a couple of words with her colleagues. After checking on the status of an at-risk mother and her twin babies, Lisa drove to her office to touch base with her office staff. On the door, it said:

Lisa Hughes, MD
Obstetrics and Gynecology

Doctor Hughes. To Lisa, Dr. Hughes was her grandfather. His having been a doctor was one of the few things she knew about him. She had in no way followed his footsteps or sought a career of prestige. She simply wanted a job where she could feel gratified for being useful. Women's issues had always interested Lisa. Her choice of obstetrics as a specialty had been natural and easy.

Lisa rented office space in the recently opened medical office building where everything looked and smelled brand new. She had chosen a blue-and-yellow color scheme for the waiting room: darker blue fabrics in various hues against the background of white walls, with oversized pieces of bright yellow modern art in black frames. Potted palms and philodendrons added a spot of green by the window. A larger-than-usual play area with wooden toys dominated one corner.

"Want some coffee?" asked Debbie, her

receptionist. Had there been patients present, she would have added "Doctor" after the word "coffee" when addressing Lisa. Lisa felt that this habit of Debbie's using titles when talking to her was complete hypocrisy. After all, Debbie had been Lisa's babysitter years ago when she was a teenager living next door to Lisa's parents' house, a large "painted lady" Victorian, in which Lisa now lived alone with her two persnickety old cats: Frasier and Niles. The house was much too large for one person, but Lisa was emotionally attached to the home and the memories in it. She had the means to keep up the old structure, and renovating the nooks and crannies had become her hobby. She paid equal attention to the gardens around the house. As a result, her house was always one of the high points of the annual garden tour to raise money for the new children's wing at the hospital.

Lisa had been born as a great and welcome surprise to parents in their forties who had reconciled themselves to the fact they would not have children. The joy of a baby had been overwhelming. Though Lisa had been adored, she was brought up with discipline and necessary order that instilled in her an endless respect for her parents, Carl and Susan. She lost them in a boating mishap on the lake during a storm, when Lisa was a first-year medical student. The news had been tragic and, for months, an endless source of various expressions of sympathy for "the poor girl, so brave, left alone so young." These condolences, although well-meaning, slowed down Lisa's desperate efforts to heal, to keep going, to build on good memories instead of wallowing in sorrow.

"Coffee would be great. Thanks." Lisa walked into

her office past one of the patient rooms with a picture of a terrified baby tiger on the ceiling above the examining table. The cat was hanging onto the corners of the poster with long, sharp claws. Her teeth were exposed with pink gums and her eyes expressed utter panic. HELP! was printed across the picture with block letters. Lisa felt the poster relaxed her patients and made them laugh while in an undignified position, vulnerable and almost naked, feet in cold stirrups. Not everyone found the tiger amusing. Her mother's friend Margaret Quinton thought it gauche and did not hesitate to tell Lisa her opinion.

The coffee, hazelnut, tasted good. Lisa sat in the expensive black leather chair and adjusted it to lean back slightly. She picked up her phone, scrolled to Alice's number, and touched it with her index finger. She was ready to have a relaxing moment with her friend on the phone.

Chapter 8

Alice hung the dry cleaning in the hallway closet for now. She had to remember to remove the plastic covering the jackets and slacks, as her mother had never failed to remind her, lest the clothing would…would what? Rot? Get moldy? She would have to google that.

She took the frying pan from the cupboard and placed it on a low flame on the gas stove. She called for Pamela and Bobby. After several increasingly louder summonses, Alice started to wonder if she was alone in the house. An investigation revealed Bobby in his bedroom wearing earphones, gyrating in the middle of the floor in a strange twisting motion with his eyes closed and his mouth in a painful smirk. Bobby's choice of music was irritating loud noise to Alice. She was thankful for the invention of headphones. Alice tapped her son on the shoulder. His body stopped moving.

"Hey, I'm just rocking on," said Bobby raising his one eyebrow, a skill not everyone had, and practiced by him frequently for its uniqueness to the point of irritation to his mother. Alice inquired about his ninth-grade homework and about his sister, Pam. Apparently, there was no homework, as seemed to be the case often lately, and, according to Bobby, there was a note from Pam on the refrigerator.

"She's eating with the Smiths again, and Dragon Lady, I mean Mrs. Smith, will take Stephanie and her to practice." Bobby smirked.

"Robert!" said Alice while trying to hide her smile. Stephanie's mother was known for her rules and regulations that extended to visitors to the Smith household.

Alice went back into the kitchen and turned up the heat under the pan. She dribbled a small amount of oil in the pan and took the meat out of the refrigerator.

"Two pork chops it is," she said, but then grabbed the other two bone-in chops. *Might as well cook them all. Life just got a little bit easier tonight. Only two of us,* she thought. While the chops fried, Alice prepared a side dish out of leftover mashed potatoes. With a fresh green salad, dinner was ready for her and Bobby.

The phone rang. Kaisa, with panic in her voice, rapidly told the story of a malfunctioning washing machine and asked Alice to come over and check it out for her. *So much for the quiet mother-son time,* thought Alice.

"I'll be right there," Alice promised her mother.

Alice told Bobby he was on his own for a bit and he could eat without her, if he wanted to. The food was ready.

The phone rang again. Lisa was now ready to talk while Alice was driving to her mother's. Almost at Kaisa's house, Alice apologized profusely for having to cut the phone call short.

"Don't worry," comforted Lisa. "Just so you know, singing together will be fun. Count me in."

From the panic in her mother's voice, Alice had imagined Kaisa's laundry room to be under water, with suds percolating from the edges of the washer door. She opened the door to the foyer, kicked off her shoes, and ran to the laundry room. She found both the washer and the dryer humming rhythmically in the warm cocoon of a room that smelled of lilac fabric softener.

"Mom, I don't see a problem here. What's going on?"

"Oh," said Kaisa, "I had accidentally set the washer on delay. I fixed it. But, since you are here, would you take a look at the bathroom window? I can only open it so far, and it seems to stick." Alice bit her tongue. She would have appreciated a call from her mother about the "fixed" washing machine. "Let's look at it," she said.

Kaisa was walking ahead of her. On the way to the bathroom in a different wing of the house, she detoured to the foyer, where Alice's shoes were haphazardly strewn about. Kaisa bent over—losing her balance almost unnoticeably for a second—picked up the shoes, and placed them neatly on the boot tray, side by side like an old couple. Alice watched her mother, shaking her head.

"Did somebody set this window to open just so far?" Alice raised her voice. Kaisa could not remember. "It should be all right now."

"Thank you." Kaisa was genuinely grateful. "Before you go, let me give you the list of songs I want you girls to sing at the memorial service." She went to her antique desk in the living room and pulled out a list of song titles from one of the numerous cubbyholes of the old secretary.

"Mom, it is a memorial service, not a concert. Let me take it to the group. Don't count on our being able to do it all."

"I know you can," said Kaisa. "By the way, I forgot

to tell you, next time you go to one of the larger grocery stores, would you bring me some cake yeast? The smaller stores only have the powder." Kaisa was a master at effortless changes in topics of conversation.

"No problem."

On the way out, Alice looked at the list of songs. Most were appropriate, in her estimation, to remember a man who was not particularly religious. "I Have a Dream" had been her father's favorite. From the songs on the list, he had also liked "You Raise Me Up," "Wind Beneath My Wings," and "Bridge Over Troubled Water." Her father's true taste in music was classical, violin concertos in particular. Whether he had, in fact, loved the Chrysalis performances was questionable, Alice admitted to herself. She would have to schedule the first practice soon after Christine came to town.

Alice threw the list onto the back seat of the car, adjusted her seatbelt, and looked in the backup mirror to check on an irritant in her right eye. In the mirror, she saw a tired, middle-aged woman whose once beautiful hair was carelessly gathered into a ponytail, with loose strands tickling her cheeks. She had inherited the typical "Finnish hair"—plenty of individual shafts of hair, all of them thin. She needed to pay more attention to herself, especially to her weight, as her mother had intimated to her on the phone a few days ago. After removing a barely visible insect from her lower eyelid, she readjusted the mirror and headed home.

Chapter 9

It was raining in Seattle, a usual occurrence in the Pacific Northwest. Christine called a staff meeting. She had, of course, spent time away from her job before, but she'd never let the ties to the office be cut entirely. Like the female in an old laptop ad, she was the epitome of a vacationing, conscientious career woman of substance, up to her knees in the ocean with a silver laptop in her tanned arms, still virtually connected to all things under her control.

This time, Christine was going to sever the ties for three weeks, go home, spend time with her mother, and bring back memories of high school days and the famous four. Her business was running smoothly with the help of her competent staff, hired not necessarily on the basis of their college grade point average or impressive resumes. She had chosen them on the basis of personal attributes of integrity, honesty, and empathy. She believed any knowledge could be absorbed, any task taught, but personal qualities were most important and mostly innate. This philosophy had served her well in building her business.

In recent years, Christine had developed a collaborative and cooperative management style. Letting go did not come naturally to her. However, she had noticed this style brought better results than her earlier authoritarian method. Christine decided to take this opportunity to delegate. She chose a substitute to take her place at an international conference in Washington, DC, and assigned a deputy to be in charge of the overall running of the manufacturing and distribution operations of the company. Although Christine found relinquishing responsibility extraordinarily difficult, from outward appearances, there was nothing to indicate that this delegation effort was painful to her.

She was going home. She thought of romantic B-movies with a predictable plot and a happy ending with the female main character returning home, where handsome Prince Charming was waiting for her. Christine wasn't looking for a happy ending. Her short, tumultuous marriage to a Seattle politician had left her suspicious of close relationships and entanglements with the opposite sex. She felt she was strong professionally and personally, and considered herself to be in need of nothing, including romance, in her life.

On the plane, Christine sat in her business class aisle seat. Her seatmate had communicated clearly that she wanted no interaction by opening a book before the plane taxied onto the tarmac for take-off. They flew for six hours, and then Christine had a layover in Detroit before landing in Rochester, New York.

After SeaTac, the Rochester airport was ghost-like in its silence and lack of people. She rented a car, and headed south on I-390. The traffic was sparse and easy, and the feeling of relaxation and relief that had started to take hold on the plane intensified. After driving on the Thruway for a short while, Christine steered the car onto the exit for the Finger Lakes region, as if obeying a reflex. As the sun was starting to set, she followed the road south, admiring the rows upon rows of grapes growing on the hillsides sloping down to the lake. At least three new wineries had sprung up in the six months since her last visit. She saw sailboats on the clear blue water, returning to the harbors and small cottages sprinkled around the lake. Sailing here was mostly sweet and tame, unlike being the victim of the waves on the Pacific Ocean, where her ex-husband had forced her to join him regardless of her severe seasickness and fear.

Christine arrived at the bed-and-breakfast run by Mary, an acquaintance from her childhood days. Mary and her husband had renovated an old farmhouse, quaint yet majestic, overlooking the lake. They ran a small coffee house in one part of the outbuilding that had once been a cow barn. The other, larger building, once a horse barn with a hay loft, had been renovated into a venue for weddings, birthday parties, and other large gatherings.

The house itself was bright white, obviously recently painted, with black shutters kept open by visible antique hooks. The full-length windows opened to the wrap-around porch. When opened, the windows could serve as doors with a slightly higher threshold than usual. This design, Christine had read somewhere, was ingeniously invented to avoid paying higher taxes, which were calculated on the basis of the number of doors in the house. You could just as easily walk out through a window as you would through a door. The deviousness tickled Christine's funny bone.

She opened the door to the bedroom assigned to her and saw a queen-sized four-poster bed covered by a crocheted canopy, Mary's handiwork, no doubt. A chest of drawers and an antique, comfortable-looking armchair completed the room. On the wall were black-and-white framed photographs of vineyards and lakes, pictures of ladies in long gowns and coats, and men with handlebar mustaches posing by a horse-drawn sled—apparently a crowd at a winter carnival by a frozen lake.

Christine unpacked her suitcase immediately, as was her habit when traveling. She hung her dresses, skirts, slacks, and tops in the small closet, and put other clothes and various travel items in the drawers of the large Victorian dresser, an ornate piece of furniture showcasing the skilled carpentry of days gone by. It had a smell of old wood, a slightly musty odor, a scent of things in an old attic. She decided to leave the drawers open part way.

After her shower, Christine went downstairs, exchanged pleasantries with Mary, and picked out a book from the downstairs library. She was impressed with the choice of books on the built-in shelves on both sides of the massive wood-burning fireplace. In addition to a collection of classics, there were also newer books, prize-winning fiction and non-fiction, and voluminous novels that had been on the bestseller list for weeks or months. Christine sat in a wingback chair with a book by a new author whose work was not familiar to her. Before long, she felt her neck snapping back, as if her brain was telling her to remain awake and in an upright position for reading. The relaxing atmosphere had seduced her, and her body and mind had relented.

Christine wondered what would be an appropriate time to visit her mother in the morning. She wanted to surprise her. A call to Long House clarified that any time would be fine, and Christine decided on midmorning.

Chapter 10

Christine slept in. She deliberately had not set the alarm on her phone. Breakfast was a delicious cheese-crusted pastry cup with cubed ham and a poached egg nestled in it, followed by a dish of colorful fruit: strawberries, blueberries, pineapple, and kiwi. After finishing her culinary indulgence, Christine grabbed her purse, car keys, and the box of well-known West Coast chocolates for her mother, and started to drive toward town. She felt the odd sensation of being in surroundings that were simultaneously familiar and comforting but also strange and distant.

The road led straight from the bed-and-breakfast to the Long House assisted living facility. Long House was named after its developer and benefactor Ansel Long, a businessman whose family had roots in Haudenosaunee Hills. To couple the last name with "House" served to point out the Iroquois Nation's history in the area. Christine had always liked the name Haudenosaunee, the nation's own word for Iroquois. The rather unusual name for a hometown was often a topic of conversation with those who heard it for the first time.

When Christine passed the street sign for Maple Street, her childhood home address, nostalgia overtook her. She had decided she did not want to see the place. It was no longer the family home, and she would cause herself grief, stirring the old feelings she had for her homestead. However, as if helpless to resist, she turned around in the small parking lot of the veterinary clinic, headed back north, and turned left onto Maple Street. There was an easy curve on the street, and behind it, on the left, there it was—84 Maple Street, the home of her childhood, her youth, her first few adult years—a symmetrical, red brick, center-hall colonial. The tops of the windows were covered with trailing vine, like eyes in need of an eyelid lift. The upstairs bedroom windows were almost entirely grown shut with English ivy. The overgrowth of the invasive creeper was, to her, a sign of neglect, and her heart sank. Strangers were letting her house go to ruin! Christine was surprised by her highly emotional reaction. She drove by slowly, but it was difficult to appear inconspicuous with her car moving at a snail's pace. She stopped the vehicle a few houses up the street.

Christine got out of the car casually. She walked to the house with normal speed, as if she had a destination in mind. A green-and-white sign flat on the ground among the high grass stopped her. Stretching her neck awkwardly, she read it upside down: "Fitzpatrick Realty FOR SALE" and a phone number.

For sale! Christine's heart somersaulted in her chest. *And?* she asked herself. Her mind had galloped miles and years from where her body stood. She loved this house. She could live in it again.

Christine wrote down the phone number of the realtor. It could be that the sign had fallen down and the house was still on the market. Or, perhaps the realtor had forgotten the sign after selling the house. Wouldn't it, in that case, have had a "SOLD" sign added on it?

Was someone living in the house? Maybe the previous owner had moved out, and the new owner was waiting to move in? Waiting for what? A loan to go through? Renovations to be completed? Christine was getting anxious. *This is not me; Christine Thurston, the cool, calculating, clear-thinking CEO. Calm down!*

Her heart was still pounding when she got back into her car. In the driver's seat, she put her forehead on the steering wheel's smooth leather. "Get hold of yourself!" she said out loud. She turned around and drove by the house one more time.

It was nearing eleven o'clock. Christine was excited about seeing her mother and surprising her. Long House, a two-level modern structure, had wings resembling the historic dwellings of the area's Seneca tribe. The building occupied a large area by the lake, with walking trails leading to peaceful spots by the water. In the lobby, residents were involved in various activities. Two ladies were waiting for the shuttle service to take them to downtown's new Italian restaurant for an early lunch and to a matinee showing of the latest action movie. According to them, the staff had suggested something tamer, but the action choice, the ladies said, would keep them awake after a pasta lunch. A gentleman was reading a newspaper in the corner, and just behind Christine his friend walked in, having taken his Bassett hound for her morning walk. Christine was surprised and pleased to find pets were allowed in Long House.

Upstairs, Christine knocked on her mother's door, which she found narrowly ajar.

"I'm not ready yet," Christine heard her mother respond to the knock.

"Hi, Mom!" said Christine, and she walked in and saw her mother sorting receipts and notepapers that had fallen out of her purse, now empty on the chair, with its mouth gaping open.

"Oh, my!" said Carol and came almost running toward her daughter with her arms wide open for a warm embrace.

"Did you tell me you were coming, and I forgot?"

"No, Mom, I thought I would surprise you. It's so good to see you." Christine gave Carol another squeeze, kissed her on the cheek, and handed her the box of chocolates with a drawing of a grandmotherly woman on the cover.

"You remembered!" said Carol, opening the box. "My favorites. You know, she looks a lot like my mother, round glasses and all."

Christine looked around the room. It was a miniature version of the old living room on Maple Street. Some of the furniture was the same, although the large sofa had been replaced by a loveseat with similar features and fabric. The familiar artwork hung all around the room, almost covering the walls completely. Carol had had a difficult time deciding which paintings to keep and which to "discard," a cruel, savage word, hostile even to inanimate objects. On the desk, in a silver frame, was a black-and-white photograph of Christine's father, John Lindqvist, as a younger man—a tall, blond Nordic god dressed in a tuxedo, holding a short glass with liquid and ice cubes. Those ice cubes were always there, as far as Christine could remember, whether he was having a cocktail, a glass of water on a hot summer day, or orange juice for breakfast. Hot weather brought on an interesting tic in his left eye, making it appear as if he were winking at you. A cold drink seemed to relieve it. As a young child, Christine had thought these neurological quirks were meant for her, an affirmation of her father's love for his young daughter. Christine smiled and touched the frame with her fingertips.

"What were you getting ready for?" Christine asked her mother.

"Oh, Margaret and I are going to a piano concert in another part of the building. Modern music, if I remember right. Margaret probably won't like it. Is it time?" Christine remembered that a local musicians' group practiced at Long House and didn't mind if the residents came in to listen.

"What time are you supposed to go?"

"I think she said after lunch. Well, I didn't have lunch yet, so… Don't mind me."

"Do you do a lot of things with Margaret?"

"I do. She's right next door."

Christine was aware of some details about Margaret's past, but to most people, Margaret was an enigma. By most calculations, she was in her late eighties. Information online regarding her birthdate varied by four to five years, and Margaret liked the aura of mystery around her.

Margaret Quinton was an opera singer. Her voice was commendable but had never been good enough to lift her to the top ranks of opera divas. She had had a great career in New York City, singing for various opera companies, often in a major role. Her soprano arias had received some laudable reviews. Margaret had retired to her roots in the quiet countryside, first in a townhouse, and, when her eyesight started to fail, to Long House in order to "feel included."

Margaret spoke with a British accent. Her father had come to the United States at the turn of the twentieth century, and, although her mother was American, Margaret had assumed British ways as her modus operandi. She preferred the British pronunciation of words (to-mah-to), the British spelling (theatre, colour) and she used British vocabulary—lift for elevator, lorry for truck, and bumbershoot for umbrella. Most people found this pretentious and snobbish. On Margaret's coffee table was an oversized book about the British royal family a few years back. On the cover were Queen Elizabeth II, Prince Philip, and their children, Charles, Anne, Andrew, and Edward, all looking rather uninterested.

Margaret was proud of the fact that she was named after Princess Margaret, the Queen's younger sister. This tidbit was helpful in determining that Margaret Quinton could not be older than her namesake, who was born in 1930. It tickled Margaret that the princess had been a rebel among prim and proper family members, and she often talked about the royal's woeful romances as if identifying with her.

"Margaret is good to me, and I can help her. She can't see well enough to read fine print. You know, like on a medicine bottle," said Carol, then adding out of nowhere, "I thought you said you were going to Washington, DC."

"I was, but Kaisa Weston wants Chrysalis to sing at the memorial service for her husband. I'm actually doing this for Alice. I got a substitute to take my place at the DC conference."

"A substitute," said Carol and recited,

"I'm a tute.
I'm a substitute
for a prostitute,
who's destitute
in an institute.
I'm a tute."

Carol turned back to categorize her assortment of papers.

"Where did that come from?" asked Christine, trying to decide between laughing and crying. This was an old ditty, one of many that had been handed down in the family from the time Carol's Uncle William attended Cornell University. Ever since the 1800s college boys had recited naughty little poems not usually shared with their families.

"I remember the darnedest things, old things, but not what happened yesterday."

Christine wasn't sure whether her mother was concerned or just making light of her memory loss.

"How about if I come back later, after the concert, and we'll go out to dinner?"

"I'd like that," said Carol.

Christine was not as much interested in Carol's schedule as she was anxious to make a phone call to the realtor.

Chapter 11

Crystal and Gavin were having dinner on the large balcony of Crystal's condominium overlooking the lake…organic early vegetables from Gavin's farm, and salmon he had caught in the local creek the first day of fishing season in April. The salmon were working their way into the lake, and, if unlucky, ended up in a fisherman's net with a hook in their gills. It was the season of grilling and smoking.

Skipping dessert, Crystal prepared some strong coffee. The couple was discussing disturbing current political issues when the doorbell rang.

Through the eye in the door, Crystal could see a short woman with an abundance of curly hair, once black but now on the way to white, a pleasant salt-and-pepper medley. Crystal opened the door to her mother.

"You're back!" she said. Tears ran down her cheeks, leaving visible trails behind them. "I've missed you so."

With her arm around her mother's shoulders, she led her to the balcony to be hugged by Gavin.

"Have you eaten?"

"Cardboard. You know—airplane food."

Gavin got up. "You two catch up. I'll fix you a plate."

"Thank you. Aren't you sweet!" Lola and Crystal sat down, and Lola put her hand over Crystal's. "You are looking fabulous."

"Thanks. It's the good life, Mom. We just got back from the Adirondacks. Climbing keeps you in shape, and there is nothing to beat fresh air."

"I know it. I can't believe I lived in New York City for so many years and did it without being forced to. Don't get me wrong. The city was good to me in many ways, but I am basically a country girl."

"You, a country girl?" Crystal laughed.

"Well, not in a country music kind of way, but you know what I mean."

"I hardly ever know what you mean, Mom. You keep me on my toes."

Gavin stepped onto the balcony with a plate of salmon, tomatoes, sweet peas, and new potatoes, the largest the size of a golf ball.

"This is heaven!" Lola exclaimed, putting her right hand flat on her chest. "Thank you, dear," she said to him, and then to her daughter, "Tell me all the news."

"Well," started Crystal, "the car dealership went bankrupt, Chrysalis is singing at Richard Weston's memorial service, and a new Italian restaurant opened in town…" Crystal stopped. "But you are just coming back from amazing adventures. Why would you even be interested?"

"Of course I'm interested. Don't be silly. Yes, I actually flew home from Venice. They are having terrible trouble with rising water."

The discussion then led to flooded gondola canals, global warming, and the fate of mankind.

"Well, I'm getting depressed. You know, I haven't even been home yet, and I have to return the rental car."

The news of the small town of Haudenosaunee

Hills was forgotten.

Crystal hugged her mother.

"Awww, you came to see me before you even went home! I love you, Mom!"

Lola arranged for the car rental company to pick up the car at her house. As she drove down the long curvy dirt road to the cottage, she considered how it always felt strange and awkward to return home after a long time away. She stood in the yard for a while, anticipating an unusually stunning sunset. The white roses were in full bloom, and the clean, light green of the trees by the water's edge indicated the summer was just beginning.

Although it was clear to Lola that Crystal had done some raking and getting rid of the worst of last year's dead plants, she realized the cleanup job was not a task for just a couple of days. Lola didn't mind yard work. She could already imagine the glorious sea of flowers in her garden later in the summer. Lola walked in the door of her small house, opened some windows, and laid the duffel bag aside.

It's amazing how light you can travel when you put your mind to it. She thought of the gigantic suitcases in large numbers lugged around by tourists all over the world—unnecessary baggage.

Chapter 12

This time of the year, Lisa spent a big part of her free time in her garden. She had made an assessment of the condition of her perennials, and noted that the irises, some having just finished blooming, needed to be separated later in the summer. Several of the iris plants were gorgeous and rare. Perhaps some of the staff at the hospital would like a few tubers. The forsythia bush needed major surgery, and now was the time to do it. Cutting the long branches back now would allow new growth to take place. Next spring, ahead of the leaves, yellow flowers would appear, sometimes as early as March, probably to be covered by snow again in a surprise spring snowstorm.

Mr. and Mrs. Hughes had had a strict division of duties. Susan was the queen of the indoor space of the house, in charge of cooking, cleaning, and decorating. She had traditional female hobbies of sewing, knitting, crocheting, weaving, and quilting. She also tried out exotic recipes, the final product often ending up in the composter accompanied by well-meaning chuckles from Carl and Lisa. Susan's choice for hobbies was a clear opposite of her college education in physics.

Carl's passion, outside of his insurance business and his sailboat, was the garden. In addition to his variety of colorful bushes and the flowerbeds, he always had a large plot tilled for vegetables. Every year, among the usual seeds and seedlings, according to the Iroquois tradition, he planted the Three Sisters: corn, beans, and squash—a perfect vegetable-protein combination.

At the time of her parents' death, Lisa had been in medical school. She knew she did not want to sell the house, and had rented it until she finished her education. Upon her return to Haudenosaunee Hills, Lisa had given up on the idea of a vegetable garden. It had not been tended to and had grown over, leaving only a rectangular area in the back yard clearly visible due to the different type of grass growing where the previous rows of peppers and spinach, carrots and beets had been. She decided to keep a small salad garden of tomatoes, cucumbers, and lettuce in a narrow bed under the kitchen window, where it would have perfect orientation to the sun. She also grew herbs in the flowerbeds and window boxes.

Taking off her dirty gloves, Lisa hung them on a hook on the wall of the garage. She stepped out of the rubber boots, realizing she had stepped on some wet mud, now traveling up the side of the right boot leg. *These boots need a healthy scrubbing.* The contrast between the sterile hospital world and the earthy garden environment struck her as funny. She stepped into the kitchen from the garage and was disappointed to see a brown, liquid pile of cat vomit on the gel mat in front of the sink. It was the third one this week. Lisa had witnessed Frasier vomiting a couple of days ago. It was time to make an appointment for him with the veterinarian. As a doctor, she didn't trust herself to diagnose or treat her pets, feeling it would be equal to hiring the mold abatement team to remove asbestos.

After the call to the veterinary clinic, she called Alice and left a message.

"Hi, I just wanted you to know that whenever you'd like all of us to get together, I'd like us to do it at my house. I have the piano, and I also still have some of the tracks with our background music on them. Besides, I might have a sick cat, so, if I could stay home in the evening, it would be better for me." After a short pause, she added: "And for Frasier."

Chapter 13

Christine accompanied Carol and Margaret to a room where a small stage was set up on one end with a grand piano. The rest of the space was lined up with straight-backed chairs in neat rows.

It appeared Margaret had dressed up for the occasion, wearing a canary yellow suit with a rhinestone brooch on the lapel of the jacket. Christine wondered whether the stones displayed in a flower formation were real diamonds. Margaret always wore heels, the height of which had diminished proportionate to the number of instances her balance had shown signs of instability. Margaret took care of herself. Christine remembered a time during one of her visits when she had found her in a yoga class downstairs, performing better than all other participants considerably younger than she. Margaret looked royal even in her black leotard.

Once the ladies were in front row seats, Christine raced to her car and called Fitzpatrick Realty. After hearing Christine's history with the Maple Street property, the receptionist connected her with Tom, the broker, as she sensed that this case was unique. After Tom Fitzpatrick introduced himself, Christine realized she was speaking with Alice's husband.

"I don't know if you remember me. I moved away a long time ago, and I am in town only for a short time.

Alice actually invited me to sing with Chrysalis at your father-in-law's memorial service."

"Yes, I heard about that. Alice is so pleased you could make it. I am happy as well, believe me, for her sake and more so for her mother's. Kaisa is driving Alice mad with her demands."

Christine could hear the empathy for his wife in his voice. "I'm glad I came." Bringing herself back to business, she said, "I saw my old childhood home listed by you. Would it be possible for me to see it?"

"If you have time right now, I have about an hour."

Christine drove in a daze to Maple Street and was checking on the yard, walking in high, overgrown grass, when Tom's large, rugged vehicle pulled up. He stepped out of the car and straightened to his full height. Although Christine was tall, she had to adjust her neck to look up at Tom. Christine wondered if Tom had lost his hair or if he had shaved his head for ease of care. Tom had a decidedly professional handshake that matched his overall self-assured decorum.

"The house has had some bad luck. The couple who bought the place from your mother moved away a year or so ago. I guess he got a professorship in another state. In spite of all kinds of crying and bellyaching by the neighbors, they sold the house to a fraternity at the college."

Christine looked at Tom sideways from under a wrinkled brow. In her judgmental mind, she immediately formulated negative, stereotypical thoughts about fraternities and imagined the inside of the house to be a disaster of keg-party proportions.

"Now, don't jump to conclusions. It's not as bad as you may think," said Tom. "It's just that when the people who live in the house don't have the same commitment as the owner, you have, let's say, a conflict. It's often the same with rental units. This house has now been empty since Christmastime. The fraternity had some budget problems, and, when it was all said and done, the brotherhood found it best to disband. They are still going through that process." Tom went on, "We have made sure the house had some heat through the winter, so the pipes wouldn't burst, and in the summer, the grass is cut, and so forth."

Tom looked at the hayfield they were standing in, and said sheepishly, "Well, sort of. Of course, in this neighborhood, the grass is always an inch shorter than anywhere else in town. Personally, I've never understood why people want to live on golf course putting greens."

Christine laughed. "I read in a magazine that meticulous housekeeping and extremely short lawns are signs of the couple's sexual frustrations." She regretted opening her mouth as soon as the sentence escaped her lips. What was she thinking?

"Well, I'll never look at my friends the same way again." Tom grinned.

He walked to the front door with a silver key on a rough, wooden keychain piece, identical to the one that might be handed to you in an urgent situation at a second-rate last-chance gas station. The door opened with a swooshing sound of air pressure being equalized between the main door and the glass storm door, through which you could see the masterful carvings on the dark mahogany panels. Tom pushed the door open, letting Christine in ahead of him.

Christine did not observe the few pieces of worn

and broken furniture strewn around, the dirt and dust on the floor, or the juvenile posters on the walls. She saw shiny hardwood floors, oriental rugs with intricate designs in reds, blues, and yellows, a grandfather clock in the corner of the living room. In the dining room, she imagined a long walnut table set for twelve with Carol's finest Spode china, two tiers of sterling silver on each side of the plates. As a child, she had wondered why you had to have a certain shape of fork to eat shrimp and yet another for salad. All the glitter on the table and in the chandelier that sparkled and glimmered as it hung from the high ceiling blinded her in her mind's eye.

In the den, Christine spotted the shelves for wine, the elixir for the birth of the name Chrysalis. What fun they had had! What utter foolishness!

A majestic staircase led up to the bedrooms. She walked up the steps carefully and slowly, as if a faster speed would have burst the bubble, destroyed the fantasy. She counted the steps: eighteen.

This information had come in handy in her high school years, when she returned home in the dark and didn't want to turn on the lights and wake up her parents or her brother. Step number seven had had a particularly loud squeak in spite of numerous efforts by her father to fix it. Christine had gotten used to stepping over step number seven and the telltale sound, thinking every time that she had read this scene in a number of young adult books.

Out of the window of her bedroom, years ago, Christine saw the big maple tree in the back yard. The tree house, a scene of imaginary adventures in the wild jungle or the arctic wilderness, had long since rotted under heavy, wet fall leaves and winter snow. The maple tree, whose dry, gnarly limb had not held Magnus' weight, had caused her brother to crash to the ground and break his forearm. Christine wondered if she should text Magnus about the house. Maybe it was too early for that. She turned around.

"How much, would you say, it would cost to renovate this place?"

"I'm not a contractor, but you can sink a pretty penny into it, if you want to bring it back to its glory days. Of course, you can always do it bit by bit. Are you considering a move back East?"

"I don't know," said Christine. She was not ready to give a definite answer to the question. Was she following an impossible dream? She looked up at Tom and repeated, "I don't know," shook her head, and walked slowly to her car.

On the way back to the B&B, Christine bought a postcard depicting barrels of wine, waterfalls, and lake scenery, and addressed it to her brother with the message: "Visiting Mom. Good to be back in NY. Everything's fine. Chrysalis will sing again at Richard Weston's mem. service. Love, Sis. P.S. Our old house is for sale again."

Chapter 14

Christine arrived back at Long House at 5:30. She was looking forward to dinner with her mother—rich, tasty, Italian food: pasta, sauce, bread, comfort food galore!

Christine knocked on Carol's door. "I'm back," she said joyfully.

"I just took a nap a while ago. What are you up to?" asked her mother.

"We're going to dinner, remember?" Christine regretted her question even before it left her lips. Why on earth would she remind her mother that she was forgetting things! It was odd, but Christine also realized she was raising her voice when speaking with her mother. Carol was forgetful, but there was nothing wrong with her hearing.

"We are? Oh, yes, of course we are. Let me get my pocketbook."

The new Italian restaurant was on the lake. The slope was steep, and, for a few moments, before discovering the small elevator, Christine questioned the restaurant's adherence to the ADA accessibility regulations.

After they were seated and had ordered a glass of wine, Carol said, "You know, I can't handle a real drink any more, but, in my day, I used to put them away."

Christine smiled.

"I remember one time a long time ago," continued Carol, "my friend Shirley had gotten a new car, a bright red Cadillac convertible. She wanted to drive to Syracuse for lunch. We used to do that a lot. This time, it was a gorgeous day, and we ate lunch at the rooftop restaurant in downtown Syracuse, Something Hotel. I think the building was torn down a long time ago. After several drinks, I asked Shirley if she thought they were having a party on a balcony of the high-rise next door. 'Look at all the people!' I said. 'What people?' said Shirley. 'There is only one woman on that balcony.' Well, I guess Shirley got worried, because she asked for the check, and we started to leave. Only, I was dizzy as could be, and my legs didn't hold me. You know, they took me down from the restaurant in a dumb waiter, with a towel tucked into the neck of my dress. I wasn't presentable enough for the public elevator! I never did vomit, though…"

"Mom! You did that?"

"I did, and I am not proud of it. Shirley wasn't sober, either, but we got into the car, and she started driving home. On the way, she missed a curve and drove the car right into Onondaga Lake. There we sat laughing with the front of the car in the lake and me with the towel around my neck… I can't believe nothing happened to us beyond that!"

"How did you get the car out of the lake?"

"There was a good Samaritan with a truck. He pulled us out with a chain. After that day, I was careful with my drinks."

"That's crazy," said Christine. "Who knew? My sophisticated, always-in-control mother had a wild side! Maybe you still do."

"Young and foolish," said Carol and shook her head. They laughed warmly.

Waiting for their dinner to arrive, Carol and Christine exchanged everyday news of no particular importance. Christine kept her visit to the old house a secret from Carol. It quickly became clear to Christine that her mother's sense of reality was shakier than before. However, old memories of Carol's childhood in the 1950s and the early years of her marriage to John were vivid and warm to her. Carol repeated a couple more stories, stories that Christine had heard numerous times before.

The stories made Christine drift into a nostalgic daydream of days of her mother's youth, days of landline phones and regular TV channels with commercials for cigarettes, staples of her mother's youth. Ah, the sexy man with a cigarette dangling from the side of his mouth in the magazine ad, every girl's dream. Probably an improvement from the 1940s, when doctors advertised a particular brand as cigarettes they would smoke themselves.

"Mom, other than Margaret, do you ever see your old friends?" Christine wondered how much Carol's life had actually changed since her move from their house had uprooted her.

"Not much, but you'd better ask some of the staff. You know how my brain is these days. I tend to forget."

Carol cut the lettuce in her salad into tiny pieces and mixed it with her fork, loudly scraping the sides of the small glass bowl. Christine touched her on the wrist and said, "That's probably enough... You don't miss the old friends, the women in the neighborhood, the Lutheran Ladies group, the Knitting Club?"

"I guess sometimes I do. Who's in the Knitting Club again?"

The entrees arrived, lasagna for Carol and chicken Marsala for Christine. They ate without talking, concentrating on their taste experiences as if any outside distractions would spoil the enjoyment. Only the waitress kept disturbing their peace with periodic inquiries about their satisfaction or their need for anything. The inquiries were delivered by Gina, a black-haired beauty whose name was embroidered on the pocket of her blouse. She spoke with a lovely Italian accent, making sure that no word ended with a consonant.

"Any desserta?" The ladies declined the tempting delicacies presented to them on a tray, plastic facsimiles of the real cakes, tortes, and cookies.

"Where in Italy are you from?" asked Christine.

The olive-complected, brown-eyed girl burst out in giggles. She bent over with laughter, then straightened up quickly and said in a whisper, with hints of another accent, "I am actually from Brooklyn. Summer job, you know. I go to college here. Theater major."

"Well, an A+ for this performance." Christine smiled.

"She fooled me," said Carol, when the waitress walked to the next table to take an order from a family with two small boys, who sat in their chairs facing left, right, backwards, and upside down, despite their parents' attempts to have them act like adults. While giving Christine and Carol a quick wink, Gina launched into her best rendition of the Italian accent. Christine leaned toward her mother and said: "There she goes…"

With a loud voice, Carol said,

"Here she comes.
There she goes,
All dressed up in her Sunday clothes.
Nobody knows.
Nobody knows
Whether she wears any underclothes!"

The little boys looked at Carol inquisitively, and one of them lay down on the floor to take a peek under the waitress's bright red skirt.

A moment of parental corrective action followed. The boy sat back up on the chair, his face expressing visible displeasure.

Chapter 15

With a package of cake yeast in her closed fist, Alice knocked on her mother's front door and walked in. The door still wasn't locked. Kaisa was sitting at the kitchen table with an assortment of small items in front of her—safety pins, small batteries, old matchbooks advertising local restaurants, unraveled balls of yarn, and spools of thread.

"I'm cleaning my junk drawer," Kaisa announced.

"I see that. I have one just like it. When it's organized, will it still be called a junk drawer?"

"That's what I will call it." Kaisa dropped a spool of thread. It rolled across the table, onto the floor, and continued toward the hallway on the bright rag rug Kaisa had woven on her loom. Alice had noticed the spool left Kaisa's hand when she'd paused for a second to contemplate the disarray on the table.

Alice bent down, and the stripes of the rug took her back to her childhood. Whenever a rug was released from the loom's torturous medieval stretch machine, Alice would lie down on it on her stomach and sweep her hands across it as if to comfort the freed victim.

She always studied the colors and the patterns.

The twelve-year-old Alice examined the hallway rug. "Here's my nightgown with pictures of baby dolls on it. This stripe was my dress I wore to the elementary school spring concert. Here's Mom's apron from

Finland with reindeer and lynx! This one…this one is my favorite shirt with Finnish designs of bright, bold colors. Mom, I can't believe you cut it up!" Alice had run into her room, hidden her head in the down pillow and cried till she fell asleep. In the clear morning light, things had looked better. She understood her mother had been right. Why save a shirt that hadn't fit her for many years? Alice wondered where that rug was now.

"Mom, I'm putting the yeast in the refrigerator."

"You know," started Kaisa, "I am thinking that I won't be baking bread any more after all. You take it, and if you make cardamom bread sometime, just give me a couple of slices…or buns."

"Are you sure?" Alice was not about to force her mother to bake bread if she didn't want to. Of course, Alice always used yeast in the small pre-measured envelopes most recipes called for, but she could compromise and improvise.

"Alice," said Kaisa with a tone of curiosity. "What do you think about a trip to Finland at the end of the summer, after things have settled down?"

"I think you would enjoy it, Mom. See all the relatives and friends again."

"And, this time, maybe we could go north, cross over to Norway, and put our toes in the North Sea." Kaisa's face brightened. She looked at Alice hopefully.

"We? Who's we?"

"Well, you and I, of course."

"Mom…" The frustration and impending defeat overwhelmed Alice. She would worry about her mother if she traveled alone, but if Kaisa went to Finland by herself, it would give Alice a welcome break, a respite from the reverse parental responsibility.

"Let me think about it."

"Okay. You think about it. Let me know as soon as you can."

"Maybe one of your friends could come with you."

"They don't know my quirks. I wouldn't trust anyone else. I will take care of the cost of the trip for both of us, of course."

Of course. When all else fails, you can always buy me. Alice immediately chastised herself for such loathsome thoughts toward her mother.

"By the way…" Kaisa arranged the safety pins in a small cardboard box labeled Maple Jewelers. "Would you have time to help me with the sauna, if we heat it up right now?"

Alice spun events in her head—papers to correct, Pam's dress to hem. "Sure," she said, and after she texted Tom about getting a frozen pizza out of the freezer, she went over to the thermostat of the sauna. She set it at 180 degrees Fahrenheit and closed the top and bottom vents. She gathered the towels, the shampoo, the soap, and the sponges. She had forgotten to order her mom's soap. She spread the linen bench cloth with images of birch tree branches on the top level. Alice understood that Kaisa, although not hesitant about much, was apprehensive about taking a sauna by herself.

The higher bench was arduous to negotiate, and Kaisa had always wanted a sauna partner to wash her back, believing that this task was impossible to complete well by yourself. Her friends were happy to take a sauna with her, as long as the heat was kept at a "comfortable" level and they could wear their bathing suits or towels. Honestly! "Who takes a bath with clothes on!" Kaisa told her modest friends, who were intimidated by a custom entirely too liberal for them.

After the sauna was heated, Alice opened the vents and filled the water bucket, and Kaisa and Alice settled on their perch on the upper level. Alice threw a ladleful of water on the gray, rough rocks on the stove. A hot, hissing, sizzling heat enveloped them. They breathed through their mouths, so as not to burn their nostrils, closed their eyes, and let the sultry flush take over their bodies and minds.

Several throws of water later, their pores opened, and toxins poured out with pearls of liquid. It was not perspiration but pure, unadulterated sweat that, for a while, took with it the tremors and uneasy steps from Kaisa, and the annoyances, resentments, and stresses from Alice. They repeated the process of hot heat to cool shower two more times. Alice scrubbed her mother's back in confident up-and-down strokes with a natural loofah sponge, pushing down hard at Kaisa's urging.

"I will sleep well tonight," said Alice, thinking of the therapeutic effects of the sauna.

"Did you order my soap?" asked Kaisa.

Chapter 16

"Pam," Alice called to her daughter, "I need to see Gavin for a couple of minutes after dinner. We could go for ice cream on the same trip, if you'd like. You know, at the new stand on the lake."

"Sure," said Pamela, "as long as I don't have to talk to him. Well, that didn't come out right." Pam smiled. "He's okay. I just...I just...I mean...you know, it's weird talking to teachers outside of school."

"I know. It can be boring. Of course, Gavin is no longer a teacher. But, no problem. Grab your phone or a book to take with you or something."

Pamela had been quiet recently, and Alice had begun to wonder whether her own busy life was affecting her daughter. Twinges of guilt crept into her consciousness. Going for ice cream was nice but certainly could not be considered quality time between a mother and a daughter. Or could it be that these simple unceremonious moments were just what they needed?

The Pure Earth farm spread out on fertile acres of land on top of the east hill of the lake, allowing the sun to wrap the farm in its warmth for a greater part of the day. Gavin Koladziejski was growing grains and potatoes, soy and hops. In addition, he had a large vegetable garden of root vegetables, beans, and greens, surrounded by an unnaturally high fence to keep out the white-tail deer, known to jump over anything lower than twelve feet. Although Pure Earth was certified only for certain crops, Gavin used organic methods for growing everything on his farm. He acknowledged to himself that where he had previously been the teacher, he was now unequivocally the student. He patted himself on the back for having hired staff who had more expertise than he, making him the smartest of all.

Gavin's border collie, Rufus, bounded to greet Alice and Pam through the still-green goldenrod field and the honeysuckle bushes. Gavin appeared from under a tractor he was fixing, and greeted them.

"Come with me. I'd like to show you something."

He walked up a path bordered by blooming peonies and irises. Rufus ran around shepherding the three.

Alice admired the large flowers of pink and red peonies, pointing out tiny ants on the petals.

"I'm waiting for the peony rain," said Gavin. "It always comes at the end of June, just when the blooms are at their most beautiful, always before Crystal has a chance to pick some—a torrential rain that pounds them all to the ground."

They arrived at the edge of a meadow full of milkweed plants, the favorite of monarch butterflies. On the side of the field stood an old ruin of a shed, the farm's previous owner's storage for garden tools.

"I am not taking this wreck down for a reason," said Gavin. "Look!" He pointed at the eaves above the windows with only cobwebs as panes. There were several chrysalises hanging from the weather-beaten eaves—shiny, smooth, light green, oriental lanterns in a neat row, dangling by their own silk like threads of white glue.

"Wow!" Pamela was enthralled.

Alice stared at the row of miniature pendants.

"Just like us, the quartet, hanging by a thread, still waiting to peel ourselves out of the cover." Alice said it to herself too softly for the others to hear.

"For some reason, the caterpillars love to settle on these eaves and grow their chrysalises to wrap around themselves like a blanket. They also love this old apple tree and the rose bush under it." Gavin pointed at a gnarly, peeling, crusty tree whose apple-producing days had, most likely, ended decades ago. The tree spread its numerous arms out like Vishnu, the Hindu goddess, offering a sanctuary for the birth process. The chrysalises hung suspended in the air, some new and fresh, some transparent, making it possible to see the developing monarchs through the thin walls. Some hung empty, torn, and colorless, having completed their protective task as a womb. Alice and Pamela were fascinated by the stages of the metamorphosis.

"This is so cool!" Pamela couldn't contain herself.

Encouraged by her enthusiasm, Gavin explained the whole genesis of the monarch, promising to lend Pamela some books on the subject. A detail that captivated Alice the most was the changing number of legs in the maturing process. In the chrysalis, the caterpillar has three pairs of true legs and four pairs of false or prolegs. However, the fully developed monarch has only three pairs of legs. *Which one of the Chrysalis quartet is the one extra pair left behind at the emergence of the magnificent creature supported by three pairs of legs?*

"Mom!" called Pamela twice.

Alice shook her head as if waking up. "Sorry, I was

somewhere else."

Alice asked Pamela to give Gavin and her some privacy. Rufus was ready to occupy Pam's time and promptly brought her a yellow hard-cloth frisbee.

The incident in the classroom regarding the Civil War had bothered Alice enough to seek Gavin's opinion in person.

"I can understand that the statement by Beau and the interaction of the students bothers you. If it is not dealt with head on, yet with care, it can fester. Also, you may have some feedback from the parents. I would suggest you see about inviting a guest lecturer from the university to address the issue. The school year is almost over, but it's worth a try. In the meantime, adhere to the curriculum the rest of the school weeks." Gavin was able to relax her to a degree with his calm demeanor, yet Alice added the divisive issue to her list of "things to worry about."

At the "Scoop of the Day" ice cream stand, Pam picked pistachio ice cream in a waffle cone. Alice chose a regular cone with maple walnut. They sat in turquoise Adirondack chairs by the water's edge, listening to the waves hitting the rocks, a great spot for an ice cream stand, previously a rundown bait shop. The cool breeze from the lake felt comforting on their faces. The hot and humid end of June in upstate New York was almost here.

"Just imagine," said Alice, "the monarch only has three legs when it comes out of the chrysalis!"

"You mean three pairs." Pam was smiling. Both of them pictured three-legged butterflies tipping over like a row of fragile, drunken ballet dancers. They burst out laughing.

Chapter 17

Another glorious June morning had arrived. The west hill wineries' grape vines shone green and lush in the early morning sun. The long, narrow lake reflected the sun in luminous tips of the waves. On calmer surfaces, the water striders appeared to be moving erratically on top of the water.

I've traveled all over the world, but here is where I want to be.

Lola was skillful in maneuvering her kayak, paddling almost without a sound, as the blade of the paddle cut through the surface of the water. When she first started looking for a kayak to buy, a couple of years ago, she was overwhelmed by the number of choices. She was certain she did not want a kayak requiring skills of an Alaskan native, or training in turning the kayak over and back upright, her body trapped up to the waist underwater in a cocoon tied with rawhide. She had seen them in Anchorage and was terrified about using one herself. To her great relief, choices for her had been numerous, and she had chosen the open cockpit style, light enough for her to carry by herself. She needed openness, not confinement. She was as strong as her recently acquired friends in Slovenia, the much younger women heaving heavy mounds of hay into the barn and moving hundred-pound milk cans from the cow barn into the flat of a truck. Her strength allowed for vigorous paddling.

Between her feet, anchored in place by her ankles, Lola guarded an old plastic bucket that once had held wallpaper paste. The bucket was full of flowers freed from her overgrown garden, rescued from the strangling sticky cleavers and burning nettles—she had bee balm and day lilies, columbine and foxglove in a natural bouquet.

"Gorgeous morning!" Lola called as she paddled past an old man sitting in his rowboat, bent over, staring at the water a few feet in front of him, where a little red-and-white bobber sat perfectly still, attached to the fishing pole by what appeared to be green dental floss.

"Sure is," said the old man, touching his free hand to the visor of his baseball cap.

"Catch anything?"

"Ain't seen nothin' yet," said the man.

"You will. Good luck!" Lola paddled on.

On the opposite shore, she got out of the kayak, picked up the flower bucket, and set it on the dock of Crystal's condominium building. She pulled the kayak farther onto the shore and, with the colorful bouquet in her arms, walked to the door like a bride. She let herself in the hallway with a key and knocked on her daughter's condo door adorned with a wreath made of wine bottle corks. Crystal answered the knock in the yellow pajamas Lola had once sent to her from Japan, bright yellow silk with cherry blossoms embroidered in white adorning the collar and the hems of the sleeves. Her curly hair was uncombed, and it was obvious Lola had woken her.

"Hi," said Lola. She did not give Crystal a chance to respond. "Here. These are from my garden. I won't stay. Sorry I woke you up."

Lola stepped backwards, one step between each pronouncement.

"It's okay, Mom. The flowers are lovely. I'm glad to have them. Thank you." Crystal surprised herself with a corresponding staccato answer.

Lola had backed almost to the outside door. "I'll talk to you later." Lola waved and disappeared through the doorway to the other side of the door. She started back to her kayak while settling sunglasses on her nose. She would need them on the return trip, paddling into the light of the bright orb.

Crystal, her sweet child... She had almost named her Ruby, for vitality, but chose a more generic Crystal to encompass all good qualities from the rocks of the earth. Her love child. She was so fortunate to have her in her life.

Chapter 18

Margaret was waiting anxiously by her living room window with its view of the woods and the parking lot. Lola, her partner in crime in their New York City days, was back in the country. Lola had promised to take Margaret out to dinner, just like the young Lola had had a habit of doing in Manhattan. They used to take turns competing in who could find the most exotic, out-of-the-way restaurants that tested their taste buds with unknown spices and ingredients they could only guess at. They were not afraid of burning their mouths or eating vegetables that grew in dung. Margaret was, however, careful to leave out dairy for a day or two before a performance, in order to avoid a phlegm attack during an aria.

Lola drove in and parked under a large black walnut tree. Her car was neon green, and, to Margaret, it appeared to be only half a car, with someone having removed the back end.

"Brilliant," Margaret said to herself, as if envying the style with which Lola lived her life, not giving a tinker's dam about the opinions of others. She, too, had thoroughly enjoyed that lifestyle, supported somewhat by her fame, which was significant enough to give her liberties, but not so immense that the whole world knew her name, her career, and her private life.

Lola looked up at Margaret in the window and

waved to her, not just with her hand, but the whole length of her bracelet-covered arm. Margaret waved back. Her hand reflexively went to her throat, and she fingered her string of pearls that matched the studs in her earlobes. Lola was smiling ear to ear, and Margaret hoped she was in for a night that knocked her socks off. At her age, it didn't take much, she figured. She grabbed her clutch purse and locked the door behind her. Lola greeted her by the car with a kiss on each cheek and opened the car door for her.

Lola drove along the lake and took a turn up a steep hill to a group of fir trees. Under the canvas of tall pines stood a small building—constructed not as expected of lumber or logs but of straw faced with mud. On top, a thatched roof covered the house like a troll hat.

"How quaint, indeed," said Margaret, reinforcing her unexpressed thought. She knew the culinary experience was going to be equally unique.

A handsome man with the mustache and eyes of Omar Sharif came out of the building, a long white apron covering his bright red jeans.

"Welcome!" He took Lola into his wide embrace, rocking back and forth, holding tight. He repeated the action with Margaret, who had to struggle to keep steady on the uneven ground.

"Meet Yusuf," said Lola. "We all call him Joe."

"So very pleased to make your acquaintance," said Margaret.

"Come on in. I have dinner almost ready." Joe went in ahead of them, holding the door open, and as a welcoming gesture handed each a glass of raki at the threshold.

They entered the house, where the aromas of the food on the stove sent them into a different world, a world of bazaars and mosaics, evil eye amulets, and women with mysterious veils.

After a salad, a meat dish appeared. The ground meat, wrapped in lettuce leaves, was arranged around the edge of a plate like swaddled babies, surrounding a dish of lemon wedges.

"*Cig köfte!* For your enjoyment!" said Joe. "Be careful. There is hot pepper paste in it. The hot pepper cooks the meat."

Margaret and Lola looked at each other. They had eaten cig köfte before and knew the burn that was about to hit them. The two ladies each took a bundle of meat, squeezed lemon juice on it, and bit into the soft mixture. The tastes mixed together pleasurably in the first bite. Gradually, the burn started. Lola's face turned bright pink, while Margaret wiped tears off her cheeks. Both were fighting to keep the cough reflex from taking over.

"The first bite is always the hardest," croaked Lola, reaching for a piece of flat bread to calm the burn.

"Indeed," said Margaret inaudibly, with her larynx obviously compromised.

"This was one of the best!" Margaret later complimented her friend on her choice of dining establishments.

"Joe does this for friends. He does not run a restaurant."

"At least not legally..." Margaret was not quite certain about the arrangement, but that only added to the intrigue.

"Please, have a seat outside. I will bring coffee to

you." Joe showed the direction of the door to the ladies.

Margaret and Lola settled on rattan garden seats set side by side, breathing in the sappy smell of pine all around them. Soon, Joe appeared with a copper tray of small, ornate coffee cups and glasses of water, and set it on the table. The tablecloth was embroidered with threads of countless colors, a testimony of appreciation to the handiwork and diligent fingers performing it.

Joe instructed the ladies to cleanse their palates with water before engaging in another experience of the senses, the aromatic strong Turkish coffee with grounds still on the bottom of the cup.

"Did you know, ladies, that in Turkey, long ago, a woman could divorce her husband if he did not give her enough coffee?"

"That's only right and proper, to be sure," said Margaret, feigning seriousness.

"Interesting combination," said Lola, "pine forest and Turkish delights."

"Splendid!" said Margaret, shaking her head slowly. "Do you remember when we were supposed to go see *Jesus Christ Superstar* on Broadway, but got deep into a discussion about our men? We were drinking raki and missed the show entirely."

"Do I!" Lola remembered a night of laughter and crying. She was so very much in love with a man who could not, would not, commit himself to her, yet could not tear himself away from her, either. That night, in a small Mediterranean restaurant, Margaret had, for the first time, confided in her that she had had—and continued to have—a lover whom she saw only infrequently, an arrangement that suited them well.

"But," Margaret had said, "You know, no man

could stand us in the long run."

Lola looked up at the dimming sky. "Why didn't you two get married?"

"He wasn't mine to have." Margaret closed her eyes and laid her head on her friend's shoulder. Lola felt the sadness travel from Margaret to her own body, her heart, her soul.

"And why didn't you ever marry?" asked Margaret.

"I'm not the marrying kind."

Chapter 19

Alice was washing windows at her mother's house. In addition to changing curtains, Kaisa's custom was to clean windows for Summer Solstice and Christmas. She followed an old Finnish tradition of changing the atmosphere of the rooms by welcoming all possible light into the house through sheers in the summer months, and allowing for privacy and comfort in the winter with the help of heavy drapes.

Staying within the style of the house, each window had twelve panes, which meant forty-eight corners for each window. With twenty-two windows in the house, that made one thousand fifty-six corners. Each window had an inside and an outside, making it two thousand one hundred and twelve corners. *That couldn't be!* Alice's own house was a modern ranch with large panoramic windows, tall and wide, cleanable in a few firm strokes of a cleaning wand and a squeegee. Kaisa's windows were lovely but laborious, and Alice had suggested that Kaisa hire professionals to do the task.

"Professionals or not, they always leave streaks. Now, if you can't do it, I'll consider it, but nobody does the job as well as you do."

Alice was overcome with happiness, basking in her mother's approval, while also seething at her inability to put her foot down and insist that the task be outsourced.

"I'll have to do a couple of windows at a time," said Alice, getting ready to leave for the day.

"That's fine," said Kaisa, hiding her hand behind her back as unobtrusively as possible. As she stood still, saying goodbye, her hand's tremor was visible.

"I was just wondering," she continued, "When do you think you'll be making the cardamom bread?"

"I don't know," Alice sighed. "Soon." She tried not to sound annoyed.

Alice drove faster than usual and almost missed a red light, coming to it too fast, and vacillating between the two meanings of the yellow light—go as fast as you can or slam on your brakes. She stopped the car on the crosswalk. With cars behind her, she was stuck. Alice opened the car window and called out her apologies to the pedestrians who were skirting her car by walking in front of it, having to veer from the walk that was rightfully theirs.

Once in her kitchen, Alice took eggs, milk, butter, and the cake yeast out of the refrigerator. While they came to room temperature, she threw a load of laundry into the washing machine and put a cabbage-and-ground-beef casserole into the oven. Everyone would be home for dinner tonight.

Alice made the dough that would become *pulla*, a braided Finnish cardamom coffee bread. It could also be shaped into rolls of various types or round-bellied pulla boys with raisins for bellybuttons, her children's favorites a few years back. With dinner over, and the dishes done, Alice peeked under the towel covering the rising dough in the large ceramic bowl. It looked like a bloated, pale belly. After washing her hands, she scooped it out of the bowl and started working it on the large wooden baking surface. Alice punched the dough down, decreasing its size by a third. She kneaded it with her hands, working air into it, letting the elastic fibers become more and more pliable. She punched it, leaving the mark of knuckles on the bouncy softness. She punched it again, harder. She saw a tear drop from her eye into the dough. Her sight turned fuzzy. She worked the dough. More tears fell. She hit the large ball with all her might, punching it hard with quick strikes originating in her shoulder. She was sobbing with audible gasps, as the dough folded in the salt of the tears.

"Shhhhh." Tom grasped her shoulders and turned her around. Alice hid her wet face in the softness of his fleece. She cried silently, and Tom let her.

"Let me help here," said Tom. "Pam, Bobby!" he called out. "We're all going to make pulla."

As the family rolled long skinny and lumpy plats and learned to braid with four strands instead of three, Alice resisted the urge to smooth the pieces, to make them perfect. They placed the completed breads on oven sheets and set them aside to rise again, to become smoother and larger.

Tom made some coffee, took two mugs, and met Alice on the deck. The crickets and the tree frogs were chirping in the warmth of the evening.

"Are you all right?" asked Tom.

"I am now." Alice turned toward Tom. "My mom is driving me crazy! If it weren't for the memorial service and Chrysalis, I would go mad. I can't wait to get together with the girls."

"Give your mother some slack. She hasn't dealt with your dad's death yet, and her own health is questionable. She is, most likely, very scared."

"You're right. With all the end-of-school issues to deal with on top of everything else, I have a bit too much on my plate. Mom just irritates me no end. I'm sorry."

"Don't be sorry. I understand your feelings. You can always use me as a sounding board. Of course, I am not as receptive as your female friends."

"Oh, stop! You are the best." Alice gave Tom a kiss on the cheek.

"Speaking of your friends," said Tom, "Christine Thurston looked at her old house and seemed quite interested in buying it."

"You're kidding me! She would move back here? Into this little town?"

"She didn't say, but she did talk about possibly renovating the house."

"Hmmm," said Alice quizzically.

Chapter 20

Frasier yawned luxuriously on top of the ebony grand piano. He stretched his legs out straight, spreading his paws as if to air the tight warm spaces between the toes. The taupe-colored long hair danced in the air as he licked his belly to remove dirt only he was aware of.

Lisa moved the cat gently to the sofa, opened the lid of the piano, and hinged it to stay up with a lid prop. She played Dvorak's "Humoresque" lightheartedly. Chrysalis was about to be reunited in a few minutes. She looked forward to the rebirth of the group, an unlikely combination of women whose interests and careers were wildly different from each other. With next to the last bar, the doorbell rang.

There is something magically uniting about music. And on that thought, Lisa opened the front door to Alice, the first to arrive.

Alice opened her baskets, made of willow reed by a local elderly gentleman, revealing an assortment of homemade hors d'oeuvres.

"Some of these are my mother's recipes. You know, herring in sixty different ways, and cheeses, always cheeses."

"I don't know how you do it!" said Lisa, bringing out her own contribution of various local wines—rich, deep reds, prize-winning Rieslings, pink rosés, and a bottle of sparkling ice wine. Ice wine was produced only under the most favorable circumstances, when the freezing temperatures of Upstate New York turned the grapes into sugar. Although entirely too sweet for many people's taste, the unique wine was a source of pride for the few local producers, and Lisa was happy to include it in her dessert wine collection. An old small copper tub served as an ice bucket for the whites.

Alice set her assortment on the dining room table, turned around, and almost tripped on Niles, whose eyes stared at her quizzically. *I wonder if the herring will be safe.*

Christine and Crystal arrived at the same time. Christine produced boxes of chocolates from her bag, and Crystal, having walked the few blocks from her condo, dropped her backpack on the black-and-white checkered floor of the foyer. The bag revealed three albums of photographs of Chrysalis' various performances, including pictures of their earliest appearances in coordinated outfits.

"I've been meaning to digitize these, but somehow I just haven't gotten to it."

"Mine are organized and stored on iCloud," said Christine, immediately regretting opening her mouth. Her statement somehow made her sound superior, and that certainly wasn't her intention.

"I mean, I had a lot of time after my divorce," she attempted to save the situation.

"If you don't mind my asking," said Alice, "what did happen with your marriage? If you're uncomfortable telling us, I understand."

Lisa and Crystal were equally curious about what had led to Christine's divorce, but looked around apprehensively. They were happy Alice had asked the question, yet at the same time disapproving of her having done so.

"I don't mind," said Christine. This part of her past did not fit her image of the powerful executive director, but Christine felt that sharing her most regrettable experience with her Chrysalis sisters would bring them closer together. "Theodore Fairfax Thurston the Third"—Christine lifted her head and stretched her upper lip over her upper incisors while forming an "o" and looked down the bridge of her nose—"was two people. We met at a cocktail party fundraiser for Bill Bevilaqua, a colleague of his who ran for state senator. I had used Bill's expertise in legal matters in my business."

"I didn't even know your husband was a lawyer," said Alice.

"No one knows much, let me tell you. The whole affair, from the first meeting to the divorce, lasted only a couple of months."

Alice, Lisa, and Crystal sat expectantly like hatchlings waiting for food.

"When I met him, I was completely taken by the tall, dark, handsome man with the looks and mannerisms of Cary Grant at his best in the old movies. He even had the same cleft in his chin. Well-dressed, impeccable manners, showing intense interest in me right from the start."

"Well, look at you," said Crystal, "blonde, blue-eyed, tall, queenly. Can you blame him?"

"I blame him for being a phony. I was so infatuated with him that I agreed to marry him without thinking twice."

"What made you marry him so soon after meeting him?" asked Lisa.

So that I could beat you to marriage. Christine said, "I guess I thought I was in love, whatever that means."

"Who said that? Somebody famous said that once," Alice seemed to remember.

"I think it was Prince Charles. He said that to the reporters after getting engaged to Princess Diana." Crystal recalled seeing the old news clips.

Christine continued, "After the wedding, the on-the-spur-of-the-moment dinner flights to Vancouver became dinners at home. Ted shelled out constant criticism about the way I ran my business, about my habits, and about my cooking. He even wanted to send me to a culinary class for chefs."

"Geez, you are a good cook. What was he thinking?" Alice was incensed.

"Pretty soon, it became clear that he wanted a trophy wife who was perfect in every room of the house, if you know what I mean." The women exchanged meaningful glances. "I also had to sail, and play tennis and golf. Soon he let me know he was going to follow Bill's footsteps and run for office, any office and—get this—end up in the White House! He was grooming me to be the First Lady. At that point, I had had enough, and basically walked out of his life."

"Oh, man," said Alice. "Just think—Chrysalis could have sung at the White House, and you closed the door to it. How could you do this to us?"

Everybody laughed.

"I guess our glory days are in these albums," said Crystal, lifting them up.

Looking at the old pictures, memories flooded the room. They reminisced about various performances at county fairs and school concerts. The highlights were competitions they won not only in local events but several states away during school breaks. No one could remember what had happened to the vulgar, huge trophy they had won in Ohio.

"Well," said Lisa, clapping her hands together, "shall we warm up, before the wine does the warming?" She sat at the piano, and the "opening of the voices" commenced: scales on numerous levels, lip and tongue exercises with nonsense syllables, breath support techniques.

"We didn't do this way back when," said Alice.

"Have you forgotten? We did, but not every time," remembered Lisa. "only when Mrs. Jones was with us. If we practiced on our own, we didn't bother."

"Let's do something fun first," said Alice, suggesting some pieces with close harmony, such as "Don't Sit Under the Apple Tree" and "Boogie Woogie Bugle Boy." Lisa found the background tracks for the music, and the room filled with World War II tunes that could be heard several houses away.

After a few successful practice rounds of songs targeted for the memorial service, the women congratulated each other for "still having it," opened more wine bottles, and toasted themselves and each other.

Alice couldn't contain herself any longer. "So, Christine, I hear you looked at your old house. I know, I'm not really supposed to know, but I guess Tom was so surprised that he just blurted it out. Are you thinking of moving back here?" Lisa and Crystal turned to

Christine in anticipation of an answer.

Christine took a long sip of wine and swallowed it. "You know, now that the house is available, my missing the area got the best of me. I have so many great memories here, the scenery is gorgeous, and I always did love the house. And, of course, Mom isn't getting any younger or better. But what would I do here? I could possibly run my company remotely," she pondered, "although that sounds too unruly. I do like the house, even the way it looks now. I will probably look at it again."

Alice was excited.

"Why not? Of course, you can telecommute. Loads of people do that these days."

"Maybe," said Christine quietly. "I am worried about my mother and her future. Being so far away from her is not easy. Not that I could in any way slow down her dementia, but I somehow feel I am neglecting her." She stared ahead of her, seeing nothing.

"I have the same feeling about my mother, and I'm right here," chimed in Alice, pouring herself another glass of Pinot Noir. "I know the time will come when she has to move out of her house, and I know she'll do anything to avoid it. She already can't function too well. She pretends to be self-sufficient, but if it weren't for me, she'd be in trouble."

"I hate to say this," said Crystal, "but I feel that no matter what you do, your mother is impossible to please. You run yourself ragged, only to get criticism and more demands placed on you."

Alice turned abruptly to face Crystal. "It's easy for you to say! Your mother acts like she's younger than we are, trotting around the world with strange..." Alice stopped in mid-sentence.

Crystal's face fell. She looked at Alice with amazement.

Alice looked lost. "No, I mean…I didn't mean…I am so sorry. I didn't mean it like that. But you have to admit Lola is not a traditional mother figure." Alice realized she had stepped onto thin ice with both feet in heavy boots.

The old grandfather clock ticked audibly.

"Well," Crystal broke the icy silence. "It wasn't fair of me to say what I did about your mother, either. I'm sorry. Isn't it odd that our mothers have such a strong hold on us, as different as they are from each other?"

She walked over to the table, poured herself another glass of wine, filled her small plate with cheese and grapes, and settled down on a fainting couch. She almost lifted her legs onto the seat as well, but thought better of it, not wanting to look like a privileged woman in a movie about ancient Rome.

"What is it about mothers?" said Christine. "You two live in the same town with your moms, but I am miles away and still feel guilty about what I do and don't do when it comes to Mom. I thought it was a matter of distance."

"Phooey." Alice stepped to the window and opened it. "It's not about physical distance. It's about emotional distance."

"What do you mean? I'm thousands of miles away, both physically and emotionally." Christine joined Alice at the window.

Lisa looked up. "Have you ever considered that you are a distant person in general? And don't get me wrong—there is nothing wrong with it. I just wouldn't call you a warm fuzzy."

Encouraged by Lisa's assessment, Alice added, "Right. You are more of a cool cucumber. I have always envied your organizational ability and level-headedness. You have it all together. I am the opposite of you, a total ditz." Alice glanced alternately at Crystal and Lisa. "Can you believe me, I even called Christine at four in the morning and woke her up."

"Forget about that already," Christine chided Alice and hesitated before adding, "And thank you, I guess. What seems like a good quality to you may be a curse to me." After a short pause, she toughened herself and said, "For this 'coolness' I have spent years in therapy and only just lately have made some real progress. Otherwise, I would never have taken three weeks off and released control of my business."

"Good for you," said Crystal.

"Do you really feel that being in Seattle has separated you from your mother emotionally?" asked Lisa.

"I do," said Christine.

Alice was thoughtful. "You know, sometimes a little space is good. It would be for me. Like Crystal said, I am my mother's slave."

"But you can be in charge of that," chimed in Crystal from her couch. "You are allowing your mother to control you."

Alice turned to face her.

"But she has given me so much. And right now, with my father gone, I need to cut her some slack."

"Some slack is good," said Crystal, "but think about it. You are doing it at the expense of your mental health."

"Are you saying that I'm nuts?"

"Not in the least! I am saying that you are stressed. You do need to think about yourself and your family. My mother stresses me in a different way. I am constantly wondering what she will think of doing next, what possible danger she will put herself in, what questionable character she will associate with, where she will travel and with whom."

"So I was right!" said Alice.

"Yes, you were, and you know, come to think of it, I don't even remember when my mother last said, 'I love you' to me. Must have been when I was a kid. And how many times have I tried to have her tell me who my father is? I have the right to know! Mom just closes up entirely. The only piece of information she has ever given me about my dad is that I was born of a great love. That just doesn't quite do it for me." Crystal had tears in her eyes. Alice sat down with Crystal and put her arms around her.

Lisa, who had not participated much in the discussion, got up from her quiet corner and faced her friends. "You know, what I wouldn't give to have my mom back again."

A quiet stillness fell on the room.

They heard a strangled sound, turned their heads, and saw Frasier vomit on the ornate Turkish rug.

Chapter 21

Christine woke up late again. The slow pace of the countryside had relaxed her. A soft fog rose from the lake, creating a curtain of gentle invisibility. A thunderstorm during the night had cooled the air, and, strangely, Christine felt relieved. This was the weather she was used to. She was also relieved that after the storm of emotions, the evening had ended with musing about the older generation and a feeling of togetherness.

Number 84 Maple Street was on her mind, gnawing at her, ignoring her attempts to put the house out of her thoughts. It was 9:05 am. Tom Fitzpatrick would be at work by now. She pushed her index finger on his name on her phone. They agreed to meet in the afternoon.

After going through the house again and making sure the more mundane but important aspects of the house were solid—that the foundation, plumbing, roof, heating, and electric were not going to cause a large expense in the short run—Christine said, "Let's go for coffee somewhere and discuss this. I think I'd like to put an offer on the house."

"What do you think I should go in with?" Christine stirred her black coffee for no reason.

"Well…" Tom thoughtfully pinched the sides of his lower lip, making his mouth look like that of a fish, "The neighborhood is the best in town, the house is basically in good condition, just needs a few cosmetic spruce-ups, and it has a good-sized yard. On the other hand, the interior is dated and the landscaping has gotten out of hand. Also, don't forget that the financial situation of the now non-existent fraternity is pretty bleak, so they may accept a lower offer. What if we go in at about twenty thousand under the asking price?"

"Let's try even lower. It's not like buyers are flocking their way, right? They can always make a counteroffer. Thirty thousand below?"

"Thirty below it is. I'll start on the paperwork and let you know when it's ready to sign." Tom got into his SUV and drove away. Two hours later, Christine had signed a purchase offer.

She felt a fluttering in her stomach. Was she doing the right thing? Was she acting too impulsively, relying on her emotions rather than using her brain? She could still back out. She hadn't signed anything binding. She wanted to talk to Alice about this, but Alice was Tom's wife, and bringing her into this would put her in an uncomfortable situation. *Lisa has a level head.* She would talk to Lisa.

Sitting on Lisa's porch in the evening, the two accomplished, strong women felt vulnerable and hesitant. Lisa had opened the door to Christine pink-eyed and blotchy-faced. She could barely utter, "Come on in."

"Are you okay?" Christine hugged Lisa.

"I'll be all right. Just came back from the vet's office. Frasier is full of cancer—or was." Lisa's lower lip quivered. "I agreed to let him go. According to Dr. Gordon, he was in a great deal of pain. Funny thing, I would not have thought so from the way he acted, other than the stomach issues. Dr. Gordon said it would just get more and more painful." She sighed. "You know, I can look at this same issue much more clearly in my job, although cancer and pain are horrendous regardless of who the patient is. Frasier will be cremated, and I'll bury him under the forsythia bush." Lisa burst into tears, pointing to a large shrub at the corner of the house.

"I can come another time..." said Christine hesitantly.

"No, no, it's good for me to think of something else. How about some iced tea?"

A while later, they were settled on the comfortable porch furniture, amongst colorful flowers in the window boxes and hanging baskets.

"I'm in trouble," started Christine. "I made an offer on my old house, and I have no real idea why. Something came over me. I'm perfectly happy in Seattle with my job, with my personal life, and yet I decided to buy an old wreck of a house, not even sure if I could actually live in it. Of all the unrealistic plans!" She ran her hands through her hair. "I am financially comfortable, but I don't have money to burn. It's crazy to think I would move here, isn't it?" Her voice was trailing.

"It's not for me to say, and I am probably the last person you should ask." Lisa adjusted the cushion behind her. "If my mother were still alive and I had a chance to be near her, I certainly would."

Christine looked at Lisa, studying her professionally cared-for face. Lisa meant what she just said. Christine remembered the previous evening's discussion about mothers and smiled.

She got up from the wicker chair, and started pacing.

"This is difficult. My mother means so much to me, but I have created a whole new life, and somehow there hasn't been room for my family in it. Is this what happens when your parents get older? They wake you up? They make you realize what is important?"

"I wouldn't know," said Lisa. "I can only imagine."

Christine felt empty and odd. Would she feel different if her mother had died a while ago? Was Lisa being unrealistically sentimental about her potential feelings toward her mother in the event she had not died? How would she ever know?

"This is the thing," said Christine. "How on earth would I run my company from here? Should I sell it? Let go of my life's work in the prime of my career?" Christine dismissed the thought of letting go of her company as totally irrational.

"I guess you'll have to figure out what your life's goals are from now on," said Lisa pedantically. "I'd love to see you in town, but this is a much bigger decision than whether or not to buy a building."

Chapter 22

The sunset was reflected in the large windows of Long House, making the building appear to be on fire. Christine walked into the lobby and saw Margaret placing the long spout of a watering can into a flowerpot. "Hello," she said.

Margaret lifted her head from under an elephant plant frond and spotted Christine. "I know you want to see your mother, but might I bend your ear for a moment?"

You might, thought Christine, but said, "Of course," as they walked to the chairs facing each other by the fireplace.

Margaret hesitated for a moment. "I've been meaning to talk to you about this, but I don't quite know how to put it…"

Christine became curious and even alarmed. Margaret adjusted the hem of her skirt and continued, "Your mother concerns me. It appears she has lost her lust for life, let's say. Although I didn't know her very well years ago, I remember her being livelier and very particular about her appearance. Now, she just doesn't seem to care."

Christine nodded as Margaret spoke. "Mom's dementia is progressing. I realize that, but one thing you need to know about my mother is that she can be a great chameleon. She will be one person in front of you and another, totally different woman in someone else's presence. This has always been the case. She could discuss world politics with my father's friends at a cocktail party in an animated, knowledgeable way, and you'd think she, instead of my father, was the political science professor. In the kitchen replenishing the hors d'oeuvres, she would pretend a yawn and call her guests a 'bunch of bores.' The next day, she would exchange cookie recipes over the backyard fence with the next-door neighbor using a completely different demeanor and vocabulary level."

Margaret frowned. "That's not what I mean exactly. Carol just doesn't seem to care about anything. In the last couple of years, she has paid no attention to her appearance. She allows the staff to pick out her clothes and her jewelry to wear, and they just don't have the taste or the inclination to pay attention. You know, one day, I found her sitting in her chair with a pair of awful white cotton stockings rolled halfway up her leg!"

"She has been very nicely dressed whenever I have seen her," defended Christine.

"Well!" The word of indignation was uttered with a strong puff of air. "The first day you came, Carol and I were going to the concert, and I had taken care that she was appropriately dressed. The other times, it was a known fact that you were in town, and the staff were on alert." Margaret tilted her head and shook it rhythmically to show her dissatisfaction.

"You have to be an advocate for yourself around here. I can't imagine what happens in the units where skilled nursing care is required. You have heard about the bedsores and people sitting in wet diapers all day. It all starts with rolled-up cotton stockings. That is why I am keeping busy and moving my body to avoid such a fate."

Christine was thoughtful. "I don't know about cotton stockings. I admire you for keeping busy. Are you saying that my mother could have prevented her dementia somehow?"

"Heavens, no," said Margaret. "I am only wondering what could be done to make sure Carol's dignity is preserved."

"I appreciate your concern, Margaret. Maybe dignity isn't a matter of white cotton stockings. Maybe the color and material of her hose do not matter to her. Those of us who still can, we pay attention to superficial things, but, in the long run, are her stockings that important?"

"Of course they are, my dear! You let go of one little thing, and it is downhill from there."

Margaret got up, picked up her watering can, and reached up to a spider plant in a hanging basket. She quickly put down her arm, changed the watering can to her other hand, and grabbed her back.

"Are you all right?" Christine said worriedly.

"Of course. Why?" said Margaret and limped to the philodendron on the side table.

Chapter 23

When Crystal arrived at Gavin's farm, she leaned her bicycle against a split rail fence. What a joy it was to ride through the countryside in good weather, even if the last hill up to the Pure Earth farm was a test of her quads. She hung her helmet on the handlebars and looked for Gavin. He was never easy to locate, and she had to rely on the cell phone to find him.

Accompanied by Rufus, as always, Gavin appeared from behind the barn dressed in soil-covered jeans and a green-and-red-plaid shirt with sleeves rolled up.

"I have Christmas paper like that." said Crystal, poking her finger at Gavin's chest. Gavin gave her a kiss.

"I've been working on getting the upper hillside ready for grapes," said Gavin.

"So you'll go through with your plan?"

"Why not? The site is good for a vineyard. Whether I'll open a winery remains to be seen, but the new ones that come on board every year seem to be successful. Why not me?"

"Right. Why not? You're good at everything you do. I'm sure a winery would be another feather in your cap."

"I'm not collecting feathers, but it would be a worthwhile challenge, I'm sure."

"Hey, it's still early," said Crystal. "If you're

finished with worming in the ground, how about riding down to the state park?"

"Sounds like a good idea, but first, I need to show you something." Gavin, with Rufus in tow, led the way across the meadow of milkweed to the old shed and pointed to the hanging chrysalises.

"More and more peel themselves out every day. I love to follow their progress."

Crystal studied the pendants in their variety of stages of the metamorphosis.

"Look at this one." Gavin pointed at a tight roll reminiscent of a Greek dolma. "Fairly new one. But, see here. This one has already released its captive." Gavin stepped around the corner to give Crystal a better view.

"There's something in it still—not a butterfly, though," remarked Crystal, moving closer to the chrysalis hanging off the eave. She carefully moved the paper-thin shell and froze. She looked again and, baffled, pulled out a diamond ring. The stone was a small but perfect gem that sparkled in the sun. Crystal turned to look at Gavin around the corner…and saw only the shed window. Gavin was in the lower part of her peripheral vision, resting his left knee on the ground.

"Will you be a farmer's wife?' he asked, with a trail of dirt across his forehead and Rufus attempting to thrust his nose into his armpit.

"Since I look like one already," Crystal responded swiping a clump of sweaty wet hair behind her ear, "I might as well! One condition, though…" She stopped for a second. "I want to keep my name. Spelling Koladziejski for the rest of my life would be brutal."

Gavin laughed with Crystal, kissed her passionately, and hugged her so tightly that residual air was forced out of Crystal's lungs. He put the ring on her finger, and she turned her hand up to admire the new promise of a commitment for a life together.

"I feel like I'm twenty years old." Crystal shook her head in amazement.

"About that ride to the park," said Gavin. "Let me just take a quick shower and get changed."

"I'll help you," said Crystal and winked.

An hour later, Crystal lifted her head from the pillow in Gavin's bed. With Gavin in the shower, she called her mother.

"Mom, you won't believe what just happened—Gavin proposed to me!" Crystal felt like a teenager telling her friends Gavin had asked her to the prom.

"Proposed? Proposed what?" said Lola, obviously pretending to be innocently unaware of the meaning of the word.

"Proposed marriage, of course, and Mom, I said yes!"

After a silence, Lola asked, "Is that what you want?"

"Yes, it is. Mom, I love him and I know we will be happy together." Crystal cringed at her platitude.

"Crystal, you know how life is. You cannot tell what the future will be like. It depends on so many unpredictable things."

"Of course. Mom, I love you, but I am telling you, do not make this about you."

"Fine. Just know that life is so much easier when you can make all your decisions yourself, by yourself, and for yourself."

"That's your life, Mom. Not mine. I like to share. I like to rely on someone else who also relies on me."

"Crystal, you can have all that without tying yourself to the dependence of marriage."

"I disagree. I believe in commitment. You made your decision a long time ago. Now I am making mine. I am ending this phone call right now before I say things I'll regret. Bye, Mom."

Crystal stared at the ceiling light. It had dead June bugs in the globe, killed by the heat of the bulb. Why did it matter to her so much that her mother should approve of her choices? Lola had never been critical of her boyfriends in high school or college. Even now, she wasn't critical of Gavin. In fact, she liked him very much. Maybe Lola thought all along that Crystal would be like her: independent, sure of herself, marching to her own beat. Crystal felt that, once again, she had disappointed her mother.

Why is she such a bitch sometimes? I wish she would go on a long trip and not return, she thought, and regretted her thinking immediately. She did love her mother, and all the positive memories of their life together far outweighed the unkind thoughts that periodically slipped into her mind without her permission.

Gavin appeared at the door, smiling brightly, a touch of ever-so-slight silver at his temples. Crystal's heart did an affectionate somersault, her usual reaction at the sight of her love. As he was letting Rufus out to chase squirrels, he said, "I guess the park will close before we could complete a walk. Let's just eat. I have some interesting leftovers. I hope you can stay the night."

Crystal stripped the bed and got dressed.

The refrigerator revealed tomatoes, peas, rice, and a container of giant shrimp from Gavin's dinner the night before. With some chopping, spices, and a little magic, dinner was ready in no time. After dessert of strawberries, Crystal and Gavin sat on the couch, ready to watch a movie.

"What would you like to see?" asked Gavin.

Crystal frowned in heavy contemplation.

"What is suitable on the night you get engaged to be married? *It's a Wonderful Life*? *Lord of the Rings*? *Some Like It Hot*? *Help*?"

Gavin laughed, "I know one movie we won't see. *Titanic*!"

They heard Rufus bark outside. Gavin opened the door and immediately closed it.

"Change of plans. Rufus found something in the woods to roll in. Most likely a deer carcass. The boy is very odoriferous."

"Odoriferous, huh? Now, there is a word. I'll help you," said Crystal.

Chapter 24

After office hours, Lisa rushed out of the medical building. She had just had a long discussion with Kathy, an elderly patient who had come to her complaining of a sizable painless lump on the lower left side of her abdomen. She had apologized for coming to see Lisa, as she was not young and Lisa was a "baby doctor." She had explained that her general practitioner, a female, had retired, and her replacement was a male, and she was "not about to take my clothes off in front of a strange man."

After a battery of tests and a consultation with an oncologist, it was clear that Kathy had ovarian cancer that had already metastasized. Her prognosis was not positive, as the tumor on the ovary was attached to the aorta, making the growth inoperable. Radiation and chemotherapy were the only options left. Kathy cried after hearing the news. Through her almost inaudible sobs, she whispered, "I just want to live long enough to see my granddaughter get married at Christmastime." Lisa could not give definitive answers regarding the prognosis, as patients' responses to therapies differed widely. Lisa inquired about the woman's support system, and was relieved to hear that her daughter lived in Penn Yan, in close proximity to Kathy's home.

Driving home, Lisa turned on the car radio. Scanning through local news, rap and ranting political commentary, she located a classical station and listened to Mozart. Something more soothing would have worked better to slow down Lisa's frenetic speed, her need to get away, to leave behind the bad news in her job. It was always joyous to deal with young women who welcomed the news of being pregnant, to deliver a healthy baby to the arms of eagerly waiting parents, and to assist women with their annoying symptoms of menopause. Some of them even laughed about their hot flashes and moments of irrationality. It was another matter entirely to deliver news of cancer or another serious ailment. Lisa had never gotten used to being the bearer of bad tidings.

She drove home faster than was necessary or safe. She opened her front door to the strident greetings of Niles, whose forlorn meowing typical of the Siamese had increased after the death of Frasier. Niles was a lonely cat, missing his buddy. While Niles ate his dinner, a stinky bowlful of fish, Lisa nibbled on grapes and wondered how it was possible for Niles to purr and eat at the same time. She got up, went outside, watered her plants, and picked a small bouquet of peonies, bleeding hearts, and white roses. Having wrapped the flower stems in a soaking wet paper towel, she drove, this time more slowly, to the cemetery. In the pine-filled park, the oldest tombstones dated back to the 1700s, local people whose life stories would be forgotten forever. The larger and higher obelisks indicated the resting places of prominent local men and their families. There were old wrought-iron crosses, oxidized and weather beaten, the names on them undecipherable, and modest flat stones for the men lost in the wars. Here were obvious hierarchy and social class distinctions even after death.

A long row of rusty grave markers had always fascinated Lisa. Under the sod lay a family—father, mother, and seven children, ages two months to 16 years, including a set of twin girls—who all had died in the winter of 1864-1865. Through the years, Lisa had imagined different scenarios. Did the father die in the Civil War as a soldier in the Union Army? Was the family not taken care of and starved to death after the father departed to do his duty to the country? Did they all have a contagious disease and infected each other? Why did all of them perish? Alice as a history buff would probably know.

Lisa stopped at her parents' grave, a well-cared-for small plot of land, a black stone with her parents' names in relief. In front of the monument was a miniature garden spot with begonias edged by a row of dusty miller, a tribute to her father, the gardener. At the beginning of May, Lisa had brought to the spot a wrought-iron chair to sit on while "visiting" her parents. Although the chair weighed a great deal, someone must have needed it badly, for the chair had disappeared. Lisa found it outrageous that people would steal from the cemetery. She discarded the old flowers in the vase and replaced the water. She put in the fresh bouquet and touched the relief letters of the stone while straightening up.

Will someone wonder, a hundred and fifty years from now, how Carl and Susan Hughes had died? And on the same day, she thought. Today's social media and information available through the air waves provided an easy route to finding out about the tragic accident in 2002, when their sailboat capsized in a sudden storm, and her father's attempts to save his wife had ended tragically. Susan's sister Jean had taken Lisa aside at the funeral and said, "You do know, as a medical student, that had your mother taken care of herself and lost a lot of her weight, she could have saved herself, or at least made it easier for your father to save her!" If this was the opinion of her loving aunt, she would be sure to stay away from conversations with other relatives less close to her than Aunt Jean.

Lisa did not want to think about those days. She knew from the time of the funeral that she was alone in the world. She knew of members of the extended families on both sides, but they were distant to her both geographically and emotionally. The conversation that Chrysalis members had had the other night had revealed to her that closeness is relative and difficult to explain. Good mother-daughter relationships did not appear to depend on physical proximity. Thinking of her loss, Lisa realized that, with time, you tend to recall the extremes of your memories, the overly positive or the blatantly bad. Lisa surmised that she had deliberately chosen to remember the good, perhaps because she was an eternal optimist as well as an expert in self-preservation techniques. She was thinking of the Chrysalis mothers. They were all college-educated women, who, except for Lola, had chosen to stay at home, to be the engine in households with men who were engrossed in their careers and positions. The mothers were certainly not unmotivated women, nor were they of the generation where women didn't work outside of the home. She would have to talk about this with the girls.

Chapter 25

"Where's the peanut butter?" called Tom, holding open the double doors of the refrigerator. Alice peeked into the kitchen while putting on her shoes in the foyer.

"It's right there, in front of you."

"Where?"

"If you just move some things, you'll find it. Not everything can be in the front row, you know," said Alice sarcastically. *Why are all men like this? Bob is the same way, and so was my father. It is logical to look behind things—the pickle jar, the butter spread, the capers...*

"Oh, here it is," said Tom, replacing the mint jelly on the top shelf of the refrigerator.

"Can you get Bobby from practice tonight?" Alice asked Tom. "I have to take some vegetables to my mom after school. She wants to make some Finnish summer soup. Pam's going to Stephanie's."

"Sure. Now, which practice is this?"

"Soccer. Lower field behind the school."

"By the way..." Tom looked at Alice. "Your mother can still drive. Why are you running her errands? Just asking."

"Good question." said Alice, and sat on the stool in the foyer. "Why am I?"

After school, Alice drove to the Farmer's Market and bought ingredients for the soup—fresh peas and carrots, cauliflower, and new potatoes, the size barely larger than marbles.

The early summer fresh vegetables reminded Alice that it was the end of June and Summer Solstice was on the calendar a few days from now, a festival her mother was fond of and diligent about following the customary celebration each year. This year, Kaisa had not mentioned it. At least, she had not reminded Alice of it yet. Alice's father had always been the one to make sure the venue was prepared. Through the year, he had collected brush, leftover pieces of lumber from various construction projects, and discarded wooden furniture, all for a bonfire. Friends were invited to share in the meal of grilled sausages and desserts. Those with Nordic roots would dance to their hearts' content, whether the music was live or taped.

Alice drove down the birch lane, noticing that the pothole she had been avoiding was no longer there. Tom must have fixed it as a preventive measure against a barrage of complaints from her mother on that score. *He's a peach*, she thought.

Alice found Kaisa sorting through printed sheets of information about plane tickets, hotels, and car rentals in Finland. Alice felt a blanket of annoyance settle on her.

"There are so many choices. It would be cheaper to fly to Finland through continental Europe, but I have to think of the total time of travel, and, at my age, the wear and tear on the old body. It's probably better to take a direct flight from JFK to Helsinki, even if it costs a little more. What do you think?"

Alice hesitated. She had made up her mind that she was not traveling to Finland with her mother. However, face-to-face with Kaisa, Alice withered. "I'll have to study the choices. I can't tell you right now."

"Well, do it quickly. The longer you wait, the more expensive the tickets will be."

"I will," said Alice. She had a heavy feeling in her chest, silently cursing herself again for being weak in front of her mother.

"I thought we could stay a little longer and do some digging into the family roots. I have always regretted that I didn't ask my parents a lot of questions when I had the chance. A lot of information went into the graves of Anna and Matti Virtanen. Do you think Pamela would want to go with us? It's time she learns more about her ancestry."

"Mom, Pam has a summer job lined up. She wants to make money to save for a car and the expenses that go with it. I have to say, Pam's being able to drive will be a great relief for me."

"You would let her drive?"

"Yes, I would. She is very responsible, and sometimes you just have to take a risk. If not now, when would you say she is old enough to drive?"

Kaisa tightened her lips. "She's just a child, after all." The accompanying huff was audible, and Alice knew there would be no point in discussing the issue any further.

"Speaking of driving, when did you take your car out of the garage last?" Alice braced herself for an attack. "There is no reason you can't drive, is there? Your tremors are not a hindrance, are they?"

"I just don't feel that I should," Kaisa said slowly.

"I think you should try, even if just a short distance." Alice changed the subject. "I brought you the summer soup vegetables."

"Oh, that's wonderful," gushed Kaisa. "There is nothing better than the taste of vegetables fresh from the ground, especially when they are harvested early, with flavors still strong and sweet. I'll make enough for your family, too. Can you come back tomorrow to get it?"

"Thanks, Mom, I'll stop after school." With the offer of soup, Alice did not want to ruin the moment by asking why Kaisa hadn't shopped for the vegetables herself. They had already discussed the issue enough.

"Let me put these in the refrigerator." Alice emptied her basket.

Alice looked forward to the end of the school year, which would free her to pay attention to her own personal life and her family, including her mother. The next few days would still be busy with end-of-school-year activities and the graduation, which Alice always attended, although she had no formal role in the event. She strongly felt she needed to be there to honor the graduating seniors, all of whom had been in her class at one time or another during their high school years. There were students who took the cap and gown for granted, but there were also those who were the first in their families to go to college in the fall. Alice was there especially for those who would be the first to graduate high school in their families, or who had struggled with their studies and made it. She knew she would tear up when the names of those students were called. Most teachers didn't bother to participate in the graduation ceremony. They felt they had done their duty for the year, and by the time the students' big day arrived, they would be engrossed in their summer activities of golf, boating, and keeping their lawns manicured and their bushes trimmed.

Alice turned to her mother. "Are you all set with the memorial service, or do you need help?"

"I have it all under control," said Kaisa, "I trust the Chrysalis pieces are ready?"

"We'll probably meet one more time, but we're okay."

Alice had to admire Kaisa's stalwart attitude. She acted like a director responsible for a large affair, all parts of the event carefully planned, all parts of it precisely organized, all details accounted for.

"Oh." Kaisa lifted her eyebrows. "What about Summer Solstice? Could you sing there?"

Alice experienced a moment of panic. The feeling of an all-together Kaisa disappeared.

"Summer Solstice? Is that being planned? Are you doing it?"

"Well, we have always done it." Kaisa faltered. "I thought you could… Never mind. I can see you aren't interested. I just think it would be appropriate to keep up the tradition, but I understand if it's too much." Kaisa appeared confused, with the expression of someone who was about to lose control while balancing playing cards on top of each other in a pyramid formation.

A small, nagging feeling was creeping up on Alice's consciousness. When would Kaisa realize her husband would never come back? When would she realize it was okay to let go?

On the drive home, Alice began to create the guest list for the Summer Solstice celebration. She would organize it as a "bring a dish to pass" event in order to save herself some work. Tom would scrounge up some materials for the bonfire, and she would ask Chrysalis to provide the program. In the past, guests would dance polkas and schottisches to the sometimes less than solid accordion music of Mr. Lehtinen. Come to think of it, he was always known as Mr. Lehtinen. Very few knew his first name, including Alice, until he passed away around Christmastime, and his first name appeared in the obituary: Yrjö, a Finnish name, impossible to pronounce.

Chrysalis would have to do.

Chapter 26

Christine picked up her mother, who was dressed up in a navy skirt and a white blouse with a large floppy bow at the neck. She wore white sandals with small heels. Her hair was in a stylish bun at the nape of her neck, a style often seen on the red carpet at the Hollywood awards ceremonies. Christine paid particular attention to her mother's appearance after her discussion with Margaret and smiled to herself with satisfaction. Navy and white—her mother was ready for a dinner cruise. Christine had remembered to put a patch behind her ear in order to avoid motion sickness.

The two-hour dinner excursion in an old boat on the lake would be lovely on this beautiful summer evening. Her parents used to do it many times a season, even if the menu items did not vary from dinner to dinner or evening to evening.

When they were seated by the window, Carol said, "You know, I tried to call you earlier, and—this is funny"—Carol let out a chuckle—"after a while I realized I was calling you using the TV remote control!" Carol rolled her eyes at her mistake. "A lot of people at Long House said they do that too. Maybe they're just trying to make me feel better."

Christine laughed slightly and said, "Oh, Mom!" Christine almost wished her mother didn't tell her of the signs of feebleness and confusion she was experiencing. To Christine, they were reminders of time slipping by, checks on the abilities to be lost. Opposite of Christine's great concern, Carol seemed to be amused by her little lapses. *It's probably better for Mother to have the attitude she has,* thought Christine, *rather than being distraught.*

As they sipped their Chardonnay, Crystal and Gavin walked in. They stopped at the table to greet them.

"You are glowing," said Carol to Crystal. Christine realized her mother was right—a certain radiance surrounded Crystal.

"We are celebrating our engagement!" said Crystal, leaning slightly against Gavin. For a second, Crystal thought of pulling out her left hand from the crook of Gavin's arm for Christine and Carol to see, but she thought better of it. It might come across as a bit juvenile for a woman in her forties. The ring was a symbol of the connection between two people, not a sign she was now taken, she had "caught a man," or a measure of Gavin's wealth.

"Congratulations!" Christine and Carol exclaimed in unison, getting up and hugging the couple. Christine inquired about a possible date for a wedding, and got two different answers: "As soon as possible" from Gavin and "I'd like a white winter wedding" from Crystal, to which Gavin raised his thick eyebrows. "Soon" to Gavin was tomorrow.

As Christine and Carol ate their seafood dinner, Carol reminisced about her own nuptials. Christine had heard this story many times but listened dutifully as Carol recalled her winter wedding on Christmas Eve of 1972. The Lutheran church had been decorated with an overabundance of red and white poinsettias, potted flowers purchased by the family with the stipulation that they stay in the sanctuary until after Christmas and then be taken to shut-ins in town. The bridesmaids were dressed in bright red velvet gowns with their hands in furry, white muffs decorated with holly and berries. For the only source of light, all wedding guests held candles in their hands, creating a calm, festive atmosphere. This had caused a small problem, with the minister not able to see the text he was trying to read. Luckily, he was able to remember most of it, having read it numerous times before. Only the assistant pastor, sitting in the pew as a wedding guest, knew where he had improvised a passage or two.

Christine had always loved hearing about her parents' past, their wedding being one of the highlights. Her own wedding had been a short, impersonal blink of an eye in the Seattle Court House, with only her ex-husband's brother and his wife as witnesses. The coldness of the event matched the temperature of their marriage, which, to Christine's relief, had ended as unceremoniously as the wedding.

She often thought of her reasons for marrying. The therapist she had engaged to help her gain some insight had been of the opinion that she had married in order to be one step ahead of Lisa in her imagined competition with her. Christine's first reaction had been that of disbelief and incredulity. Further exploration of the relationship had proven the hypothesis to be true. She had thought of taking back her maiden name, wiping away the entire marriage, but her business was known to belong to a Thurston. Christine was trying to decipher the legal aspects of changing the name.

The boat had filled to capacity, and various familiar local people from Christine's school days were enjoying their dinners. Most of them were recognizable to Christine, with the women a little heavier and the men with less hair: her old English teacher, who was now walking with a cane; a neighbor, whose name she had forgotten; and a funeral home director's son, who was a pathologist at the hospital. Christine wondered if the family had a particular propensity for dealing with dead people through generations.

When the cruise was over, it was getting dark and clouds were gathering in the sky. *Rain is needed,* thought Christine. Amazingly, she missed it. She missed the misty rain of the Northwest, the rain that was now part of her.

Chapter 27

If Crystal and Gavin had a choice between a meat dish, seafood, or a vegetarian meal, they invariably chose the seafood, unless it was breaded and fried. They thoroughly enjoyed their engagement meal, and, afterward, decided to walk to the pier, where Gavin's sailboat was moored for the summer season. Gavin regretted he wasn't able to spend more time sailing. He had bought the boat when he was teaching. Free summer months were meant for lake activity, and the beauty of the quiet, clean sound of the sailboat cutting the waves pleased him more than the rumble of a motor craft.

Gavin's decision to become a farmer had developed out of kindness to himself. In the early years right after college, he had been an enthusiastic pedagogue, an example to others in his eagerness to share knowledge and to instill the love of learning in his students. Through the years, the job had changed. As in all jobs, the daily activities had become routine, and the curriculum was narrowly determined with little ability to alter it to suit one's teaching style. Most of all, classrooms had become spaces where authority was no longer accepted by many students and their parents, and valuable time was spent on disciplinary issues.

Gavin's love for everything healthy led him to organic farming. He found his choice to be the right one, even if his free time now was at a minimum.

They arrived at the boat, and settled on a side bench. The sky was cloudy, and the wind caused the ropes and cables to clang against the mast.

"You really need to set things straight with Lola," said Gavin. After Crystal had hung up on her mother, she had regretted her action. The discord bothered Gavin as much as it bothered Crystal.

"I know. I will. I was just so disappointed. After all, you and I are not kids. Here I am, a middle-aged woman, worrying about what my mother thinks!"

"You are a caring person. Don't degrade yourself. You worry about everybody. Why wouldn't you care about your mother's feelings?"

"Our relationship is such a strange one. Sometimes I can't stand her and her strong opinions, but I would be wounded if I lost her. You know what hurts me the most? That she has never told me who my father is."

"You usually don't bring this up, but okay, let's talk about it. Don't take this the wrong way," Gavin said hesitantly, "but do you suppose there could be some sort of a 'Mamma Mia' scenario, where she really doesn't know herself?"

Crystal snapped her head around quickly to look at Gavin.

"Really? Oh, my God! I don't think so. She knows. I'm sure of it. Maybe I'll tell her I want my dad to give me away at the wedding, like in the play, and that I absolutely have to know."

"There you go."

"Then we need to embark upon finding Mom's most secret diaries. Dot. Dot. Dot."

"Now we're getting ridiculous." Gavin shook his

head. "Maybe it's somebody famous, and she doesn't want to ruin his reputation by naming him. An actor? A politician? After all, she was living in New York City at the time."

Crystal burst out laughing so loudly she scared away the seagulls eating remnants of French fries by the garbage can on the shore. "Well, look at me." Crystal stood up. "He would have to be somebody short, with brown eyes and black, curly hair."

"You just described your mother."

"Oh, right."

"A sperm donor?" Gavin ducked, when Crystal threw a sailcloth pillow at him.

"She said I was a love child. I don't think she was cozying up to a laboratory vial."

They walked slowly to the car, holding hands.

"I'm in this with you." Gavin took Crystal into his safe embrace.

When Crystal got home, she was tired, but the situation with her mother disturbed her, and she knew she could not sleep. She called Lola in an effort to settle the issue once and for all.

"Mom," she said, "I feel horrible, and you know it. Can we get together and talk about my dad, please? I just don't understand what the big secret is. I am an adult. What do you think I'll do with the information?"

"I am not ready to talk about it quite yet. I will tell you one thing. Your father is no longer alive. You don't need to bother your head about meeting him."

"Then, even more so, why won't you tell me?"

"We all have our reasons for doing what we do. Give me time."

Crystal felt defeated. Now she knew she would

never meet her father. She knew what she had hoped for would never happen. But now she had one piece of information she hadn't had before. She decided to look at it as a positive.

"Okay, Mom. Promise we'll talk later."

"I promise."

A piece of the puzzle had been placed in its spot. Although it fit comfortably, it did not allow her to see the total picture. The shape, the color, and the detail were only a part of the answer. Without the surrounding pieces, the whole of the picture remained distorted.

Chapter 28

Summer Solstice, the longest day of the year, was important to Kaisa. It was the highlight of the summer to her, a fest to celebrate the sun that didn't set, a setting for rituals and traditions from the distant past. It had a certain allure, a magic that took you to a place long, long ago. It had also always been a day of celebration for Christine's family, who honored their Swedish roots. Alice was able to gather a comfortable-sized group together, and, when Lola received the invitation, she quickly suggested that the party take place at her house on the lake. She mentioned to Alice that the bonfire would be more spectacular on a raft on the water, and much safer away from the shore. Alice found it uncharacteristic of Lola to be concerned about safety, but she had to admit Lola was right, and gratefully agreed to her offer. Alice could already see Tom's frown when she told him that he would somehow have to get the bonfire makings to Lola's place.

In earlier years, the Westons had always hosted the gathering, with Kaisa introducing new foods and games every year after her trips to Finland. She desperately tried to portray the Finland of today to her friends as a modern country, progressive in education, arts, and sciences, not a place where polar bears walked the streets and snow covered the landscape year-round, as some seemed to think. Nor did she want to perpetuate the picture of Finland at the turn of the twentieth century and the hard times when her friends' parents and other relatives had immigrated to the United States. She was willing to compromise on holding onto old traditions of the 1800s, and she wore her colorful traditional costumes, and, although she disliked accordion music, she saw it as part of the Solstice celebration.

Kaisa had left all arrangements for Alice, and was one of the last to arrive at the lake, having been picked up by Christine, with Carol and Margaret in the back seat. They emerged from the car, Carol and Margaret casually dressed in Capri pants, short-sleeved shirts, and cardigans, just in case it became cool in the evening. Kaisa lifted up her long skirt and stepped out. The striped multicolored skirt and a scarf with bright flowers reminded everyone of the Finnish folk dancing group that had performed in last year's festivities.

Kaisa took in the view. Closest to her were long tables laden with appetizers, hot foods, and desserts, the lawn chairs neatly arranged around small, round tables with white tablecloths. Thanks to Lisa and Lola, there were large arrangements of colorful flowers on all tables. Scandinavian folk music was playing in the background.

She glanced farther away, toward the lake, where, on each side of the dock, small cut birch trees were firmly tied to the dock posts. The trunks had their cut ends in the lake, the water keeping the trees looking freshly cut. Off the end of the dock, on a raft, stood a pile of discarded wood, like a giant ant hill. There were boats on the lake—sailboats, motorboats, and small fishing boats, the expected busy traffic on the water on a beautiful June night. The dinner cruiser would be passing by later. You could count on a few kayaks and canoes, as on any given day. The lake would truly come alive after school was out for the summer.

Although Kaisa was confident walking on flat land, the uneven terrain of the lake shore and the longer skirt made her feel uneasy. She asked Alice to help her to a table and gratefully accepted a glass of local wine Lola brought to her.

Alice has done it again, thought Kaisa. She had created a lovely atmosphere with all the accoutrements needed. Kaisa was proud of her "Renaissance woman" daughter. Kaisa wondered why she wouldn't always want Alice to take charge, to organize things, to carry out complicated tasks. There was no one to match her! "She even produced these two wonderful creatures," Kaisa said aloud, hugging Pam and Bobby, who had arrived on their bicycles and made the obligatory detour to greet their grandmother before walking off with their friends, all of them with their thumbs firmly on the screens of their smart phones.

Alice brought Kaisa a plateful of appetizers—first-course fish dishes and cheeses, herring in tomato mixture, herring in garlic-vinegar solution, and gravlax. Kaisa had tried to teach her daughter the old etiquette, fish dishes and meat dishes are never to be mixed on the same plate. She had always looked in horror when people filled their plates at a buffet, mixing foods of all kinds, creating true garbage plates.

After finishing the salmon grilled by Tom, and then the Swedish meatballs and beet salad, Kaisa sat back and admired the cottage. Lola had been home for only a few days, but the place already looked lived-in and cozy. Lola joined her with two cups of coffee in her hands.

"All single girls, gather around!" Alice was organizing an ages-old "treasure hunt" of sorts. All unattached females were to go off and gather seven different blooming wildflowers. Once successful, they were to put them under their pillow that night, and a future lover would appear in their dreams. Alice handed out small plastic sandwich bags to the participants, who summarily disappeared into the woods. Pam and her friends took part, secretly enjoying the hunt, but outwardly appearing to be slightly uninterested, so as not to appear too "uncool." The teenaged boys immediately announced the activity to be "totally lame."

Margaret nudged Carol. "We are single women. Let's go." Carol gave her a look of complete surprise and then immediately got up from her folding lawn chair and reached for the bag Alice was handing to her.

Kaisa looked quizzically at Lola, who shook her head. "I am happy with the way things are."

Kaisa disappeared into her thoughts. *I am a single person as well.* She was amazed that this had not occurred to her before, and she shuddered. She sat in silence for a while.

"Tell me about your latest trip," said Kaisa. She leaned forward, and without realizing it, transmitted a nonverbal permission for Lola to be as detailed as she wanted to be in her description of her travels.

Lola was an animated storyteller, and Kaisa laughed wholeheartedly at her adventures in the Slovenian countryside, harvesting new potatoes with coworkers whose language was strange to her. For a couple of days, Lola had tried to communicate with a woman through a dictionary, only to find out that the language the woman was speaking was Croatian instead of Slovenian. Lola was thankful for Kaisa's interest, but periodically she inserted an "Are you sure you want to hear more?" into the account of her experiences.

"Yes, I do. I love to hear about people's travels, especially to places I'm not familiar with."

"We have known each other for decades, but I must say I don't know a whole lot about Finland, either."

"We can remedy that, if you're interested. In fact, I am going to Finland again in August. I want Alice to go with me, but I think she is not keen on the idea. It's sad. It's so important to know your roots. Anyway, we'll get together when I get back and talk about the wider world out there."

"That's a deal." Lola was sincere about her interest, and Kaisa sensed it.

Little by little, young and older ladies returned from the woods, victorious with their bags filled with assorted blooming plants.

Greeted with chuckles, Carol and Margaret appeared at the edge of the woods. They looked disheveled, like two women who had engaged in a torrid sexual encounter or women who had been attacked in the woods by someone or something. Carol's hair was in disarray, and Margaret had some buttons open on her shirt; a most disturbing happening for her. She turned around and buttoned herself up while facing the woods.

"Well!" said Margaret, "Heavens to Betsy! Carol stumbled and fell, and when I was helping her up, I stumbled as well. I got stuck in a batch of burdocks."

She paused. "But we got the wildflowers, all seven of them." She held up a plastic bag filled with dying greenery. Pieces of burdocks bunched up her cardigan sleeves.

Every one clapped. "Good for you!"

The teens had noisily played volleyball and *mölkky*, a Finnish lawn bowling game, yet were happy to be interrupted for dessert. Strawberry cake, blueberry torte, and thick fruit *kisel*. The texture of the kisel discouraged the young people. "I'm not eating that. It looks like snot!"

Kaisa used to be annoyed at the comments uttered without discretion, but now she smiled. She understood that it was not fair to expect everyone to have the same taste buds or to like blood pancakes or head cheese, and she had to admit the kisel did have a consistency of mucilage.

Christine was trying to get everyone's attention by clanking a spoon on her wine glass.

"Ladies and gentlemen..." She cleared her throat and thanked all the people who had made the evening a success so far, giving Alice a special mention. She then announced that Chrysalis was the live entertainment for the evening, and introduced the members of the group to people who already knew them as their relatives or friends. Christine pointed out each Chrysalis member by extending her arm toward each like a game show hostess. When she got to Lisa, she mentioned that the doctor was on call, and might have to leave the gathering in the middle of it all, should the hospital or an arriving baby need her. "We will sing a few of our old pieces you haven't heard us sing together in twenty-two years."

There was discernable whispering in the audience about how fast time goes by—"It's been that long? How wonderful to have them together again!"

Lisa turned on the accompanying soundtrack, and Chrysalis launched into "The Longest Time." After a few more pieces, and suggestions for them to become professionals, (to which they gave polite but declining answers), the group gathered on the dock for a picture to be added to the album. While Chrysalis posed for the last pictures, Lisa's cell phone rang with the tune of "Ode to Joy"—her sign to leave.

While cleaning up the tables, Christine ran into Tom at the garbage can and inquired whether he had heard anything about her offer on the house. Tom encouraged Christine to be patient, promising to let her know when he had any news. Christine realized she had given them a deadline date and time, and it wasn't up.

As the sun was setting, Tom jumped into Lola's kayak, paddled to the raft, and set the bonfire ablaze.

Kaisa stared at the flames, mesmerized. In her youth in Finland, the sun hardly set on Summer Solstice, and the bonfire, although impressive, had never been as awe-inspiring as it was here. The contrast of the flames against the black sky created a majestic sight worthy of the fire's original purpose, to ward off bad spirits.

After most people had left, Alice and Crystal, Tom and Gavin, and the Fitzpatrick teens stayed behind to help put Lola's yard back to normal. Lola offered the adults a glass of the special wine she had brought from Italy. Pam and Bobby enjoyed a soft drink. Lola usually would not serve foreign wines in this wine-making region, but made an exception for a close group.

Everyone raised their glass and realized that Alice was not in the room. After a short search, Tom found her, exhausted, sound asleep on Lola's sofa.

Chapter 29

Lisa left her car in the staff parking lot, feeling oddly bothered to slide into an empty spot marked Doctors Only. She justified the special privilege only at times when she was rushing in the face of an emergency. She hurried to the obstetrics suite. Another obstetrician's patient, who had chosen a midwife to assist with the birth of her baby, was lying in the labor room bed with her worried husband by her side. The baby was in breech position, and Lisa had been called to assess the situation. Lisa ordered an ultrasound to confirm the position and orientation of the baby. She determined that a vaginal birth would be risky due to the size of the baby's head in proportion to the size of the opening of the pelvis of the mother. She advised the couple of her findings and walked to the desk where the OB technician was sitting.

"Are you calling it?" the technician asked—"it" meaning the Caesarean section.

"I am," said Lisa. The activity level in the unit increased. The operating room filled with people, all with their specific tasks to complete. The labor nurse asked the husband to don what they lovingly called the "bunny suit," a sterile outfit for the occasion. Nurses and technicians directed by Lisa performed an intricate ballet of movements, polished and practiced.

Lisa was at home with the family-centered C-section regimen, where the atmosphere was warm, calm, and less clinical than might be imagined. Music was turned on, drapes and mirrors were set in a fashion to allow the parents to see their baby as soon as possible, and, in most cases, the baby was given to the parents immediately, with the umbilical cord still intact, if possible. The staff called the method a "stork drop." The staff took pictures with the parents' cell phone, allowing the father to concentrate on the baby.

As the staff all sang "Happy Birthday" to the newborn, Lisa left the operating room to check on the progress of another mother. After helping bring a second baby into the world, Lisa left the hospital when her on-call duty ended at 7:00 a.m. With luck, she could sleep about six hours.

She arrived home to be greeted by emptiness. Niles stretched on the divan and partially opened one eye to acknowledge her presence. Lisa made herself a cup of chamomile tea and picked up a book to take upstairs to the bedroom.

She woke up at 2:30 p.m. with the open book on the floor upside down, pages folded unnaturally, and cold tea on her night table. She removed the pillow from behind her back, punched it, and laid her head on it, adjusting the summer covers over herself. Lisa thought of yesterday's celebration, the camaraderie, the closeness of family members with each other. She did not have that. She had memories of her parents only from a child's and a young woman's point of view, but as an adult she had been deprived of the privilege of knowing them. She realized she had superficial knowledge of her mother and father, their hobbies, their interests, and the routines of their everyday lives. She did not know them as unique people. What were their joys, their fears? How had they felt about having only one child? Was her mother satisfied with her life? Was her father ever emotional? She could no longer remember the timbre of their voices or the way they smiled. Lisa's grandparents had died before she was a teenager. She felt that her other relatives did not consider her part of their extended family. Lisa didn't know the reason for it, and she couldn't ask them.

She turned over and gave her pillow a couple more punches. She stared ahead into the room darkened by blackout shades, and a feeling of insecurity, a sense of floating in a vast void, overwhelmed her. Was this it for her? Very little knowledge of her past and an equal lack of awareness of what the future would hold? By outward appearances, Lisa had it made. She was a prominent, well-respected member of the community, an educated, beautiful woman in her prime, a talented musician. Lisa had dated a great deal, yet she had not met anyone for whom she had felt great love and affection. She was happy for and jealous of Alice and Crystal for having found a love, a life partner. She was also envious of the fact that they, as well as Christine, still had their mothers, no matter how difficult those relationships appeared to be.

Lisa turned over onto her back. She threw the covers off, got out of bed, pulled up the shades, and opened a window. She could hear a railway crossing signal in the distance and knew a cargo train was passing through. However, the rhythmic sound of the train cars running over the crossing made her feel a wanderlust of sorts. She felt she needed to get away for a while, to get a new, fresh perspective on life. Lisa went back to bed and let the light sheet settle on her body. She checked on the time: 4:17 p.m. Her mind was galloping. What were her choices? She wanted to be of help to mankind, not just to take time off and spend time away.

With her thoughts in full slow simmer, she fell asleep, only to wake up to a clear solution, an answer to her dilemma. She would join Doctors Without Borders for a year, travel to an area where skillful medical professionals were desperately needed, and acquire experiences she could only imagine. Lisa jumped out of bed and into the shower. The clock on the night stand showed 7:03 p.m. She had slept way too long.

****

Margaret was expecting Lisa and had brought out tea and crumpets on her beautiful blue-and-white china tea set. When Lisa moved her crumpet in order to spread orange marmalade on it, she read on the surface of the plate: "God save our Queen."

"Thank you for allowing me to bend your ear," started Lisa. She gathered her hair in her left hand and used a "scrunchy" in her right hand to twist it into a knot on her neck, as if getting prepared for a fact-finding mission and removing all possible hindrances from its path.

"I know that you and Mom were friends and that Mom treasured her friendship with you. I am wondering—did my mother ever talk about her innermost feelings with you? I know you didn't grow up together, but other than the busy woman with many skills, who was she?"

"Well," said Margaret, tilting her head slightly, "Susan was lovely. She was kindness personified, a woman who seemed to see through you, someone who understood you and your problems even before you opened your mouth to talk about them. She was loyal, honest, and always ready to listen. If she had a critical thought, she never let it show. Come to think of it, she was you!"

Lisa felt touched and fought the tears that had pooled in the corners of her eyes.

"Dear, why are you asking? Why do you want to know now?"

Lisa confided in Margaret her plan for a year away.

"Splendid!" said Margaret. "They need people like you. By the way, your knowledge of French will come in handy, with French being the official language of Doctors Without Borders. You do speak French, do you not?"

"I read that mastering French would be a benefit, and I've decided to take a refresher course in French Literature in the fall semester at the college. The small seminar will force me to speak French again in discussions about any given book. I'll have time to improve, as I won't be going anywhere for a while. There is a waiting period of a few months."

"Brilliant!" said Margaret and poured more tea into Lisa's cup. They continued their discussion about Susan. Through numerous anecdotes and stories of her mother's friendship with Margaret, Lisa gained a wealth of knowledge beyond the mundane and the superficial.

"This has been invaluable." Lisa got up from the sofa. "I am so grateful to you. If it's okay by you, maybe we can continue our chat on another day."

"By all means. You need your rest." Margaret

walked her to the door.

As Lisa was leaving, Margaret said to her, "If it's not too much trouble, send me a note now and then from wherever you are."

"You bet. But I'll see you through the summer and the fall before I leave."

Chapter 30

Christine grabbed her laptop on the way downstairs to the breakfast room. She had grown increasingly concerned about the lack of communication from her staff on any level, although she had given them instructions not to contact her during her trip. She was simultaneously proud of her company's personnel for handling things on their own, while feeling a slight bit ignored and even unnecessary. She had made a promise to herself not to give in to the temptation of checking on the situations she had left for others to manage. She would honor that promise and check on the local weather report instead. Seventy-two degrees and sunny. Perfect day. She decided to rent a bicycle and tour around for a day or until she got tired. Half the way through her yogurt and berries, Christine's phone buzzed.

"Tom here. I promised to let you know when I heard something new on 84 Maple. The owner turned down your offer." Christine almost choked on her mouthful. She felt deflated, but tried to keep up a positive demeanor.

"Did they counter with something?"

"Well, in a way. There is another offer on the house, well above the asking price."

"Above the asking price!" Christine's voice had jumped up an octave.

"I guess a counter to you is a number over the offer they got."

Christine was quiet. She wasn't about to get into a bidding war for a potential money pit. Thinking of the work needed to make the house hers, Christine said, "I have to be realistic about this. What fool would pay over the asking price for that wreck? Don't get me wrong, I do love the place, but I know that I'm against the wall. I'll let it go. By the way, who is the buyer?"

"You know I can't tell you that. If the seller accepts the offer, if the buyer is interested, and, more to the point, if you are willing, I can arrange a meeting where you can go through the house with the buyer and point out details pertinent to its history. Some people are very much into that sort of thing, where others could care less. This is a little contrary to the norm."

Christine hesitated. "I hate to say it, but I am curious about who will be sleeping in 'my' bedroom. I just hope it's a family that will take care of the place. I am so afraid it's another fraternity, not that all of them are bad..." Christine caught herself being judgmental and felt the sooner she could put the house dream behind her, the better. Perhaps this buyer had been the entity needed to save her from herself and her emotional decision making.

"Is Tuesday morning okay for you at the house?" Tom was ready to move on.

"Works for me," said Christine.

Christine was peddling on a path following a creek, uphill most of the time, it appeared. She stopped to rest on a large stump and watched squirrels chase each other up and down a tree trunk in front of her. She was trying to convince herself that the house deal had gone exactly the way it should have. It was interesting to her that Tom wanted her to tell stories about her old house to a buyer with whom she had competed in the bidding. This was, most likely, not going to be very pleasant. Did Tom have a mean streak?

Christine set out to ride back to town. This time, it would be all downhill. She put her left foot on the pedal next to her and, kicking the ground softly with the right for momentum, swung her right leg over the saddle and the frame. As she settled on the seat, it was quickly evident that her derriere was painfully sore. She had not imagined bones could hurt. The pain ruined a large portion of the enjoyment she would have felt otherwise. Once home in Seattle, she would take advantage of the bicycle club. *Behinds get used to hard seats, just as hands will develop callouses from rowing.* Or so she hoped.

I guess I got kicked in the butt in more ways than one today. Christine chuckled to herself and peddled the rest of the way in a standing position.

Chapter 31

Lola decided that the birch branches and small trees, fresh and aromatic at the Solstice festivities, had lived their better days, and contemplated disposing of them in a brush pile by the road, to be picked up by the town. She then had second thoughts. Reminiscing about the magical evening, she decided to save the birches as a nest egg for next year's Solstice celebration bonfire. She knew she would volunteer to host it again, and she could build a large collection of brush by next June. Recycling at its best! She had just finished piling them neatly under a cover which also housed her kayak when her cell phone rang.

"Ms. Giordano?" A female voice was serious and professional.

"Yes?" said Lola.

"This is Kim Vanderpool. I am the Executive Director of Long House."

Lola was familiar with the staff at the office of Long House, but Mrs. Vanderpool mostly kept her office door closed. Lola remembered Mrs. Vanderpool from the one and only local fundraising event she'd attended in town. Like a bat, the woman in charge had flitted about the large room in a wide, flowing black cape, sure to be noticed by all.

"Yes?" Lola repeated.

"It is my most regrettable and unpleasant duty to

inform you that Margaret Quinton has died."

"Excuse me?" Lola found the news inconceivable. "When? I can't believe it. How did it happen?"

"We don't know. It appears that she died in her sleep during the night. Are you family?"

"No, no, I am just a friend. I don't believe Margaret had any relatives. Her siblings died quite early, leaving no children."

"I wondered, as I have seen you visiting Ms. Quinton quite often. There is a letter here addressed to you by her. We had instructions to share it with you upon Ms. Quinton's death."

"A letter for me?" Again, Lola was taken by surprise.

"Ms. Giordano, do you want me to mail it, or will you stop in to get it?"

Lola was thinking that Margaret would describe her state of mind as being gobsmacked at the news.

"I will come and pick it up. Thank you. And… thank you for calling."

Lola went inside, walking in a fog.

News can come to you with a force that paralyzes you. Margaret had been so happy-go-lucky at the party, having fun with Carol and enjoying the food, the music, and the atmosphere.

As Lola came out of the steamy hot shower with her hair still in a large bath towel turban, her phone rang again. She was not in the mood to talk to anyone but picked up the phone when she read "Grant & Grant" on the screen.

"Mrs. Giordano, this is David Grant of the Grant and Grant Law Office. We have sent you an official letter in the mail, but I wanted to talk to you as well. I am assuming that you have been notified of the death of Margaret Quinton. Please, let me express my condolences."

"Thank you. Yes, I have."

"Mrs. Giordano, I would like to schedule a meeting to discuss the issues at hand."

"Meeting with me? To discuss what issues?"

"You are the person Margaret Quinton named in her will to act as executrix of her estate. Of course, you will need to be legally appointed, and that will take about five to ten days." Lola was thinking hard. She would know if she were to execute anyone's will. She had no knowledge of anything like this, except… Lola stopped mid-thought. *It can't be…* There was one time in New York City when she and Margaret had enjoyed a lovely dinner at a high-class restaurant near Central Park, including a couple of Manhattans. Slightly inebriated, Margaret had expressed to her that she was like a daughter to her and that she felt comfortable with Lola taking care of things after she was gone. Although flattered, Lola had dismissed the statement as cocktail talk. Margaret had meant it! The heavy turban fell from her head onto the hardwood floor of her bedroom.

"A meeting is fine. What do I need to do now?"

"That is what I will tell you at the meeting."

"Is it all right for me to go over to the apartment and see that everything is all right? I have a key."

"That's fine. I would recommend that, until you are legally appointed, you don't remove Ms. Quinton's possessions."

"That's fine."

They agreed on a meeting date and time, and Lola dried her hair with a hair dryer, an unusual action reserved only for the most hurried moments.

Lola walked up the steps of Long House. She was wondering if Carol Lindqvist had been told the news. She entered the Executive Office suite, only to be told that Mrs. Vanderpool had gone to a meeting and would return in an hour or so. Lola asked if she could go into Margaret's apartment using her own key.

"Certainly," said Evelyn, who was familiar with Lola as Margaret's friend. "Go ahead."

Everything was in meticulous order in the living room, not counting a Batman thermos cup on the coffee table, obviously forgotten there by a person responding to the emergency call.

Lola sat in a comfortable chair with a good reading lamp, Margaret's reading corner. On the side table were several books with bookmarks in them: a book on the Duke of Windsor and Wallis Simpson, a work on Queen Victoria and Prince Albert, and, to Lola's surprise, a recent accounting of the trials and tribulations of the current British royal family. On top of the pile of books was a pair of Margaret's glasses, thick goggle-like spectacles that would make most people nearly sightless. It looked like Margaret was reading several books at the same time, with a rather narrow subject matter. Lola took in the room. She could feel Margaret's presence. Margaret was regal. She was a royal, a monarch. Lola was overcome by a feeling of loss. She had never taken the opportunity to tell Margaret that she, in turn, had felt like a daughter to her. Lola wiped away her tears of sorrow and regret.

Feeling awkward but wanting to follow David Grant's suggestion, Lola opened the desk drawer. It contained invoices with accompanying signed checks with the due dates for mailing written on envelopes on the spot designated for the stamp. She opened an ornate jewelry box next to the bills. Either Margaret had inherited the pearls and gems, or she had received the jewels as gifts, sparkling diamonds, rubies, and emeralds. She was too frugal to have spent her own money on expensive jewelry. *These should be in safekeeping somewhere.* Lola reminded herself of David Grant's advice not to remove anything.

Lola stepped into the bedroom, where the bed still had the bottom sheet and the pillow in place. The top sheet and blanket had been thrown to the floor. From under the pillow, a corner of a plastic bag peeked out. Lola pulled on it and saw shriveled, broken wildflowers in the bag, Margaret's findings from the Solstice caper. *I hope she saw her true love as the last thing before passing.*

She turned and looked at a chair by the bed. It had underclothes—called "unmentionables" in Margaret's vocabulary—a pair of white slacks, and a bright red blouse neatly arranged, obviously the chosen wardrobe for the next day, a day that never came for Margaret. Similar underwear could be seen in the top drawer of the chest of drawers. The drawer was half open, forgotten by Margaret. To the left of the bras and underwear, she saw several photographs, mostly unfamiliar faces with no indication of the people's identities. When she lifted up a picture of a 1920s house, underneath it was a 5x7 black-and-white photo of a handsome blond man with a drink in his hand. John Lindqvist. Carol had the same picture on her desk in her living room. Lola quickly looked for a picture of Carol. Perhaps the photos were taken at one of the numerous cocktail parties they were known to attend. She could not find a picture of Carol. Lola felt puzzled, and, looking for a date, turned the picture of John Lindqvist over and read aloud:

> *To Margaret, the love of my life*
> *My everything*
> *With my deepest devotion*
> *I will always love you*
> *Jack*

Lola felt like running out of the apartment, out of the building, out of town, but her legs would not obey. Did Carol Lindqvist know? Margaret was a great deal older than John. She felt cold sweat gathering at her brow. She was feeling faint. She ran into the bathroom and purged her stomach.

After collecting her thoughts and washing her face and her mouth with cold water, Lola went back into the office area. Mrs. Vanderpool approached her with an envelope in her hand.

"Can we sit down to talk for a while?" Mrs. Vanderpool suggested.

"No. I can't. Not now." Lola was rushing through her words. "I'll let you know." She grabbed the envelope from Mrs. Vanderpool's hand and thanked her quickly. She ran out of the building, grabbing a peppermint candy from a dish on the desk on her way. She popped it into her mouth. Mrs. Vanderpool and her assistant director looked at each other, unaware of the turmoil raging in Lola.

Chapter 32

Lola ran to her car, hands shaking, body shivering in the warm June breeze. She fumbled for the car key among the numerous keys, some of which were no longer keys to any door in Lola's current life. A crowded, heavy key chain in need of weeding. She located the black fob that allowed her to unlock the door with a push of her trembling thumb. Lola threw her purse and the envelope on the passenger seat and backed out of the parking spot. Without noticing it, she backed into a boxwood bush, put the car in first and then into second gear, and sped out of the parking lot into the street, boxwood greens sticking out of the bumper. She glanced at the envelope on the seat next to her and switched the car into third gear. She had planned to read what was in the envelope when she got home, but she wanted some answers now. She wanted answers in Margaret's own, beautiful, Palmer-method handwriting. Lola steered the car to the first available parking lot, an empty space left behind by an Ames store that had vacated the location years ago. She stopped the car in the middle of the large parking lot, taking two separate parking spaces sideways. It was typical Lola, going against the grain, ignoring painted lines that were meant to keep people in order, in their small designated corrals.

Lola picked up the envelope, business size, for an

official sheet of paper. She ripped open the envelope, straightened out a paper folded in three and read:

Haudenosaunee Hills, NY
May 1, 2019

My dearest Lola,
You are the closest friend I have ever had and, as I told you many years ago, you are like a daughter to me.

When you read this, I am no longer on this earth. Where I have gone, your guess is as good as mine.

I have stipulated in my will that you are to be the executrix of my will. I have also indicated that, as I have no family left on this earth, everything I still own at the time of my death is yours. It won't be a great deal, as a part of the assisted living costs have had to come from my savings. I have tried to live my life modestly when it comes to possessions, so as not to leave a large workload for you.

When you go through my things, you will find a surprise, a secret I had planned to take to my grave, but I changed my mind. We had talked about the loves of our lives on many occasions. As I told you, I was never free to marry the man I loved, as he was already married. Jack Lindqvist and I saw each other every time he came to New York City to lecture. Sometimes I met him in other cities, wherever his lectures took him. I don't know how well you knew him and his family, but they were all lovely people. When Jack got sick with cancer, my life collapsed, and when he died five years ago, I decided to move back home. At that point, I could not run into him, yet I felt I was closer to him. I loved Jack deeply and I mourned him deeply.

Gradually, I started to look back at my life, and realized that although Jack and I had been illicitly happy, our togetherness was a betrayal of Carol. It was as if my life was being directed by an outside force when Carol moved next door to me three years ago. Perhaps it is guilt or maybe my true fondness of Carol that has made Carol and me good friends. She is unable to be out and about alone, so I am happy to help her. Carol thinks that she is helping me with reading tasks. She does not realize I can see properly in most tasks, using my strong glasses. Carol's dementia is getting worse. Her daughter is in Seattle, and the son in Florida. They can't make it here to visit very often. Therefore, I am asking you, please, take care of Carol for me.

As to my remains, it would be unique to become a diamond or a tree, but I am happy with my ashes buried somewhere beautiful. I don't want to pollute a body of water anywhere.

I hope that by the time you read this, you have found what you are so desperately looking for in all corners of the world, and have settled down.

I wish you and Crystal all the best. It has been a complete joy having had you in my life. Thank you for everything.

Your friend,

Margaret

Lola sat quietly. *When did Margaret write this letter? Two months ago? Was she sick and she knew it? Why now?* "Take care of Carol for me." Lola pinched the bridge of her nose and closed her eyes. She needed to go home and think about it all. She pulled out of the parking lot and drove up the street. She followed a line of cars in the right lane before realizing she was in a queue of cars for an old-fashioned automated car wash. She was stuck with cars in front and in back of her. *The car needs to be washed anyway.* She got a ten- and a five-dollar bill out of her purse. She followed the directions given—put money in, get a receipt, drive forward, stop, put car in neutral, take foot off the break, take hands off the steering wheel. The soapy water hit the windshield in globs like soft, wet snowballs. The car was moving slowly on a conveyor belt, following the program with an occasional boxwood branch hitting the body of the little car. The sound of the water spraying made her feel she was underwater, drowning. This small but mighty woman who always thought of herself as a sequoia, strong forever, was sensing that her branches had been cut down, and there was nothing left but a stump. *I am nothing but aging, graying driftwood. Take care of Carol...* Lola felt betrayed by Margaret. She felt betrayed by Crystal. They had both left her, each in their own way. To Lola, getting married closely resembled death.

Chapter 33

Alice sat on an uncomfortable metal folding chair on the forty-yard line of the high school football field. Lined up in the same row were the few teachers present, with the principal and those giving scholarships and awards in the first row in front of them. The Haudenosaunee Hills High School's graduation ceremonies were traditionally held outside if the weather was favorable. The band was playing the school song. The absence of the many graduating senior band members, now in their caps and gowns in the field, was discernable with squeaks of the clarinets, vacant sounds in the brass section, and obvious clashes with the rhythm.

Alice's thoughts wandered. She clapped robotically for the performances of the band, the scholarship recipients, and finally, for all eighty-seven graduates, who, as instructed, took the diploma from the superintendent of schools in their left hand, leaving the right one free for a handshake. Alice missed the message of the principal and the speeches of the valedictorian and the salutatorian of the class. She was thinking of Kaisa and her insistence that the trip to Finland become a reality. Her compulsion had become stronger after the Summer Solstice celebration and had come to a head the previous night when Alice had finally told her mother that she had no intention to go to

Finland this summer, and that if Kaisa wanted to take the trip, she was on her own. Kaisa's reaction to her daughter's decisiveness had been one of disbelief, yet she had recovered quickly. She stated she needed to make the trip now, while she was able to move reasonably well. She added there was no way of predicting how long she would be able to move at all. Alice had bitten her lip and remained steadfast through the rest of the discussion.

Since her moment of courage, she had spent a sleepless night drinking decaffeinated tea and trying to mull in her mind a way in which to tell her mother that saying no to the trip was not a proclamation of an end to their relationship. For all Alice knew, her mother had a mind to disown her. The thought shook her, and she brought herself back to the football field. Alice looked at the joyful young faces of the students with their lives ahead of them. She was happy she had decided to attend the ceremony again this year.

Alice had spent several evenings writing personal notes of congratulations to all eighty-seven graduating seniors, a custom she had adopted early on, as soon as students who had been in her class had reached their goal of receiving a high school diploma. Although not a positive development for a small town, the number of graduating seniors had not grown in recent years, making Alice's gesture doable for her. She felt she could handle eighty-seven notes, but not many more. Every year, the students looked forward to receiving a note from Mrs. Fitzpatrick, one of their favorite teachers. Alice always included personal anecdotes for each student, funny little clips from their long high school reel. Through these snippets, Alice showed the students she was interested, that she knew them more intimately than as just another student among many.

After the ceremony and countless handshakes and hugs, the crowd dispersed for celebrations of many types and sizes, from backyard cookouts to country club dinners.

Alice drove home to change her clothes. Gavin was taking the Chrysalis members sailing. The death of Margaret Quinton had shaken everyone. Lisa had just spoken with her a few days ago and found her to be in great condition both physically and mentally. Christine was upset that Carol could not remember from day to day that her friend had died and relived the shock of the news each time Margaret's passing was mentioned. Crystal was worried about her mother. Lola had taken the news the hardest; she was beside herself. Alice was curious about Lola, as her reaction had been almost too raw, too disconsolate. Alice knew Lola and Margaret had been good friends for a long time, but Lola usually took life as it came, able to deal with its twists and turns rationally. Gavin felt that a sailing excursion up the lake and back would lift everyone's spirits.

When Alice arrived at the pier, everyone was boarding the boat, all wearing their bright orange life vests. Gavin handed one to Alice. She apologized for their having to wait for her, and was grateful her attending the graduation had not cancelled the outing. Crystal helped Gavin with cans of soft drinks and bottles of wine, as well as various finger foods.

Alice was upset she hadn't had time to make anything to snack on, and apologized for her inadequacy numerous times, while the others rolled their eyes. As the sailboat left the pier, the wind picked up, and in a few minutes, the four women were taking in the sun and the wind.

Christine had been hesitant to agree to sailing, but with her trusty patch behind her ear, she almost forgot about her motion sickness. With the strong wind in the sails, Christine did feel slightly uncomfortable. She remembered the times her ex-husband had belittled her ability as a sailor. She imagined tasting salt in the lake water sprays that landed on her skin and lips.

Lisa had felt uneasy around water ever since her parents' death, but now she knew it was time to convince herself that her fear was unreasonable. She relaxed.

Chapter 34

Gavin was sailing the boat to Beech Point, a quiet bay known for its good fishing. At the destination, he dropped the anchor near the shore and got out his fishing gear, including a multipocketed vest with choices for tackle. He donned the vest and moved to the bow of the sailboat with the intent to ignore his passengers. Crystal brought out crystal goblets from the cabin.

"You sail in style!" said Alice.

"Crystal by Crystal. Nothing but the best for my friends." Crystal poured white zinfandel into each glass. "I picked white zinfandel because, of all wines, it's supposed to have fewer calories than most wines."

"That's considerate of you," said Alice. "You were most likely thinking of me."

"Nonsense," said Lisa, feeling the very beginnings of a bad topic turned worse. "It's interesting that a pink wine is called white."

"It's actually made of red grapes, but the skins that give the color are removed early in the process. You didn't know I was such an expert, did you?" Crystal grinned and lifted her glass. "To Chrysalis!" she said.

"To Chrysalis!" repeated everyone in unison.

"And here's to Margaret," said Lisa, adjusting her sunglasses.

"To Margaret!" Everyone raised a glass once more.

"How is your mother doing?" Christine directed her question to Crystal. "I know she's taking Margaret's death very hard."

"She's not okay, I know it. She puts on a good show, but inside, she's hurting massively. She won't talk about it, either. I have offered to help her take care of Margaret's things, but since our relationship isn't the closest right now, I hesitate to get into a discussion with her. She may think I'm being pushy and will shut down even more." Then she added, "You probably don't know that Margaret named Mom to execute her will."

"I didn't know Lola and Margaret were that close," said Christine.

"They were in New York City at the same time for many years. Although they were a generation apart, they seemed to click. When I was a child, I remember the two of them having a great time together." Crystal became wistful. "Sometimes, when you find a person from your hometown in your new surroundings, call it homesickness maybe, it's enough to form a friendship. Mom and Margaret had that, but they also were genuinely close friends. They would have been friends regardless of where they came from."

"I know what you mean. Sometimes it works in reverse, as well," Alice offered. "People say to my mother all the time that they know a Finnish person and the two of them should get together. It may work, but it may not. Just because you were born in the same geographic location does not automatically make you friends. In any case, my mother is so demanding, it's hard to be her friend, I'm sure. Even I find it hard to be friendly with her. You wouldn't believe what she is pulling now." Alice held out her empty glass for Crystal to fill. "I told her last night that I was not going to Finland with her, and…"

Everyone yelled "Yay!" in unison. Alice smiled slightly. "Mom was clear in her answer to me that she wants to go now, she needs to go now, she has to go now, because she doesn't know how long she will be in good enough condition to travel."

"And you caved," said Lisa.

"No, no, no, I didn't. I just left it at that. I didn't know what to say. I didn't know what to do. I can't let her go alone."

"Why not?" asked Christine. "She's sharp. She can take care of all the arrangements. All she needs to do is request special services by the airline. They will accommodate her, meet her at the door of the airport, get her to the gate of her connecting flight, and on the way back, reverse the order."

"I know, but if I let her go alone, I'll be a nervous wreck, wondering how things are going with her. I'll be pacing the floor each night."

"Alice," said Crystal, "you have to stop thinking of yourself as your mother's guardian or her servant, or, worse yet, her mother. Your mom is one of the strongest people I know. She is taking advantage of you—but we've talked about this before."

"I know, I know," Alice agreed and emptied her glass.

"How did your mom end up here, anyway? I guess I never heard the story," said Lisa.

"Well, originally, she came as a high school exchange student. Mom and Dad were in the same class in Manlius. After the school year, she went back to Finland and was studying at a university. Mom and Dad corresponded through the years, and when Mom graduated, Dad proposed, and they got married in Finland, in a medieval castle, I might add. So, I guess, she came here for love."

"Awww," said Crystal.

"Mom was fine until recently, when my dad died. I think being alone with the Parkinson's diagnosis scares the living daylights out of her."

"Did she rely on your dad like she relies on you?" Christine was curious.

"She ruled the roost like she still wants to do, but when it came to truly big decisions like buying a house or accepting a job and so on, she left it to Dad."

"Kaisa worked?" Crystal was surprised.

"No, I mean my dad's job. But come to think of it, none of our moms except Lola worked outside the home. Why do you suppose that was?"

"I'm glad you brought that up. I've been wondering the same thing," Lisa said. "I think it's rather curious."

"I know my mom loved her role as the party hostess, the wife of the Political Science Department head," said Christine. "She did volunteer work through the church, but I know it's not in the same category."

"Only a CEO of her own company would say that," piped in Lisa, now animated. "Come on, just because she didn't get paid big bucks for the good she did, it doesn't mean her work wasn't important." Lisa surprised herself for having reacted so vehemently. Her own frustrations and decisions for the future were now reflected in her conversation.

"Do we need to look at our moms' mothers?" continued Lisa. "I don't know a whole lot about my grandmother, but I wonder if our moms were trying to prove to their mothers that they had made it by marrying well, that they didn't have to work, that they were super wives?"

"Well, that sounds downright Victorian!" said Christine. "Marrying well! Is that still a thing?"

"Hey, I plan on doing it!" Crystal sensed the conversation's serious direction, perhaps a little too uncomfortable for the moment. Gavin looked over his shoulder and shook his head, smiling.

"Lisa, you might have something there," said Crystal. "Of course, who knows what my mother is trying to prove and to whom. I wish I could break through the wall between us.'

Crystal filled the wine glasses again.

"I guess we all have our own walls." Lisa put a pillow behind her back. "Walls that we ourselves have erected, partitions for convenience and independence. We've made walls for self-preservation, self-defense."

"I guess that's all I do, defend myself for acting like a wimp, but I can't…" Alice started crying, unable to talk. She got up and walked to the bow, where Gavin was pulling in a fish too small to keep. He took it off the hook and released it. He looked uncomfortable in his attempts to have Alice settle on the bow. Alice was quiet as others continued their discussion. After a while, Gavin realized Alice had nodded off. He caught Crystal's attention and tilted his head toward Alice.

"Well, what do you say?" Crystal looked at her friends. "Should we head back?" All looked at Crystal, then at Alice, who had woken up and was wiping her nose.

"Probably a good idea." Christine nodded at

Crystal.

Gavin set the sails, and the boat set out to tack and jib toward the harbor. They glided through the water, passing Lola's white cottage, each of them trying to discern whether Lola was in the yard, when they heard a splash. Alice had disappeared from the bow. Her life jacket floated on the waves. Christine jumped into the lake and swam with strong strokes to Alice, who was treading water but frantic in her attempt to stay afloat. Christine was able to get her arms around Alice from the back and gradually succeeded in calming her down. Once back in the boat, Alice shook her head.

"I shouldn't have loosened the ties of the jacket," she said, feeling sheepish.

They docked at the pier in silence. After the boat was secured, Christine helped Alice out of the boat, Alice still shaken and slightly inebriated. Gavin offered to drive Alice home. Lisa looked at Christine and Crystal and said, "You don't suppose she jumped, do you?'

Chapter 35

Alice started to shiver even though it was warm in Gavin's truck. Her wet clothes stuck to her. She gathered the beach towel tighter around her and started to laugh.

"I can't believe I did that." She looked at Gavin. "Then again, I have always been a bit of a ditz, and the wine didn't help."

"Don't worry about it. We'll get you dry and warm."

Tom met them at the door. "What on earth?" Furrows appeared on his forehead. "You decided to go swimming instead?"

Alice rolled her eyes and walked into the house. Tom looked at Gavin.

"You know, Tom, no good deed goes unpunished. I had realized from what Crystal was telling me that all the women in Chrysalis were going through some difficult times, each in their own way for different reasons. I thought going sailing might be fun, an activity to take them away from their problems, but what do they do? They take the opportunity to moan and groan about their moms! It got quite heated at times. I guess they needed to get their feelings out, but c'mon, why not enjoy a beautiful moment handed to you?" Gavin shook his head. "Don't get me wrong, I don't want any accolades for taking them on the water, and I don't resent that the day didn't turn out like I thought it would, but geez! Putting those women together is like an invitation for trouble."

"So you couldn't distract them from this mother discussion?"

"Me? What am I, a recreation therapist? I just sailed the boat and made myself invisible by fishing in my own little corner."

"Well, after the memorial service, maybe their lives as well as their mothers' will calm down a bit. I know Kaisa's life will be less hectic, with no more planning and plotting. And, if she gets her way somehow and goes to Finland, she will be recharged for a long time. Alice finally told her point blank that she was not going with her. Now we just need to find Kaisa a traveling partner—you know, like a governess for a kid, or a social companion for an elderly lady in the olden days."

"Yes, Alice mentioned that on the boat. That issue seems to be causing some raw feelings."

Alice appeared at the door, now dressed in a skirt and a sleeveless top. She was pulling her hair into a ponytail and asked, "You guys want some iced tea?"

"No, thanks," said Gavin. "Crystal is waiting for me at the dock, so I'd better go." Tom suggested he go with Gavin to pick up Alice's car.

"I've been thinking." Gavin backed his truck out of the driveway. "I would still like to do something special for all of them. How about if we take them to Letchworth State Park and have dinner at the restaurant there?"

"Sounds good. Christine will probably leave shortly after the memorial service, so sooner would be better than later. We'll just make sure you and I are in charge of the conversation and steer them clear of certain topics. Could you see guys talking about their mothers like that?"

"I guess not. I'm sure mother-son relationships can be equally troublesome, though."

They drove in silence. When they arrived at the pier, Tom said, "For sure," as if the conversation had continued without a pause. "Mother-son relationships, that is." Tom got out of the truck and realized he had not brought the keys for Alice's car with him. He wondered if being scattered was contagious.

Chapter 36

On the day of Richard Weston's memorial service, New York's Finger Lakes region competed with the country's more tropical states in heat and humidity. Early in the morning, a blanket of oppressive, heavy air settled on the hills and valleys with no relief from the slightest breeze.

Alice was getting dressed and supervising the whole family's choices of clothing for the occasion. The event was to take place in a park. However, the attire was, as per Kaisa's expectations, to be more sophisticated than casual. Pam objected to the idea of wearing a dress, and agreed to do so only after Alice pointed out the benefit of something less form-fitting on a hot day. Tom was reluctant to wear a tie, but realized his slight discomfort was worth avoiding any disapproval from Kaisa and Alice. Meanwhile, Bobby uncharacteristically said, "Whatever," and put on slacks, dress shirt, jacket, and tie, only to take off the jacket immediately when the family exited the house and the sauna-like air hit their faces.

Kaisa was waiting for them to pick her up. She had spent the morning on the phone ironing out last-minute details involving catering. She was worried there would not be enough food for everyone, and the temperature was of great concern to her. All she needed was a crowd of people coming down with food poisoning from dishes that sat out in the heat without refrigeration. She regretted her decision not to reserve the community center for the event. The caterer assured her the food would be kept in trucks built for the purpose, and served from hot or cold dishes as appropriate. In case of rain, the tables could be moved into the pavilion.

The seating area of round tables was set by the tall trees. A string quartet was playing as people gathered to greet Kaisa and her family with expressions of condolences. The guests commented to each other on the beauty of the setting and the oppressing humidity. Between two tall yews stood sturdy easels holding large, framed collages of Richard Weston's life in photographs. From left to right were displayed pictures of his childhood in Manlius with his parents, his brother Carl, and his dog Nellie, summer days spent on the beach at Green Lakes Park and winter ski trips to Gore Mountain. There were candid shots of Richard at Syracuse University, playing the violin in the orchestra and football in protective gear, an unlikely combination of skills that kept his mother worried about the possibility of the sport maiming his delicate fingers and ending his passion for the violin. Graduation and wedding pictures were included, with pictures of little Alice with Richard on the golf course or by the pool, both of them with books open on their bellies. In the middle collage, there was a large assortment of Richard shaking hands with dignitaries, including three Presidents, and receiving or giving out awards and certificates. And, finally, on the right, the father of the bride with Alice on his arm, and next to the formal picture, Pam and Bobby from birth to teen years. A life lived fully and happily.

She went into the attic anyway, thought Alice, admitting that the collages were artistically constructed and served to evoke fond memories in the guests. *I should have remembered to do it for her.*

Richard Weston's friend and colleague Henry Clark gave the eulogy to a tearful audience. Alice held her mother's hand. Kaisa sat motionless, glancing now and then in the direction of the catering company's vehicles. Tom read a touching memory written by Alice, as Alice knew she could not get through it without breaking down. Chrysalis sang "You Are the Wind Beneath My Wings," perspiration glittering on each of their foreheads, Alice with swollen, puffy eyes from crying. Guests were asked to offer their tributes, and many of them offered their memories and anecdotes.

Chrysalis sent Richard on his way with the words "I cross the stream" from ABBA's "I Have a Dream." The four women sounded as good as any professional group, although their performance was an odd juxtaposition of sadness and joy. The small amount of practice had brought results, and their voices blended better than ever before. Alice was pleased she was able to provide for her mother what she had looked forward to. Christine and Crystal wished life's circumstances were different, so the quartet could keep singing together. Lisa thought of Mrs. Jones, who had identified the potential of this group of girls twenty-two years ago. She would have been proud to hear them today, but breast cancer had taken her life ten years earlier.

As the food was being served, Crystal rushed to get a glass of ice water. She had a noticeable twitch on the left side of her face, which gradually disappeared when she pressed the glass against her cheek.

"This darned thing," said Crystal.

"My dad had a tic like that," said Christine. "It went away if he just drank something cold, without even putting anything cold on the outside of his face."

"It doesn't last long. It's just annoying, but luckily comes only in hot weather. It's nothing to worry about. I've had it checked. Sometimes it happens when I sing, and I hate that."

Kaisa had a very small plateful of the numerous salads, and a dessert of fresh berries and whipped cream, Richard's favorite, simple and healthy. She was too warm to eat warm dishes. She circulated from table to table, thanking everyone for their presence and kind words. With the last lingering guests leaving, a rumbling of thunder was audible in the distance on the north end of the lake. The musicians quickly and protectively packed away their instruments. The catering staff showed how a smoothly running operation works with efficiency, gathering dirty tablecloths, collapsing tables and chairs, and making the venue pristine in record time.

Alice was growing increasingly concerned about her mother's stoicism, her apparent lack of emotion. When they were back in Kaisa's driveway, Alice suggested that she stay overnight at her mom's, and Kaisa did not object.

"How about a glass of cognac, Mom? I think you could use it. I know Dad had a nice collection."

"Sounds good, but maybe I shouldn't. My medicines and all. That reminds me, I don't think I took them today."

"I'll get them," said Alice. She opened the closet door in the foyer. Facing her were Richard's medications, the ones Alice had offered to dispose of and Kaisa had insisted on doing so herself. Kaisa's almost full amber-colored plastic medication bottles were hidden behind Richard's containers that were half empty.

"Mom, come here," called Alice. Kaisa looked at the bottles and started to open one of them.

"Mom!" Alice grabbed her arm. "Which ones are you taking?"

"I am taking these small yellow pills and the larger, white capsules. These." Kaisa handed the two bottles to Alice.

"Mom, these are Dad's pills!"

"They are? Oh, my!"

Kaisa was not usually forgetful and had most likely only paid attention to the size and color of the medications without checking the name of the drug or the person for whom they were prescribed. Alice put Richard's medicines in her purse.

"Here, Mom, these are yours. I think we need to get you the blister packs with days and times. It will be easier for you."

"Okay. I agree," said Kaisa, feeling tired and defeated all of a sudden. Alice wondered how many of Richard's pills Kaisa had taken. His blood pressure medication worried her, the proton pump inhibitor not so much.

They sat at the kitchen table and watched the lightning and the torrential rain.

This is Gavin's peony rain. Sad.

"Mom, this won't hurt you." Alice handed Kaisa a cognac snifter big enough to be a flower vase and sat down. Kaisa looked at the syrupy liquid on the bottom of the glass and took a sip of the burning alcohol. She wrinkled her face and said, "So, now what?"

"What do you mean 'Now what'?"

"You know, like what Scarlett O'Hara said when her husband left her. She, too, was wondering about what she should do and where she should go."

"Well, your husband did not want to leave you, and, if you ask me, you're a lot more resourceful in an honest way than Scarlett ever thought of being. We won't think about that today. We'll think about that tomorrow," Alice winked at her mother, who started to cry, first softly, then harder and louder, until she let all her pent-up emotion loose in a flood of tears.

Alice moved closer to hug Kaisa, letting her cry until her sobs eased. They got up and walked out onto the patio in hopes of smelling the fresh air the storm had cleansed. What met their nostrils was an earthy odor. The patio stones were covered with large night crawlers and toads of many sizes. The pink peonies lay flat on the ground.

"I need more cognac," said Kaisa.

Chapter 37

I wonder if I should cancel the house tour? Christine fashioned her long hair into a large chignon. She looked in the mirror and saw a young version of Carol. She needed more gray hair and many more wrinkles to catch up with her mother, but she was generally satisfied with her future appearance. What would she tell the buyer? That one summer there had been bats in the attic? That under the large maple tree by the fence in the back of the property, three pet dogs and two cats were buried? That the back bedroom was so cold in the winter months that a supplemental heat source was needed to sleep comfortably in the room? Figures on the amount of natural gas used in a year? The year the roof was last replaced? Tom would probably have the data on measurable things.

Christine decided to pay her mother a visit prior to heading out to Maple Street. She had noticed Carol was reading the same book each time she visited. The bookmark was now placed toward the beginning of the book, although a few days ago, Carol had said she was almost finished with it. Maybe she was done with it and had slipped the bookmark between the pages haphazardly.

"Did you finish the novel?" asked Christine.

"No," said Carol. "I get to a point and, for the life of me, I can't remember what happened in the story earlier, so I have to go back and reread it. Imagine that! I might never need another book, just buy the same one, when this one wears out completely." Carol chuckled. "It actually belongs to Margaret. I'll probably give it back to her before finishing it. She might wonder why I'm keeping it so long." Christine was alarmed. Carol still could not remember that Margaret had died.

"Mom," Christine started hesitantly. "You remember Margaret passed away, don't you?" Carol acted baffled for a moment. "Oh," she said. "Oh, yes. I remember now." Carol sat down on the sofa. "She was a good friend, but Lola and Margaret were even closer friends. Lola was not around much. I think she traveled a lot." Christine could hear a small hint of jealousy in her mother's voice. Carol obviously had wanted the closeness Margaret and Lola had enjoyed. Christine felt sad but was uncomfortable about pursuing the topic further, and, abruptly, changed the topic.

She straightened the pink summer shift she was wearing. "Linen always wrinkles, but it's so comfortable in hot weather," she said as much to herself as to her mother. Carol looked up and recited,

"A little pink petty from Peter
A little blue petty from John
And one that is yellow
From some other fellow
And one that I haven't got on."

Carol smiled slightly while putting the tip of her tongue on her upper lip, as if to express awareness of her naughtiness.

"Okay, Mom. I need to go. I'll see you tomorrow."

Christine drove to 84 Maple Street. Tom's large SUV and a showy European luxury car were in the driveway.

Well, the buyer is certainly not short of funds, but I knew that from the offer above the asking price. Christine walked to the door and rang the doorbell, a familiar tune from the past. Tom opened the door with a wide smile. He looked overly happy for the occasion.

"Hi, come in and meet…"

A very tall, blond man stepped into the foyer from the living room.

"Magnus!" Christine was confused. "What are you doing here?"

"Hi, Sis, I'm buying a house." Numerous scenarios ran through Christine's mind. Was this a big joke, cooked up by Tom and Magnus together to derail her? How was it possible that Magnus was in New York? He was usually buried in his job, and very aloof and noncommittal.

"So, Magnus," started Tom. "What would you like to know about this house? Christine is ready to tell you in detail."

Christine was still off balance, but succeeded in telling Tom that she and Magnus could take it from here. She grabbed Magnus' arm and dragged him outside.

"We have a lot to talk about. It's you who needs to give me some information. I cannot get over this. Let's go somewhere to talk. It's almost dinnertime. How about Italian?"

"Sounds good. I'll drive."

"Fancy car." Christine admired the expensive sedan.

"It's a rental. If you remember, I can't fit into just any car. My legs are too long." Magnus gathered his legs inside the car like a daddy-long-legs.

Tom stood as if he had been jilted on the steps to the front door, watching the Lindqvist siblings drive away. He then nodded his head. He had succeeded in keeping a secret and surprising Christine.

"Not bad!" he congratulated himself.

Chapter 38

"I think this is now my favorite restaurant in town," said Christine to Magnus after they had been seated by the window with a view of the lake.

"Is the food as good as the view?"

"Absolutely, if not better," Christine assured him.

Gina had appeared by the table to take their drink orders. Waiting for their wine, Christine started to unravel the mystery of her brother's presence.

"So how did this happen? Are you really buying the house, or was it a joke?"

"I'll tell you what's going on." Magnus proceeded to tell Christine the events of his life for the last few months, the succession of occurrences that led him to Haudenosaunee Hills again after years of short, infrequent visits.

About ten years before, Magnus had invented and finalized a metallurgical process for the company he worked for. It was patented under the company name, which granted him a small bonus for his efforts. Magnus had always been interested in experimenting with things such as substances of all types, movement, temperature, et cetera, and had a small laboratory by the swimming pool in his yard, a structure that was meant to be a pool house. It was a perfect location for his experiments, and had come in handy a couple of times when an exploration with an intensely hot metal item had forced him to throw the gadget into the pool in order to prevent a burn or a fire.

As a result of his studying and experimenting, he had come up with a new invention. It had started out as a hinge but had developed into a newer and better artificial knee joint. He had been successful in patenting it a year ago, and, in April, he had sold the patent to an orthopedic device company for millions of dollars.

As Magnus smiled widely, Christine's mouth gaped open. She had been aware of the first patent Magnus had worked on for the company, but the private invention was news to her.

"I am so proud of you!" said Christine. "Not because you have loads of money, but because you made it by coming up with something to help people."

"Following in your footsteps, Sis." Magnus patted her on the shoulder.

While they ate their dinners, they caught up with the news both near and far. Finishing his tiramisu, Magnus said, "About the house. I knew the house was for sale again, even before you sent me the postcard. I've been checking the real estate offerings since April, but when I found out you were in town, I thought I would schedule my visit for the same time and surprise you."

"Did you ever! In many ways. Did Tom tell you?"

"Tell me what?"

"That I had also put in a bid for the house."

"No, he didn't. You did? He said there was an offer on the table when I last contacted him."

"I did, but I can't pay what you apparently offered, so I gave up."

"If you really want the house, we can negotiate."

"No, no." Christine shook her head. "This changes the whole thing. I am excited!"

"Just so you know, I feel great for having quit my job. Enough of sitting in an office or a lab. I have become quite handy at construction and renovation work, so I'm looking forward to restoring the house to look like it did when we were kids."

Christine laughed. "Oh, my, orange and olive-green linoleum on the kitchen floor, mustard-colored appliances, and all?" She cringed.

"I am counting on your taste in this endeavor. I believe in authenticity, but within reason. I am thinking more of redoing the wood floor, painting, landscaping, and the like. Bringing the house back to life."

Christine saw the final product in her imagination.

"Tomorrow, we'll go see Mom," said Magnus.

"Sounds good. She will love to see you. Just be warned that her memory is even worse than before. She is still her sweet self, at least to me, but you can't tell from one day to the next. The staff members tell me she can be 'ugly,' as they put it.

"At least she's better off than some of the people at Long House. It appears to me that people are medicated quite easily. I've seen what I call the psychotropic shuffle in people's gait, and some have the pill-rolling going on in the fingers. Of course, there needs to be a consent for medications… I don't know. It is so bothersome to think you are given drugs because you are diagnosed as depressed. Wouldn't you be depressed if your freedom and independence were gone?"

Christine had talked to her plate. She lifted her head and said, "Enough of that! Where are you staying?"

"I'm at the old motel with the little white cottages by the lake. Not luxurious—in fact, the opposite, but clean and quaint. There isn't even a TV set, just a radio. Very 1950s."

Christine burst out laughing. "That's why millionaires are millionaires. They don't spend their money!"

Chapter 39

Magnus had been surprised to find the competing bidder for the house was Christine. He felt awkward about snatching the house away from her, but he also knew Christine was not a person to shy away from any competition, to give up something she wanted, at least not without a fight. He was looking forward to the restoration project and felt good about involving his sister as a partner in the planning process. He was hoping perhaps this collaboration would bring them closer together in spite of the geography between them. Distance had always been accentuated by their eight-year age difference. As a child, he had thought of his sister as a much older person, someone who was almost an adult, not a playmate for him. Their personalities and interests were also different—Christine a goal-driven, self-assured woman, and he himself a quiet introvert, happy in his world of research and experiments.

Magnus locked the cabin door with its old key, almost a relic in the world of hotel or motel room keys, these days mostly electronic detection systems of one kind or another. He drove up to the wine country and Mary's B&B to pick up Christine. He found her in the kitchen, talking to Mary about the great surprise she'd had the day before.

Magnus mimed to Christine that he would wait for her on the porch and went outside. He sat in a rocking chair and took in the view of the vineyard and the lake beyond it. How different the scenery was from his Florida patio with palm trees and sandy soil. Even the sounds were different. It was clear the bird species varied from state to state. He had never thought of that. This would be something to study in the winter months, with crackling logs in the fireplace and soft music from the whole-house sound system, when a brutal snow or ice storm was raging outside. He could even put out bird feeders like his father had done.

"I'm ready," Christine said, interrupting Magnus' daydreaming. "Isn't it gorgeous here?"

When they arrived at Carol's door, Christine knocked on it gently with the knuckle of her bent index finger.

"You go in first." She said to her brother, putting her hand on his back.

Carol opened the door and took two steps back.

"John!" Carol's face showed a variety of emotions, from disbelief to joy to confusion. In her eyes, there stood a man with whom she had spent half a century, a man she had loved, the father of her children, someone who shared feelings, interests, and mundane everyday concerns with her, the handsome blond man with brilliant blue eyes, whose face was able to express the smallest nuances of feeling.

"Magnus, Mom," said Magnus, remembering Christine's warning about Carol's fragile reality.

"Magnus? Oh, yes, Magnus!" Carol's face lit up. She put her arms around her son and laid her head gently on his chest. Carol was a tall woman, but Magnus towered over her.

"You came back," Carol whispered. Christine

wondered if Carol was talking to her son or to her husband.

"It's a beautiful day. What would you like to do, Mom?" asked Christine.

"Oh, I don't care. Having the two of you with me is enough." Carol opened her arms to her children and pulled them into a triangle of a hug.

"A walk in the park?" Magnus was eager to see the majestic waterfalls and the deep ravines. Carol agreed, noting she needed to put on sturdy shoes. Although she was in good physical shape, she made sure she didn't risk falls. So many of her friends and acquaintances had fallen, broken a hip, and never been the same again.

The ancient ravine, carved by water through countless years, provided a refreshing coolness. As the morning advanced, more and more people appeared on the trails, most of them appropriately dressed for a walk in the semi-wilderness on rough terrain. However, when a large tourist bus spewed out its passengers, all bets were off as to the variety of "country attire"—men in wingtips and women in stilettos. It was obvious they had not paid attention to the item in their itinerary describing walks on wet, slippery stones and the need to avoid mud puddles near the waterfalls.

Magnus suggested a visit to the playground and pool area, his favorite part of the park in his childhood. The large pool was open, and now, with school out, the dissonance of children's yelling and splashing filled the park. They sat at a picnic table.

"Mom," Magnus started carefully, "what would you think if I moved back to Haudenosaunee Hills?"

"What do you mean?" Carol was squeezing her eyes, looking into the sun. "You mean, to live here?"

"Yes, that's what I mean."

"Well, what about your job? What would you do here?"

Magnus hesitated. It was almost as if he were a child in front of his mother, about to confess some transgression. "Mom, I quit my job. I sold a patent and have enough money to live for a long time with the money invested. I need to tell you something." Magnus raised his eyes to glance at Christine. "I am buying the old house."

"The old house? *Our* old house? The house on Maple? I think it's in bad shape. Somebody told me that. I was surprised, because the young couple seemed so responsible."

"The house changed hands after that, Mom," said Christine. "The young couple moved out of state."

"Oh, I guess I remember that." Carol shifted to look at Magnus again. "You are buying it? Isn't it a little large for one person?"

Christine and Magnus shared a quick look. Carol had not found the house too large for one person when she reluctantly sold it.

"Granted. I want to renovate it…no, that's the wrong word…" Magnus hesitated. "I want to restore it to the house we all knew."

"Well, good for you! It will also be nice to have you closer. You will visit me more often, won't you?" Guilt grabbed Magnus' heart.

"And, Magnus, it's nice you have money, but remember that's the thing that impresses me the least." Carol smiled. As they walked toward the trail, tears slowly flowed down her cheeks, and she whisked them away with the back of her hand.

The trail was getting crowded—families with children, all of them with colorful backpacks, older couples, groups of teenagers with their attention directed at their cell phone screens, and of course the stereotypical tourists with their shorts and visors, some with real cameras, a noisy chatter of languages, some less recognizable than others.

They were descending a set of steep stone steps when they met up with Lola Giordano. She was walking up the steps with her head down, as if concentrating on a determined placement of her feet on each step.

"Hello," said Christine. Lola lifted her head and saw Christine and Carol. Then she looked to the left, and her face registered surprise, almost shock. She stared at Magnus in disbelief, shook his hand, commented on his looking a great deal like his father, and expressed her surprise at seeing him back in New York State. Her surprise was even greater at the news that Magnus was moving back into town.

After Lola's initial remark about Magnus resembling his father, the man in the picture, they exchanged some pleasantries and expressed regrets about Margaret's death. Then they parted ways. Carol, with her children, continued down the path toward the park gate, and Lola emboldened herself to walk on up the hundreds of steps that required strength and fortitude. She wanted the burn in her muscles, the pain in her body, the feeling of accomplishment at the top. She decided she would go through rock if she had to.

Chapter 40

Lola half walked, half ran up the stony stairway. Her heart was beating hard, sending blood rapidly through her veins. She sat down on the ledge of a large boulder and took a bottle of water out of the loop of a belt specifically designed to hold containers for liquids. She took a large, loud swig, wiped the sweat off her face with a tissue, and lifted her head. Across the ravine was a wall of shale, layered in many shades of gray. Miraculously, small trees grew horizontally from between the layers, a witness to nature's unending urge and need to take root, to reproduce.

Shady areas were covered with velvety moss in multiple shades of green.

Lola remembered when, as a child, she had often hiked the trail with her parents and her siblings. She had her favorite place a few steps from the trail, hidden behind a rock under a large pine tree. She always sought out the spot, and would lie down on the soft, cool moss, breathing in the earthy smell of the green carpet. On a windy day, the air hummed through the treetops. Life was so simple then, the three generations of a close Italian family all living together. Nonna's cooking, Sunday dinners after church, when the aunts, uncles, and cousins came to join the family at the table. The loud laughter and even louder arguments accentuated by hand and arm movements like so many orchestra conductors all leading the same musicians. Hugs and kisses, exclamations in Italian. Nonna's performance when she became irate and stormed out of the room, first making sure everyone was watching.

Lola sat listening to the waterfall below, until the squeals and happy shouts of children interrupted her reverie. She felt that her happy-go-lucky, simple life had become severely complicated. She had tried to digest the relationship between Margaret and John. And now, out of nowhere, Magnus had appeared. There was John personified, alive, in front of her, right out of the black-and-white photograph on Carol's desk and in Margaret's underwear drawer. Lola bent her head back and let the sun warm her face.

She felt uncomfortable. "Please, take care of Carol for me," Margaret had asked of her. What did that mean? Visit her periodically? Take her on excursions like Margaret had done? Margaret had felt an obligation to Carol for having betrayed her, a reaction born out of guilt.

Guilt was a feeling Lola had not allowed for herself. She felt that guilt served as brakes on your life. It was a power that halted your forward movement, a useless waste of energy. Lola had always prided herself on the fact that she lived her life without artificial restrictions, concrete boundaries that held her back in her development as a human being and as a woman.

However, she now sensed that feeling trying to invade her psyche.

"Take care of Carol for me." For me. Why for Margaret? Carol, perhaps, was in need of a good, steady friend, but Margaret had somehow assumed ownership of her.

"Take care of her for me." You would say that about a pet. "Would you take care of my cat while I am on vacation?" Margaret had looked at her relationship with Carol as a responsibility. Lola did not feel the same sense of duty and accountability, especially since Carol had children. With Magnus moving back to Haudenosaunee Hills, wouldn't that duty be his?

Margaret had written her request to Lola only. No one else was aware of the contents of the letter. Could she just ignore it? Pretend she'd never read any of it? How could she ignore a request someone made as her last wish?

Guilt. There it was with full force! She had to deal with the issue somehow.

Home again, Lola looked at the clock on her stove. This afternoon, Margaret's remains would be cremated. The inevitable autopsy had revealed that Margaret had died in her bed of a ruptured aortic aneurism. Whether Margaret had been aware of the aneurism would probably never be known. There was no reason to investigate her medical history. With bittersweet feelings, Lola had chosen a simple dark marble urn with an engraving on one side; a woman holding up a heart, as if adoring it. She would hold onto the urn until she decided on a suitable place for her friend's ashes.

Margaret had saddled her with the worst predicament Lola could imagine. She did not want to be Margaret's confessor posthumously. Of all people, she was the last person to give her absolution. Lola started to feel resentment and anger toward her friend. She resented Margaret for putting her in this difficult position. She resented her for having betrayed her and so many other people. She made a pot of coffee, poured herself a cup, and said to herself, "Face it, Lola. This is not about Margaret. This is about you."

Chapter 41

Magnus wanted to see the house one more time before returning to Florida. He was pleased with his decision to buy the old house and wanted to start the renovations by taking measurements of cabinets, cupboards, shelves, and so on, to supplement the figures in the floor plans Tom had given him.

Tom assisted Magnus, holding down one end of the measuring tape or handing him a marker or a pen. Magnus accepted the assistance gracefully, although the job was easily accomplished by one person. His anxiousness to get started led him to push Tom in the real estate proceedings to have everything completed in record time. He was excited to own the house outright and to begin the long endeavor. He was not in a hurry to have a finished product to admire as soon as possible, but rather wanted to work on the house slowly, carefully considering every choice in materials, styles, and designs, always keeping authenticity in mind. He was looking forward to the plan, first a dream in his head, then on paper, and finally, as actual labor, with likely changes as he went along.

Telling Magnus about the planned outing to Letchworth State Park, Tom blurted out, "Why don't you come with us? We need to even out the group. It's Gavin and me against the four women." It had been years since Magnus had been at the park, when the

Lindqvists had made a trip there most summers and sometimes in the fall to see the colors in the trees.

"That sounds good," said Magnus. "What can I bring?" He remembered the preparations for the picnic lunch his family enjoyed at the destination—hot dogs and hamburgers, chips, and soft drinks only allowed on occasions such as picnics. Carol would pack blankets to sit on, silverware and dishes all kept in place by tight, specially designed elastics on the inside of the lid of a wicker basket. No paper plates, ever, for Carol Lindqvist. It was his father's job to do the grilling, and, after forgetting the charcoal one summer and resorting to twigs and small, dead branches from the surrounding woods, the family came to the conclusion that they preferred the wood fire and the taste it gave to the meat.

"You don't need to bring a thing. We'll be eating at a restaurant."

The next morning, Tom and Alice met the rest of the group at the parking lot of the grocery store.

"This reminds me of the days we used to rent a large van to go on a winery tour for a day. Somebody wanted to call it a limousine. Who was that?" said Lisa, not really wanting an answer to her question. She climbed into the twelve-passenger white van.

"It was probably my mom," said Christine. Tom and Gavin looked at each other. Mom, the magic word had popped up. They would survey the situation of potential mother-talk commencing. As Magnus climbed into the van, he reintroduced himself to everyone. It had been years since he had last seen some in the group. On the way, he and Christine let everybody in on the restoration plans for 84 Maple Street, the surprise change in the buyer, and the resultant fact that Christine would not be moving to Haudenosaunee Hills, and that, instead, it would be Magnus.

At the park gate, they purchased a pass and started the seventeen-mile ride through the park, following the Genesee River on one side. They stopped periodically to take in the beauty in the overlook areas, where majestic eagles flew effortlessly through the air. In order to see them, you had to look down where the birds were gliding with motionless wings, with the opposite wall of the ravine as the backdrop. Far below was a snake of a river following the ancient path it had eroded for itself through the last twelve thousand years.

They admired the vegetation, the birds, and the workmanship of the numerous stone walls erected to keep visitors safe. The topics of conversation varied from old memories to climate change. Whenever the talk leaned dangerously toward a topic involving mothers, Tom and Gavin were masterful in redirecting the discussion.

After lunch at the old inn, they lingered, admiring the koi pond and its fountain on the grounds. They descended to the waterfalls below. No wonder this was a popular site for an outdoor wedding. On sunny days, the rainbow would reach across the ravine in the sparkling pearls of the water from the falls. The noise of the falls made them appear even more powerful.

"I wonder how they deal with the sound of the water in weddings. You can't hear a thing." Lisa was always the practical one.

"Sound systems," said Magnus, and winked. He started to discuss the intricacies of how man could overrule nature in this case by using technology, continuing to wink with his left eye as he spoke. Crystal had noticed the wink and thought it did not fit the discussion. When, after a short break, Magnus winked again, she realized it was a tic. Christine had said her father had had one. It was obviously inherited. Magnus went on and on excitedly. All but Lisa disappeared from the near vicinity.

On the ride back, each Chrysalis member made a comment in one way or another about Christine's departure for Seattle being a clear sign that Chrysalis's reunion was about to end.

"So this is it?" said Alice, with a question in her voice. "Will we ever sing together again?"

"How about my wedding?" asked Crystal. "I know it's not customary for the bride to be part of her own wedding's entertainment, but I would like that. Gavin and I have agreed on a Christmas Eve wedding."

"It's likely that I will still be around in December," said Lisa.

Christine felt that five or six months from now would be a good time for her to visit her mother again and to collaborate with Magnus about the progress on the house.

"I'm going nowhere," said Alice.

Chapter 42

Lola rummaged through her pantry for the strongest roast of coffee she could find, and chose espresso. She needed strength to go through Margaret's paperwork: possible unpaid bills, bank statements, and miscellaneous documents Margaret seemed to have saved for decades. It appeared she had been an organized hoarder of sorts.

After Lola returned from the park two days ago, she had poured herself a strong Scotch and sat on the kitchen stoop staring at the lake. After a "dividend," as her father used to call topping off a glass, she felt a panic pushing down on her. She was trapped. In order to feel exonerated, she needed to be truthful. She needed to admit she was not as strong as her outer armor. In reality, she felt a mess, a human ruin, who had thought herself to be above it all, untouchable. She was still astonished at Margaret's betrayal, and had miscalculated her ability to deal with life's twists and turns with indifference and detachment.

Lola had been unable to sleep well since she had come face-to-face with Magnus, a younger version of his father.

She could no longer see the lake. She was crying. The cries turned to sobs. She hung her head and let sounds of desperation escape her throat. She wailed, with phlegm pouring out of her nose onto her shorts and bare thighs.

Lola needed to get hold of herself. She stood up and wiped her nose on a red bandana in her gardening bucket, the only thing she could find within reach. She breathed deeply and consciously and walked into the kitchen sneezing uncontrollably. She had inhaled some dirt from the bandana into her sinuses.

After having been officially appointed executrix, Lola had felt the responsibility heavy on her shoulders and had asked her daughter to help her sort out Margaret's belongings. Lola lifted five boxes onto the kitchen table, waiting for Crystal to arrive.

Crystal had just kayaked across the lake. She put a bag of cookies on the counter. "I made these last night, one of Alice's recipes, walnut chocolate chip."

"Mmm." Lola opened the bag, removed a cookie, and took a bite, then repeated more loudly, "Mmm."

Cookie finished, Lola nodded her head toward the boxes and said, "Well, here it is. I'll dive into the bills and such. Maybe you can go through the other half of the boxes."

They discovered Margaret had kept very organized and detailed records of all aspects of her life. There were only two bills to be paid, cable and telephone. Margaret had had a simple checking account and one savings account. Neither had funds in it beyond what would be expected of a person her age and situation. Margaret was comfortable, but not wealthy.

Lola sorted out old receipts, outdated insurance policies, bank statements, old correspondence from investment companies indicating closed accounts. She saved anything that had to do with taxes, intending to seek advice from David Grant as to what should and should not be destroyed. The "to discard" pile was getting higher.

Crystal looked through a box of programs from various opera houses and theaters with Margaret in larger or smaller roles, birthday cards, and wedding invitations from decades ago. She perused the wedding invitations, realizing that Margaret had been invited to the weddings of several famous people, all of them in New York City or close proximity. In another box were letters from Margaret's parents, written to her in the sixties and seventies, the time when she was at the top of her career.

In the box were also newspaper clippings, mostly from the *New York Times*, featuring critiques of operas performed somewhere in the city. Although Margaret's name was not always mentioned, Crystal made the assumption that she had been in the cast. She leafed through papers in a large envelope: travel brochures, city maps, used plane tickets.

As they worked, Lola and Crystal carried on a lively conversation about the value of keeping memorabilia. In the end they agreed that, in a case like Margaret's, items that had emotional value only to their owner were worthless to others. Crystal felt satisfied putting most of the ephemera into the discard pile.

Concentrating on the last of her boxes full of photographs, Crystal found old black-and-white pictures from the 1930s through the 1950s, some with notched edges, bundled together with now faded silk ribbons unraveling at the ends. The earlier photos had sepia tones which, to Crystal, were products of ancient times. Other pictures, equally bundled, were of more recent vintage. Photos after 1960 were in color, many of them candids, square in shape, with dates printed on the side. Most of the pictures from all decades depicted people and parties, with an occasional landscape or a tourist shot of a famous landmark.

It appeared Margaret's childhood had been happy and calm in a family with loving parents. Her adult private life was not in the forefront in the pictures. Margaret the opera singer monopolized the collection.

The few albums were dedicated to photos of her career as well. In the smallest box were a few loose pictures. Crystal picked up a black-and-white five-by-seven.

"Interesting. John Lindqvist."

Lola froze. She was putting the insurance policy for Margaret's condominium back into its folder and stopped mid-motion.

Crystal continued, "It's odd that Mr. Lindqvist's picture is among Margaret's belongings, and so large and official, of all things." She took another look at the photograph. John had a glass in his hand, filled with what appeared to be alcohol on ice. Crystal remembered Christine telling her at the memorial service about her father's tic, a twitch similar to Crystal's, and that he was able to get rid of it by using a cold drink in a cold glass.

She then thought of Magnus' tic, a twitch in the same place as hers. She let the puzzle pieces circle in her brain for a while. The puzzle was coming together. She had had an inkling, a hint of what might be the truth, since the memorial service. However, the idea was so reckless, so wild, she didn't give it space in her thoughts.

So reckless, so wild, like her mother. Crystal

toughened herself.

"Mom, look!" Crystal held up the photograph for Lola to see. "Mom, do you know if tics are inherited?"

Lola surrendered.

"Crystal, let's go and sit on the sofa." They settled on the soft cushions facing each other, each aware of the other's discomfort.

"Crystal, I guess you have deciphered the biggest mystery of your life. I think you can see how difficult this is for me."

"John Lindqvist is my father, isn't he?" Crystal said directly and calmly.

"Yes, he is." Lola took Crystal's hands in hers. "But can you see how complicated this is? As the back of the picture shows, John was the love of Margaret's life, also."

Crystal raised her eyebrows.

"And now, in a letter Margaret left for me, she has asked me to take care of Carol, the wife of her lover. And my lover! Margaret did not know about my relationship with John, and Carol knew nothing. Sweet, kind Carol…" They sat quietly while Lola cried softly.

Crystal's mind was whirling. She had a million questions for her mother. She was relieved that the most important question in her life had been answered. She now knew for certain who her father was. As good as it felt for a moment, Crystal started to understand the intricacies of all the relationships. Not only did she know who her father was, she also knew she had two half-siblings, Christine and Magnus, two people she was very fond of. Crystal touched her dark brown hair, thinking of the lack of resemblance between her and the other two. They obviously didn't know anything.

Should they be told? For what purpose? The knowledge might destroy their good memories of their father. She would never want that.

Crystal could understand the dilemma her mother was facing regarding Carol.

"Mom…" Crystal looked at Lola. "Thank you for telling me and reinforcing my suspicion. I have had a hunch ever since Mr. Weston's memorial service, when Christine described her father's tics to be exactly like mine. I feel better for myself, but I feel very sad for you. I am not accusing you of anything, but you really have created a Peyton Place for yourself."

Lola tried to smile. "I'll figure it out. Thank you for being understanding. I am so, so sorry, Crystal."

Crystal reached to hug her mother. "I think we are done with the boxes for today, Mom. I have some things to sort out in my head. Will you be all right?"

"I'm glad you know the truth. The rest is my own doing, and I have a lot to figure out."

"I love you, Mom."

"I love you, too."

Crystal got into her kayak and started paddling slowly across the lake. She felt strangely happy. Lola had said she loved her. The words redeemed all that had been wrong between her and her mother. As she replayed the conversation in her mind a few times, she deciphered the details of the discussion, wondering what Lola had meant by what she saw on the back of the picture. Crystal could not remember having seen anything.

Lola watched from her front steps. Crystal's figure got smaller and smaller as she neared the far shore. Finally, she went back inside and looked at the empty boxes and the disarray all around—Margaret's mess cluttering her house. She picked up the picture of John.

"If only I hadn't put the picture in with the others, Crystal would not have had to find out for sure, not yet." The photo fell to the floor on its face. The back side was clear, an empty space of white paper without writing of any kind. A duplicate!

There was no message on the back for Crystal to see. Lola covered her eyes. Crystal did not have to know about Margaret and John. She could have just dealt with her paternity and been blissfully unaware of Margaret's affair with John. Now Crystal knew clearly that John Lindqvist was not only her father, but a first-class dishonorable cheat and scoundrel.

"So be it—I am so good at ruining my life!"

Chapter 43

It had gotten dark all of a sudden. Lola had no sense of time's passing into late evening. She sat on the sofa in the darkness, trying to reason the events of her life—Crystal's knowledge of the identity of her father, Margaret's dying and choosing Lola to deal with the tidal wave of issues, saddling her with the responsibility for Carol. What a cruel twist of events!

When Lola had first read Margaret's letter, her thoughts and feelings had rushed in all directions. The strongest response was a sense of betrayal, of Margaret letting her down in her trust in their friendship. She caught herself thinking hypocritically. She herself had not divulged her relationship with John to Margaret. She was equally secretive, equally untruthful. Had Lola known who Margaret's great love was, they would never have been friends.

That would have been a great loss, thought Lola. Margaret was her idol, a woman she wanted to be in her older years. Yet she now resented her vehemently. It did not bother her as much to know that John was married. She had known it from the moment she met him. Carol had been neatly tucked away in Haudenosaunee Hills during the years Lola stole her wonderful moments with John in New York City…but Margaret! Lola felt catty as a feeling snuck in where she questioned the age difference between Margaret and John. Margaret was almost twenty years older than John. If John found Margaret appealing, what about his attention to Lola? Was she only the sex partner he wanted and Margaret the intellectual stimulation he craved? Didn't sweet, intelligent Carol meet his wants and needs? Was Margaret a better sex partner than Lola? Had John ever loved either one of them?

Lola found her thoughts primitive and ugly and inappropriate toward both Margaret and John. Lola had idolized the man to the point where she had not allowed herself to get deeply involved with anyone else. She had had relationships, but they had been superficial in nature. What about Carol? The whole affair...Lola smiled at her choice of the word...was now distasteful to her. Anger bubbled in her. Who was to say that Margaret and Lola were the only objects of John's affection outside of his marriage? "The love of my life," he had written on the back of his picture for Margaret. Lola felt cheated. John hadn't given *her* his picture with that dedication.

Why was she so severely affected by the turn of events? After all, the affair had started ages ago. Lola closed her eyes. She imagined herself with John in Central Park, John walking fast with his long legs and Lola taking two steps to his one. They rented a rowboat, and John showed off his skills with the oars to the city people and foreign tourists, who invariably rowed around in circles or had to retrieve an oar that had gotten away.

She pictured the two of them in Little Italy, hidden away in a dark corner in a restaurant, enjoying homemade pasta and meatballs. A candle, stuck in a Chianti bottle, dripped down the sides of the bottle, adding to the already thick layers of old wax in many colors.

She saw them in the audience of an out-of-the-way theater production, and sitting on a park bench in Greenwich Village, talking until the early morning about what they had just experienced.

She remembered them in her apartment, John reading the *New York Times* in her Eames lounge chair, a piece of furniture she had had to have, a chair that now sold for over six thousand dollars! While John read, Lola painted, usually colorful abstracts with powerful strokes. If she had some wine, she would slow down and produce still-lifes and scenery, most often depicting a lake and vineyards.

She recalled intimate moments they shared—the furtive glances from one to the other, the acknowledgment of the strong pull in each other's direction from the first of John's lectures Lola attended, the attraction that grew both on the intellectual and the raw physical level.

Lola had been enamored with everything about John. In addition to his intellect, she loved his build, the body of a marathon runner, a lanky, tall, sinewy body the opposite of her softness. She had always found bulging muscles to be vulgar.

Lola could still feel the overpowering delicious ache in her lower belly that waited for fulfilment, times when she saw nothing, heard nothing, until John, very skillfully and lovingly, brought her to the highest ecstasy and the divine resolution.

They made love in unexpected places. After breakfast, there was, at times, no time to consider comfort, and the breakfast nook table accommodated them, as her cat Whiskers licked the cream on the floor from the knocked-over pitcher under the table while furtively looking up, concerned about the noise and the movement of the table above him.

For variety, Lola liked to surprise John by jumping out of the hallway closet, wearing nothing but heavy, musky perfume, when he unlocked the door to her apartment with his key.

Lola smiled at her memories and cried as she weighed her choices. She knew she could pretend to be a friend to Carol. She would be reminded of John every time she ran into Magnus—in a small town, avoiding him would be impossible. She had deliberately avoided John all those years after she and Crystal moved back to Haudenosaunee Hills, an exhausting game of hide-and-seek she had tired of quickly.

Lola's leg had fallen asleep. She readjusted herself among the pillows on the sofa and rotated her foot from the ankle to bring it back to life. What if this was a joke on her? Had Margaret been aware of Lola's relationship with John, and this was a cruel act of revenge on her part toward Lola?

Restless and uncomfortable, she decided to risk waking up Kaisa. Her friend answered on the first ring. After some necessary small talk, Lola inquired whether she could take Kaisa to lunch the next day. Kaisa agreed, but wondered to herself about Lola's sudden show of friendship. Was this just lunch, or did Lola have something special to discuss? Kaisa was not a person who would call other women just to chat, nor was she a person women would seek out for that purpose.

The next day, Lola picked up Kaisa, who looked at

her bright-colored small car with suspicion and managed to lower herself onto the seat.

"This is like sitting on the ground," she announced. "I may never be able to get out of this trap." She gently rubbed her knees.

"Let's talk about Finland," said Lola as soon as they sat at the table in a cozy coffee house.

"One of my favorite topics, as you know." Kaisa smiled. Lola had a litany of questions, from food culture to art, climate to customs.

"Kaisa, I heard you will be traveling to Finland in August and that you are looking for a traveling companion. What if I came with you?" Lola blurted out. "I think we could get along. I have never visited the Nordic countries. You know I am not a tourist. To experience a country with a native of the land is an entirely different and better experience."

"By far," said Kaisa, hiding her shaking hand in her lap. "If you're serious, let's decide on the dates of our trip." Kaisa was beaming.

Chapter 44

Mary's Bed & Breakfast was busier by the day. Christine enjoyed meeting new people at the breakfast table or chatting with them on the porch at the end of the day with Mary's homemade candles providing the only light to compete with the fireflies. With New York State's schools out, the B&B was filling with families, who added to the liveliness and the noise level.

Christine had packed her bags except for items needed for the next twenty hours or so. She had a flight to Seattle at six o'clock the next morning. Christine looked back at the events of the past three weeks, amazed at how much had happened in a short time. She felt satisfied. On her previous trips back home, leaving had always been difficult, with ties to the old hometown loosening with every visit. It was different now. With Magnus' plans, there was a feeling of hope for the future rather than a sense of winding down, an end of an era coming closer and closer. Optimism colored Christine's attitude, and she felt a rush of energy. The house project would be exciting as a "family affair," and, Christine admitted reluctantly, it was time for Magnus to take more interest and spend more time with their mother.

Christine thought of Carol, who had given so much to her family. It was very difficult to pay her back for her devotion, dedication, and love. She did not need anything, nor did she want anything. Carol had always been a storyteller, and she was grateful for an audience. Carol had lost Margaret, so Magnus would need to step up to be a support. Christine made a promise to herself to visit more often as well.

Carol had wanted to visit the University Art Museum. Today would be a good day for that. Christine dressed for the air conditioning in the museum.

When she arrived at Long House, she saw an ambulance at the entrance. Her heart fluttered with uncertainty. As she walked in, she found her mother in perfectly good condition. Odd how she had immediately personalized a potential disaster.

Carol had been reading her book. Christine checked on the bookmark. It had been moved slightly toward the back pages.

"I'm going shopping!" announced Carol with a bright smile.

"You are? With whom?"

"Elizabeth. Her daughter is taking us."

"Who's Elizabeth?"

"Elizabeth moved in last week. We were in elementary school together before her family moved away. I used to dislike her. She bragged a lot in those days. Of course, she always had more than anyone else—clothes in the newest styles, the best toys, you name it. I was jealous, to be sure. What a stupid feeling! Well, I don't envy her anymore. She's in a wheelchair and has had some sort of cancer. I don't dare pry, but she'll probably tell me eventually." Carol was on a roll. "You know, it's funny, but Margaret only wanted to be called Margaret. Elizabeth took an aide's head off for calling her Betty!"

"That's fine, Mom." Christine chuckled to herself. From Margaret to Elizabeth, Princess to Queen. Christine had been concerned about the void left by Margaret. Elizabeth might just be the answer for her mother. Instead of being taken care of by someone, Carol would now see herself in the role of a helper for someone else.

Although disappointed she wasn't able to spend the last day with her mother, Christine understood the importance of Carol's chance to strengthen a new friendship. She also knew Carol would be tired after a shopping trip, and said, "Well, Mom, you have a great time. I'll be flying out very early in the morning, so I'll say goodbye now." She hugged her mother, gathering Carol's warmth.

"I'll be back before you know it. With Magnus' project with the house, I may be back sooner rather than later. You never can tell."

"You never can tell
From where you sit
Where the man in the gallery
Is going to spit."

With that, Carol winked at Christine.

She was obviously happy, which allowed Christine to walk out of Long House with a light heart.

Chapter 45

Lola had invited Crystal and Gavin to dinner. She had fixed a simple meal of chicken, broccoli, and a tossed salad with homemade, light dressing. She had no energy for creating anything more exotic, although her daughter was used to sitting down to platefuls of colorful dishes created on the basis of a new ingredient, something Lola had been served on one of her countless trips abroad, or a complicated dish she had made up.

As she cleared the table after the meal, she hesitated. The dinner conversation had been slightly strained, but Lola quickly realized the atmosphere had been tortured due to her own unwillingness to speak openly about John, even in the face of Crystal's yearning for details. Gavin's presence curtailed Lola's ability and desire to be candid, as well.

"Mom?" Crystal looked at Lola sideways. "I feel you're not quite at home with what has been going on. I want to reassure you that I'm fine. I'm relieved and thankful all secrets are out. You've had your reasons for keeping things from me, and that's okay. You can relax."

"Thank you for understanding," said Lola out loud. *You have no idea how my life has been turned upside down.*

Lola's phone rang. She saw Kaisa Weston's name on the display, made her apologies to Crystal and

Gavin, and left the room to take the call.

Crystal and Gavin were finishing the dishes in the kitchen when Lola returned.

"I'm sorry. That was rude of me." She looked at the clean kitchen sink and counter. "Oh, thank you for doing the dishes. You didn't need to. I have all night. That call did come at an opportune time, though. I was just about to tell you I will be going to Finland, and now I know the date—August seventeenth."

"And I thought you were back home to stay," said Crystal.

"So," said Gavin, "this is obviously related to Kaisa."

"Yes, she's a bit reluctant to travel alone, with her symptoms of Parkinson's, and I offered to go with her and hopefully be of some help while I experience yet another culture."

"That's great, Mom." Crystal was honestly happy for Lola. "I'm just being selfish. Now that we have the unspeakable issues resolved, I was hoping to have you around for a longer time."

Lola smiled. Unspeakables. Unmentionables like Margaret's underwear. In this case, dirty garments.

"Don't worry..." The phone rang again with its tone of an old-fashioned landline ring from the 1940s. Kaisa wanted to tell Lola to pack for both warm days and cool nights.

"As I was saying, don't worry. I'll be back soon enough. It's only a three-week trip."

The phone rang again. Kaisa informed Lola that she had reserved economy comfort seats on the plane for better leg room, and she wondered whether that met with Lola's approval.

She could understand Kaisa was excited, but all these calls were alarming. Hopefully, this was not the way it would be until they left. Then again, as they say, For a short time, you can be in a loose noose. Her time with Kaisa would be limited.

No wonder Alice was sometimes anxious, dealing with this woman, thought Lola.

Chapter 46

Lisa had methodically addressed the paperwork needed for her application for Doctors Without Borders. She met all requirements easily, and had e-mailed her application, feeling confident about her acceptance into the program. Now she waited for the next steps—interview, training, starting her French classes. She was already reading French works in the original language, currently *Le Petit Prince,* easing into French with an easy-to-read novella. She had previously read it in English, and familiarity with the content allowed her to experience success with the task.

Lisa was tending to her parents' grave when she saw Alice nearby, kneeling down by a cemetery plot covered with soil and obvious grass seed under protective straw. Lisa walked over.

"Oh, hi," said Alice. "I'm just looking at what I should do here. Mother doesn't know. Can you imagine? My mother knows everything." Alice rolled her eyes sarcastically.

The gravesite of Richard Weston was bare and looked forgotten.

"The gravestone is on order, and I don't want to plant anything before it's in place. Maybe I should also wait until the grass has taken root and grown a bit. What do you think?"

"Sounds like a good idea. It's not a matter of a

great hurry, after all," Lisa responded.

"Exactly. It will be here forever."

"By the way, that reminds me," said Lisa. "Do you know the history of all the members of the one family buried by the lilac bushes? The Barlows. They all died inside of a few months: mother, father, and seven children." They walked over to the simple rusted cross markers.

"1865," noted Alice. "I've never noticed this before, but I do remember my parents' talking about this family when I was a child. It scared me, as I had never thought children could die. It was probably an epidemic of some kind that killed them all, typhoid or diphtheria, most likely. They were common in those days. Hah! I am telling this to a physician!" Alice shook her head.

"True," said Lisa, disappointed that Alice did not have more detailed knowledge about this unfortunate family.

"Why are you so interested in these people in particular?" Alice was wondering.

"I don't know. They have, in a way, become a symbol to me of our lack of permanence. Everything we produce, build, and create is temporary. These people have been reduced to their names and the dates of their birth and death. All the rest, we have to imagine and guess. I have wondered about the father's occupation, the place where they lived, their religious and political opinions. Judging by the crosses, they were not people of means, but not such paupers as to have no monument at all."

"Interesting. I haven't really delved into local history, but when I retire, I'll have to research this," promised Alice.

Lisa laughed. "I guess I'll wait a while then."

"Right now, I can't even imagine retiring. What would I do with all the free time on my hands? I'm afraid my mother would quickly determine what I ought to do and steer my life in a direction suitable for her."

"Only if you let her," said Lisa.

"Right. Mom is leaving for Finland for a few weeks. I am so looking forward to a break from her. I know, I know, you would rather have a mother to fight with and to annoy you than no mother at all." Alice sighed. "Did you know Lola is going with her?"

"Really? Well, that's an unlikely pair to travel together, isn't it?"

"I guess. I'm just glad Mom isn't going alone. She is stubborn enough to have tried that, had Lola not offered."

"Lola just can't stay in one place for too long, can she?"

"Appears that way."

Lisa was quiet, staring blindly at the cross of Abigail Barlow. She looked at Alice. "I'm leaving, too, most likely at the beginning of the year, if you remember. I've been meaning to ask you, do you think Pamela would be willing to take care of Niles for a year or so while I'm gone? With your approval, of course."

"I have no objection. Pam loves animals. I'm sure she would say yes, but go ahead and ask her. Her cell number is…" Alice recited the seven digits, which Lisa entered into her phone's contact list.

Alice was already picturing Niles lurking around her house. She had never cared for short-haired cats with long, skinny legs, especially ones whose behavior clearly indicated that humans would need to live on the cat's terms. Frasier had been a different story—a long-haired, fluffy, cozy cat, ready to cuddle with you wherever you alighted. Alice saw herself feeding Niles, cleaning the litterbox, giving him his flea treatments. She needed to be definite from the beginning that the cat was Pam's responsibility, not hers.

Alice acknowledged that she was a magnet for things in need of organizing and taking care of, flypaper to tasks calling for a responsible person. Very similar to Kaisa, Alice realized, a thought that did not come to her as a surprise.

Chapter 47

Kaisa opened her eyes and viewed the intricate carving on the face of the bottom drawer of her secretary in the living room. She was disoriented and lifted her head from the floor. She saw clasped in her hand a small notebook, and it came back to her that she had been in search of phone numbers for her contacts in Finland. Kaisa moved her head from side to side, and tested the rest of her body parts to make sure she hadn't sustained any major damage in her fall, the cause of which appeared to be a corner of the carpet, slightly turned upward to catch an unsuspecting sandal. When she realized no permanent harm was evident, she relaxed. Although she must have hit her head, to lose consciousness, she felt normal. She got up from the floor with one hand holding onto the door handle, and carried on with her plans.

Kaisa had forcefully directed all her energies to organizing the trip. She had made the same trip almost every year and, although she felt comfortable in her native land, she sensed that where the country had developed and modernized—to extremes, in some ways—she herself had not. Her Finnish self was stuck. She was anxious to share information about her place of birth and proud to sing the praises of the arts, technological advancements, and the unique qualities of her homeland. But what she still longed for was the romanticized, idyllic place of her childhood and youth.

In a concrete effort to hold onto the days gone by, she had maintained ownership of her family's summer cottage on a small island in the Baltic Sea, a tiny, two-room hiding place with no electricity and no running water. Although, a few years ago, the neighbor cottage owners had opted to sign up for the offered conveniences, Kaisa insisted on keeping the cottage as she remembered it from the 1950s. She looked forward to sharing the cottage experience with Lola, who was the perfect person to accompany her, someone who had never been afraid of less-than-perfect accommodations, "perfect" being a relative term.

Kaisa had contracted with the son of a high school friend to keep an eye on the island property through the years. She had notified him of her upcoming trip, and had asked him to have the chimney cleared and the privy cleaned. He should ensure there would be drinking water, and store enough firewood for the sauna, the fireplace, and the outdoor cooking pit. She'd also need a fresh bottle of gas for the rest of the meal preparations. Primitive summer places were viewed as work camps by young people today, but Kaisa was thrilled to keep the tradition alive.

July had been fairly uneventful for Kaisa. She was worried about her daughter, who seemed to be dealing with loss on many fronts. Alice was mourning the death of her father, to be sure, a feeling Kaisa did not allow for herself except on quiet nights when she was unable to sleep. Alice had said goodbye to Christine, and was already anticipating the emptiness left behind by Lisa's departure in a few months. Crystal's upcoming marriage was a loss of sorts as well, for Alice. Even if

Gavin was in no way restricting Crystal's independence, the couple's tentative future vineyard plans would be time-consuming.

Through July, Lola told her she had read up on Finland, its history and its culture, and seemed to be eager to leave "the sooner the better," according to her own words. Kaisa was both flattered by Lola's enthusiasm about the trip and, at the same time, curious about her motives. Lola seemed almost too anxious to start the trip. Kaisa attributed it to the loss of a good friend and the general restlessness of a world traveler.

For the past month, Lola's life had involved the systematic organization and settling of all things legal with Margaret's estate, as well as dealing with the disposition of Margaret's belongings. She had been able to store some of the larger items and boxes in Gavin's farmhouse or barn until she was able to decide what to do with them. Lola felt the trip was exactly what she needed, as she told Kaisa, a chance to take a break before the next chapter in her life. Kaisa hoped to find out during the trip what that chapter might be. With Lola, anything was possible.

Chapter 48

"Täällä kapteeni Nikula. Olemme pian valmiita laskeutumaan.

Lämpötila Helsingissä on kaksikymmentäyksi astetta Celsiusta ja taivas on pilvetön. Toivomme, että teillä oli miellyttävä matka ja että näemme teidät lennollamme pian uudelleen."

The announcement jarred Kaisa, who was starting to nod off. Lola looked at her, baffled, until the announcement was repeated, first in Swedish and then in English.

"We will be getting ready for the final approach momentarily. The temperature in Helsinki is seventy degrees Fahrenheit, and the skies are clear. We hope you have had a pleasant flight and will fly with us again soon."

Lola looked out the window and twisted around to see as far as she could both behind her and ahead of her in the frame of the small window.

"We can't be landing." Lola looked at Kaisa quizzically. "I see nothing but forest."

Kaisa smiled knowingly. This was the expected response from a foreigner every time. Lola gathered her few belongings and put them in a bag she pushed under the seat in front of her. Kaisa had prepared herself several minutes ago, in her eagerness to be in her native land again.

As the wheels of the blue-and-white Finnish airline's plane touched the ground, Kaisa's tears flowed freely in spite of her heroic efforts to hold them back.

"Welcome to Helsinki," said the captain. "It's now eight-oh-three a.m. local time. We wish you a pleasant stay in Finland."

"Damn it!" huffed Kaisa. "I don't know why this happens every time I come to Finland! And, let me warn you, it'll be twice as bad when we leave. I have no reason to cry. It's just, it's…I have no idea what it is. You don't cry after being gone from the States for a while, do you?"

"No, but I have never lived away from the States for over forty years, either."

After clearing customs in record time and picking up their luggage, the unlikely traveling companions took a taxi to their hotel, a quiet place for recuperation from exhaustion and adjustment to the seven-hour time difference. They would take in the sights of Helsinki for a couple of days before heading out to the countryside.

Confused about the time and feeling heavy-headed, Kaisa and Lola looked around Helsinki. They visited museums, ate fresh berries at the marketplace by the sea, and after figuring out the intricacies of public transportation, toured the city to give Lola a better idea of Finland's capital.

On the last night in the modern hotel, Lola said, "Here I am with a native of the country, but I feel like a tourist. I'm ready for the less cosmopolitan areas."

Kaisa laughed. "Cosmopolitan! I guess. Compared to the days of my youth, you might say that."

The next day, they picked up the reserved rental car, a midsized sedan, huge to Lola and small to Kaisa.

"Want to drive?" Lola looked at Kaisa with raised eyebrows. A moment of truth for Kaisa. She rapidly thought of reasons why she could say no, but other than feigning helplessness, did not come up with any.

"Sure, unless you want to." Kaisa hoped secretly that Lola had only asked her to drive to be polite.

"We'll take turns. You first," Lola offered. Kaisa agreed. She had completely forgotten to teach Lola about some traffic rules that differed from the ones in the United States.

Kaisa sat behind the wheel and felt oddly confident. As they left the city area, the scenery quickly turned into the woods Lola had viewed from the air.

"Look at those trees. They grow straight up like large sticks, both pines and birches."

"I never thought of that. I never saw that before," said Kaisa, wondering how many other new things Lola was going to point out to her during their trip.

"When you take your turn driving," Kaisa began, "there are a few rules you are not familiar with, so pay attention."

"Yes, ma'am," said Lola and pretended to write on her hand as Kaisa talked.

"Pay attention," Kaisa repeated. "This is an important list. It is absolutely against the law to turn right when the traffic light is red, no matter what. There are "metal police"—cameras on posts—that film you and catch you speeding. You'll get a ticket in the mail. The amount of the fine is based on your income. You have to yield to traffic coming from the right, if you are not driving on a road that has the right-of-way, even if you think you are driving on a major road. Buses have a right to pull out in front of you from the bus stops.

Using your horn is considered extremely rude, unless you are in a dangerous situation. And, of course, stay alert. There are deer and moose around. Got that?"

"Got that," said Lola.

After driving for a few hours and stopping at the local grocery store, they drove onto a small yellow ferry, operated by Mauno Kuusinen, Kaisa's elementary school classmate. A sea captain's hat covered his silver hair. A white, well-cared-for beard completed the obviously intended nautical look.

"And you are still working?" Kaisa asked the man over the loud noise of the ferry motor.

"Not ready to be shelved yet. I have the best job, a total opposite of my previous banking world scene. I'm outside all day and meeting interesting characters, especially foreigners." Mauno looked at Kaisa sideways. "Like you," he added and flashed a row of bright white teeth.

I bet he has used whiteners, said Kaisa to herself.

Kaisa wasn't sure whether this was Mauno's brand of humor or if he really viewed her as an outsider. She decided not to take the bait.

At the destination, Lola stepped out of the car onto bedrock on a high hill amidst pine trees overlooking the Baltic Sea. With no neighbors in sight, nestled in the woods and halfway down the hillside was a red cottage with white trim. The only sounds she heard were a symphony of birds and an undecipherable low frequency murmur, the cause of which quickly became evident. An immense cruise ship approached from the left, almost hugging the shoreline, an eleven-story hotel gliding by slowly toward Sweden. It was like looking up at the spaceship in *Close Encounters of the Third*

Kind. To steer the ship among islands sprinkled close together in the sea must be a navigational miracle. Lola's mouth hung open in awe. The juxtaposition of the almost virginal nature all around and the enormous modern community traveling on water struck her as incongruous. Lola turned to look at her friend. Kaisa was sitting on a lichen-covered boulder, wiping her eyes. At that moment, it became clear to Lola how difficult it must be for Kaisa to belong to two different worlds, how impossible for her ever to be truly at home.

Chapter 49

After dropping her mother and Lola at the airport, Alice drove home in a leisurely fashion. Now was her opportunity to do things for herself. She would have three long weeks to finish projects she had put off and to concentrate on classwork preparation before school started.

The busy season of spring and early summer real estate boom had passed. Tom was working shorter days and kept a more regular schedule. He allowed time for lending Magnus a hand as an "apprentice" in the house restoration project at 84 Maple. Tom and Alice had even thought of stealing away for a mini-vacation, just the two of them.

Pam greeted Alice at the door, in uniform for her fast-food restaurant job.

"Mom, I need to ask you something. Do you think, if you taught me to drive, I could get my license before winter?"

A few months after Pamela had turned sixteen, she had started to show an interest in driving. Unlike her friends, who had applied for their learner's permits on their sixteenth birthday, Pam had not been eager. When questioned about her hesitancy, she confided in Alice that she was held back by two things. For one, she understood car insurance costs would go up with a teenage driver in the family, and also, a memory of a bad accident haunted her. In a car crash a year earlier, four Haudenosaunee Hills High School seniors had been killed. Their vehicle was traveling at a high speed down the hill and careened over the guard rail into the ravine below, killing all of them instantly.

Thoughts churned in Alice's head. *If Pam were able to drive, it would relieve me and Tom from the taxi service we now provide for both of our teens. A sixteen-year-old, most likely, won't be allowed to have passengers without an adult in the car, if I remember right. We would still chauffeur Bobby to and from practices.*

"You feel you are ready to drive now?" asked Alice, reminding Pamela of her earlier wavering. "I never believed you were concerned about the insurance costs."

"I've checked into that and know it's true." Pamela was earnest. "With my job, I have the money saved, so I can help."

My concerned, sweet, old-soul daughter. "You do know we can easily afford the cost, right?"

"I know, I know, but it means a lot more when I can contribute."

"So what exactly has made you change your mind? I thought you were going to take driver education in school in the fall."

"Going to work by bike has been okay. They promised I could continue to work on weekends during school, but using the bike in snowstorms would suck."

Alice smiled. "I guess it would. Whose car will you use?"

Pamela looked shocked. She had taken some things for granted. "I…I could… We could arrange our schedules so I could drive your car or Dad's, couldn't we? I don't have enough money saved to buy and maintain a car of my own."

"I'm sure we can work it out." Alice was pleased with herself for steering her daughter toward thinking responsibly.

Pamela continued excitedly, "I've studied the manual, gotten a hundred percent on the practice tests, and I have my eighty dollars ready. What do you say, Mom? Will you teach me?"

How could I say no to this enthusiasm, this initiative? "Of course."

"Mom, you're the best!" Pamela jumped up and down, squeezed her mother, and took her phone out of the pocket of her uniform. She pushed a number. "Stephie, she said yes!"

Alice walked into the kitchen, took the calendar from the wall, and crossed out a penciled line "Maine trip with Tom?" in squares covering the next two weeks.

Chapter 50

Lisa drove up to the Pure Earth farm. She planned to pick up some vegetables and to find out when apples would be ripe for picking.

The view of the lake from the top of the hill was breathtaking. The lush greenery with water views would most likely be among the things she would miss, wherever she ended up in her assignment. She found it cumbersome to try to plan for a long trip without knowing the destination.

I suppose it's like life in general. You can make plans in one direction, and events will take you on an entirely opposite path.

From childhood on, Lisa had been levelheaded, pragmatic, and, some might say, predictable. Her youth had been steady and secure. Her parents worshipped her. Until Lisa was eighteen and legally an adult, her parents had never traveled together in one vehicle. They had visited friends using two cars, and taken separate flights to go on longer trips, making sure at least one parent was still around for Lisa, should the other perish in an accident. Lisa was sure Susan and Carl had felt victorious having survived until Lisa's eighteenth birthday. It was ironic they would be killed on the lake only a few years later. Fate had a curious sense of humor.

"Hi!" Lisa greeted Gavin and Crystal, both on their

knees in the flowerbed.

"Hey, what's up?" Crystal sprang up from the ground.

"I'd like some fresh beets and carrots, and maybe some chard. Do you grow them?"

"Absolutely," said Gavin. "I'll get them. How much would you like?"

"It's just me. Enough for a few meals, and some carrots for snacking, as well."

Gavin started for the vegetable garden.

"You snack on carrots, too, huh?" said Crystal. "They're the best, sweet like candy. I should take some over to Alice. She's gained a lot of weight in the last couple of years."

Lisa looked thoughtful. "Weight is a difficult topic to bring up to a person. In my job, I struggle with that all the time. People, especially women, react to issues with weight so strongly. I do mention it to those whose weight is already a detriment to their health, but it's a gamble. I've had swear words flung my way, and some of my patients have found a new doctor for themselves."

"Really?" Crystal was amazed at people's ignorance and rudeness.

Lisa continued, "Although it happens very seldom, I've received thank-you letters from women who somehow couldn't figure it all out on their own and took my advice with good results."

"I'm not about to go to Alice and tell her to lose weight," said Crystal. "Her life is so very stressful. That alone can make her body hold onto the fat. To add a weight-loss program to her already full life might be the last straw. I'll take some carrots and apples to her, though, just as a friendly non-occasion gift."

"That reminds me," Lisa said, "When will the apples be ready?"

"Honeycrisps are ready now. We also have some old Cortland trees. You can pick the apples in October."

"Looks like I'll be making a few trips up here. Did you notice, by the way, that you said 'we' have apples? Are you living on the farm now?"

"Not full time. Call us old-fashioned, but we want the first few weeks after the wedding to feel different, that we are truly a married couple."

"I get that." Lisa nodded.

Gavin returned with a paper bag full of chard and another with root vegetables still covered with dirt and smelling of healthy, rich soil. "You want me to wash them?'

"No, no. This is a true earth experience, not a trip to the grocery store."

After paying Gavin, Lisa turned to Crystal. "What do you hear from your mother?"

"Nothing yet. She travels without a phone and only sends news via snail mail. I expect to get a letter any day now. I'm sure she's fine. Kaisa would have somehow contacted Alice if she weren't."

"I bet they're having a ball," said Lisa and drove away.

Chapter 51

Magnus had driven without an overnight stop from Florida to New York. His head was heavy, and he realized that the marathon drive had affected him more severely than similar trips in his younger days. Eager to spend the night in his old family home, he settled an air mattress and a sleeping bag in what used to be his parents' bedroom. He realized he had not brought a pillow. A rolled-up bath towel would have to perform double duty.

Magnus strolled through the house slowly, and now that the house belonged to him, he felt pride in the worn-out floors, the outdated wallpaper, and the old appliances. Every scratch, every dent and gouge had a story to tell, if not of his childhood and youth, then a story of another young family or of fraternity brothers.

The moving van would arrive in the morning. Magnus looked around with an eye to placing what little furniture he had decided to keep. He would use the dining room for storing items while the restoration advanced from room to room.

After restoring the house, Magnus wanted to furnish it with pieces appropriate to the colonial time period of the house. At the moment, he did not own anything colonial, except for the antique cobbler's bench, unique in its style, with a rounded seat and holes of various shapes for tools around the low surround at the opposite, square end of the bench. Underneath was a drawer for storing the numerous tools when not in use, the hammers, knives, and awls. Magnus had used the bench drawer most recently for storing coasters and cocktail napkins. The bench had reportedly belonged to John Lindqvist's eighteenth-century forebear, a shoemaker who immigrated to the United States from Sweden right after the Revolutionary War. The bench had been passed down in the family from eldest son to eldest son, and Magnus was proud to have it.

He woke up early the next morning and thanked his lucky stars it was not raining. When he returned from breakfast at the old corner restaurant, where everything was the same as it had been twenty years ago, the moving van was in the driveway. With three movers, it took no time for the van to empty and the house to fill up with professionally packed boxes. Magnus was in awe of the men strapping large chests of drawers to their backs and walking up a flight of stairs like turtles upright on their hind legs.

A couple of days later, Magnus had emptied most of the boxes. His abstract paintings already looked out of place. He wondered if there was a decent way to pass them on or to sell them without hurting the artists' feelings. Most had been given to him as gifts by his neighbor in Florida, an eccentric art teacher at the local community college.

Magnus had decided to make his meals at home, but opening the door of the gas oven was enough to discourage him. Fraternity boys apparently had no knowledge of how to clean an oven—or anything else, for that matter. He had always been under the impression fraternities had paid cooks. It seemed not so, especially if they were having financial problems.

After contemplating the wisdom of inviting his mother to see the house, Magnus called her. He felt slightly awkward presenting Carol's old house to her as his own, but Carol was delighted. She walked through the rooms, reminiscing about dinner parties and quiet TV nights, a house full of Magnus' and Christine's friends, and the eerie silence the day Magnus left the house for college.

When Carol saw the cobbler's bench, she sighed. "Well, welcome back home!" she greeted the bench, then lifted her head. "I think this old piece has been in the Lindqvist family for seven generations. Do I have my math right? I'm looking forward to the eighth generation to appear, but you and Christine haven't worked at that too hard now, have you? Christine's marriage gave me a small ray of hope, but you know how that ended."

Magnus was thoughtful. How does one know when it's a good time to bring up a topic that's apt to cause surprise, puzzlement, and, in Carol's case, confusion?

"Mom," Magnus began, "there's no reason to circle around the issue. I may not be producing the next generation to inherit the cobbler's bench. I'm gay."

"Well, I knew that," said Carol matter-of-factly. "Your being gay and producing an offspring are not mutually exclusive. Haven't you heard of 'partner parenting'?"

Magnus stared at Carol. Was this his old mother, who needed assistance with activities of daily living? The little old lady whose memory and understanding of simple things had faded considerably? He couldn't decide what surprised him more, the delightful fact that

Carol found his being gay an everyday issue, not worth discussing, or that Carol knew of the newly popular way of parenting. Magnus had studied the "social experiment" and it interested him—sharing a biological child without a marriage or even a close personal relationship with a partner, an arrangement where the child had two parents equally committed to the child.

"Well, you need to do what's best for you," said Carol.

"Love some,
Kiss a few,
Always paddle your own canoe."

"Right," said Magnus, looking sideways at Carol from under his brow. He shook his head and grinned.

Chapter 52

A white envelope with stamps depicting swans appeared in Crystal's mailbox. She was used to Lola's mail from all corners of the world and noted that this one was, yet again, slightly different from the others. The rectangle's shorter side was slightly longer than in standard American envelopes. Crystal opened it, making sure she didn't disturb the postmark or the stamp. She pulled out a letter, several pages long, written in Lola's artistic, yet easy to read handwriting.

August 27, 2019

Dear Crystal,

I am so grateful for a chance to experience this trip with Kaisa. Finland is amazing! I could describe for you pages and pages of sights in Helsinki and compare them to other places in countries I have visited, but the time in the countryside is what makes this experience extraordinary. There is a "hush" in this place, a quiet peace I have not felt anywhere else.

Kaisa's summer place is a nostalgic scene from long ago, a little two-room cottage making you breathe in the richness of the past. Time stands still in this place. Every item in the little house has a story. Kaisa knows most of the history and, of course, it is more meaningful to her than it is to me.

This tiny nest is surrounded by great, tall pines and a few birch trees, juniper bushes, and wildflowers.

We have no modern conveniences, and that suits me fine. With Kaisa's balance issues, I am the one to carry water into the sauna from a large barrel collecting rain water from the roof of the building. Drinking water was brought to the cottage before we arrived.

One early morning, I needed to use the toilet at about 5:00 a.m. As I was sitting on the composting toilet in the outhouse (completely clean, odorless, and sanitary, by the way), I heard rustling outside, followed by a strange sound of air forced out of a tight opening. I got up and peeked out of the small heart-shaped hole in the door. (Funny how the Finns have hearts and we have moons on the old outhouse doors.) Up the hill, on the bedrock a few steps from me, stood a bull moose, a tank on stilts, with majestic antlers silhouetted against the hazy light of the sky. The sound I had heard was a snort of the moose. Unsure whether the sound was a warning to me or an indication of fear on his part, I chose to wait him out. I did not dare yell for Kaisa, as a moose can, most likely, mow down a skinny, tall outhouse. As the moose settled down on the soft moss, showing no signs of leaving, I decided to meditate. I know when I am defeated. When the sun rose almost an hour later, he finally sauntered away.

In addition to the creatures familiar from home, I have also seen hedgehogs scampering around and heard a cuckoo bird that distracted me when I tried to concentrate on a book.

Tomorrow, we will go to Naantali, a small city closest to us, where I will buy some art supplies. It's been a while since I painted, but I am inspired by the beauty and serenity around me.

Kaisa also found a place in Naantali where we can participate in water aerobics for seniors. I don't feel like a senior, but I realize that vanity makes me fool myself. Kaisa's limbs can benefit from the gentle exercise and, in addition to my daily yoga, it will do me good as well.

I hope you and Gavin are well. You are, most likely, working on the farm with him. He truly is a gem among men!

My dear Crystal, I have decided that my days of trying to tell you what to do with your life are over. Kaisa and I have had heart-to-heart conversations about mothers and daughters. As she has helped me see that it is useless and completely wrong of me to tell you what is right for you, I believe that I have made a dent in convincing Kaisa that she should follow her own advice and admit that her relying on Alice for everything is detrimental to her daughter. See, old dogs can learn new tricks!

I am looking forward to painting. The colors of the red granite bedrock and the lichen-covered boulders are fantastic. I will do my best to duplicate their earthy beauty.

Be well. My best to Gavin.

I love you,

Mom

Crystal put the letter back in the envelope and hugged it to her chest. She decided to buy a binder and organize Lola's letters in chronological order. Lola's amazing adventures the world over. Someday, her own children would read them in wonderment. Her children… Crystal was ready to be a mother.

Chapter 53

A child needs a tub. Magnus made the first hit of the sledge hammer on the hallway bathroom wall upstairs. He had ended up with a walk-in shower model in his restoration plan for the room, but as often happens, restoration plans themselves require renovation.

Although a newborn could be bathed in the kitchen sink if need be, a young child loves to play in a tub. Magnus pictured a toddler covered in suds, endlessly pouring water from one colorful plastic dish into another. The original clawfoot tub was still in the garage, left there by Carol and John after the latest renovation project in the late 1980s. It could be restored. Christine could advise him whether a deep tub was suitable for bathing a child.

Magnus caught Christine on her drive to lunch with a friend.

"Hi, Sis, what do you think about a clawfoot tub for bathing a kid?" Magnus jumped right into the matter without the usual preparatory small talk.

Finding small talk nonsensical herself, Christine jumped right in after him. "A special kid or children in general?"

"Any child, I guess, but let's say he's mine."

"He? What if it's a girl? You are really serious about becoming a dad, aren't you?"

"I am. I found a co-parenting group in Rochester, not a support group, but a group for finding a suitable partner. This fall, I'll go to a meeting and see what develops. There are also groups online."

"I'm actually surprised you're progressive enough to entertain an unusual arrangement like this. Hah! Magnus, the quiet scientist!"

"Yeah, you know what they say, still waters and so on. I find the concept solid. I could adopt, of course, but I want a child who is biologically mine. Also, let's say I father a girl. It's only fair that she has a mother figure in her life as well."

"So tell me, what criteria will you use to pick a mother for your child? A raving beauty, a "brainiac" with an IQ over 150, an athlete, an artist, someone politically on the same page with you?"

"You've got it." Magnus laughed. " 'Musical,' 'artistic,' and 'beautiful' are not words describing me, so it wouldn't hurt for the mother to have those qualities."

"Sounds like you're setting out to create a perfect being." Christine's voice reflected a hint of concern.

"No, I place more importance on soft values like kindness and a sense of humor."

"To figure that out, you'd have to know the person pretty well."

"Granted. I intend to spend a lot of time with the potential partners. With romance out of the picture, you can concentrate on the essentials as platonic friends. We need to agree on the basics—living arrangements, finances, legalities, child-rearing practices. It's like stepping into a divorce but without the marriage behind you and bad feelings about your partner gnawing at you."

"Would you consider a co-parent of a different race or religion?"

"Why not? Race, definitely. Religion…if she were fanatic or rigid about it, probably not. She would also have to accept the fact that I'm an atheist."

"Right. I'll be curious to see how your search advances. I wouldn't mind being an aunt to this amazing child. This really is a project for mature adults, and you do meet that requirement, dear brother."

"Gee, thanks. But about that tub, what do you think?"

"A clawfoot tub will go well with the house. After all, it was there before, and you know it's light enough for the floor. It'll be a major pain to bring it upstairs, right? As far as safety, you'll be right there when the child is in the tub, so I wouldn't worry about that. The design you showed me could be left as is, using tiling all around the tub. In other words, wallpaper is out."

Magnus laughed.

Christine continued, "In the old days, a bathroom was not an actual wet space. Especially with children, you'll want it splatter-proof. You'll want a hand shower, as well. I can just imagine a six-year-old learning to use it."

"You're right," said Magnus, while he pictured himself getting an unplanned shower along with his child.

Chapter 54

Lola stepped into the car, taking care she didn't trample the heather growing in the nooks and crannies of the small rocks. The car was parked on bedrock, an unusual phenomenon for Lola, who was used to cement parking lots and, at her own cottage, a gravel-covered area specified for her little car. Here it seemed people adjusted to their natural surroundings, not the other way around. She looked forward to their trip to Naantali, a quaint medieval town on the sea. There she could buy paints, brushes, and cleaners. She saw productive painting days ahead.

Lola experienced an uncomfortable feeling of fear as Kaisa drove onto the first of the two ferries on the day's journey. The ferry's bow in front of them had only a heavy iron chain across it, indicating the spot for stopping. *What if Kaisa's foot on the brake didn't hold? What if they drove right into the sea?* Lola's body was alert with an undeniable adrenaline rush. When the car stopped a few inches from the chain, Lola sighed audibly. Her hands were wet with sweat, similar to the reaction she'd had on the ferry the day of their arrival. She contemplated a way to be at the wheel herself on the way back to the cottage. Approaching the second ferry, Lola noticed, to her relief, that this one had a wave guard across the bow, giving at least an impression of containment and safety.

In Naantali, they walked around the little town in the shadow of the convent church from the 1400s. The yards of the wooden buildings were filled with an array of blooming colors of the late summer.

Lola peeked into a square courtyard set between three dwellings and an outbuilding. Opening the gate slightly, she saw a colorful flower garden and a clothesline filled with equally colorful garments. Kaisa mentioned that, when possible, Finns preferred to dry their clothes outside in the wind.

"I remember when I was a child and winters were colder, we brought in frozen clothes from the line. They looked like the cod dried stiff on wooden racks on the Norwegian shoreline. Instead of folding the clothes into a basket, we stacked them like stiff sheets of cardboard. The moisture from the cold made them perfect for ironing."

Lola laughed. "I wonder if anyone irons anymore."

"I do," said Kaisa.

Lola was sure she would return to this picturesque town to paint.

Sitting on a seaside park bench admiring the boats of all kinds, from small fishing boats to large yachts and sailboats, Lola realized water was a surprisingly important element to her.

"You know…" She looked at Kaisa and then into the sun, which made her squint. "I thought I would only be at home on my lake in New York, but now I feel that any place with water can be home to me."

"Then you'll be right at home in the water aerobics class in the pool," said Kaisa. "It's time to go."

Climbing out of the pool after the vigorous class, Lola said, "This is so healing." Kaisa's balance was affected more than usual, stepping out of the water. She held onto the railing with a strong grip. With loud, rhythmic music blaring from a boombox, the seniors in the water had tried their best to follow the directions and the example of an athletic young woman on the side of the pool. Lola was two steps behind everyone else. Not understanding the verbal instructions in Finnish, she imitated the movements of the instructor and the participants in the pool.

After the session, Kaisa told her to take a shower before going to warm and relax their hard-worked muscles in the sauna. Lola stepped out of the open shower stall still wearing her bathing suit and saw Kaisa in front of her stark naked. The two of them had taken saunas unclothed at the cottage, but this was a fairly public place. As Lola looked around, other women came out of their shower cubbies wearing nothing. Kaisa pointed to a sign on the wall—a picture of a one-piece green bathing suit in a circle with a diagonal red line drawn across it. "Bathing Suits Prohibited." The text under the picture was in plain English.

"When in Rome…" said Lola, and she took off her bathing suit and followed Kaisa into the sauna, this one a large room with tiers of benches. The bravest souls sat on the top perch to catch the heatwaves at their hottest. Lola looked around, half expecting to see men file in from their locker room. Kaisa quickly pointed out that mixed bathing only happened in a family setting.

The women, all sizes and shapes, had a lively discussion going about something, taking turns lifting their arms, pointing to both sides of their lower abdomen and their breasts, all accompanied by sounds that Lola could only interpret as admiration and reverence. One of the oldest women turned her body from side to side to ensure that everyone had a chance to view her back.

Someone threw more water on the rocks. The women on the top bench reacted to the sudden heat wave. They closed their eyes into tight squints, and, holding their jaws closed, exposed their teeth and gums. *Tasmanian devils,* thought Lola. *Either that, or they are in the transitional phase of labor.* The odd thing was how they appeared to enjoy it!

"What's going on?" asked Lola quietly.

"You know how, at our age, talk inevitably turns to illnesses and medications. They are comparing surgery scars."

The younger ones, with laparoscopic gall bladder removals or vaginal hysterectomies, were obviously not leaders in the category of "most conspicuous scarring," nor were they winners for the "most pain endured."

The final winner in both categories was a woman in her late eighties who had a scar reaching from the middle of her back to her front, ending by the belly button—removal of a cancerous kidney in the nineteen-sixties. The scar looked wide, with each stitch mark still visible decades later. The woman also had a Caesarean scar running from her belly button to her pubic bone, cementing the winner's spot for her. Second in the competition was the winner's contemporary, who had to lift her belly to display an appendectomy scar about six inches in length. For the operation, she had been hospitalized for a whole week.

"Aren't we lucky?" said Kaisa. "Our bodies are intact."

Lola nodded. *My scars are invisible.*

Returning to the car for the trip back to the island, Lola casually said, "My turn to drive," and held out her hand for the keys, which Kaisa handed to her without objection.

Back on the ferry, Kaisa and Lola, now tired and relaxed, were approached by Mauno. "I'm having some people over on Saturday. I'd like you to join us."

"We'd love to," said Kaisa without hesitation. "Wouldn't we?" She looked at Lola.

"Absolutely. We'd be honored. Thank you," said Lola.

Chapter 55

Crystal put apples on the bottom of her backpack and filled the top with carrots, leaves sticking out. She grabbed the letter from Lola. Alice and she had agreed to compare notes on the information sent by their mothers from Finland. Although Lola refused to travel with a cell phone, Kaisa always had one with her in case of an emergency.

Crystal stood her bicycle on its stand and read a note on the front door of Alice's house: "Crystal, I'm out back. Come around to the deck."

Alice was reading a magazine article about the importance of sleep. "Hi, Crystal. You won't believe what I just did."

"Hi, I probably won't. I never know about you."

"I was reading about sleep's rejuvenating powers and looking at the picture that goes with the article." Alice had a Finnish ladies' magazine in her lap. Kaisa had made sure Alice had at least a rudimentary knowledge of Finnish. "It's referring to our busy lives, with the picture showing an anthill of people in the street, all looking hurried, all without a personality. I wanted to look at a face in detail, and you know what I did?"

Crystal raised her eyebrows.

"I put my thumb and my middle finger together on that face and slowly moved the fingers apart from each other, 'enlarging' the picture." Alice demonstrated as she spoke. "I'm so used to doing that on the phone!"

Both burst out laughing.

"I know what you mean. I catch myself looking for the 'thumbs up' icon after reading an email."

"It's imprinted in our brains," said Alice. "It's probably also a sign that I spend way too much time staring at a screen of some sort. Addictive personality, I guess. I should sleep more."

"Speaking of things good for you, I brought you some carrots and apples." She pulled out the bunch of carrots. "These beat potato chips every time!"

"Thank you," said Alice. "I really need to pay attention to my diet. My mom is always harping about my weight, but you know, the more she preaches, the less I want to do anything about it. Weird, isn't it?"

Crystal was not about to step into a deep discussion about Alice's relationship with Kaisa.

"Hey, I wanted you to read my mom's letter. She's having some interesting experiences in Finland."

Alice put on her glasses. She burst out laughing as she read about Lola's hiding from the moose.

"My mom was talking about that. You know Mom calls me sometimes after Lola has gone to bed? 'Lack of a phone keeps Lola's experience pure,' she says." Alice read to the end of the letter and set her glasses on her lap. She was tearing up. "I know I complain about my mom a lot, but I also love her over the moon. Every time I complain about her, I think of Lisa and the emptiness she must feel without a mom in her life."

"True," said Crystal quietly.

Alice continued, "Mom is so glad to see Finland through Lola's eyes. Things she's taken for granted all her life now have new meaning." She looked pensive. "Lola made it possible for Mom to make the trip safely. For all we know, this may be her last trip to Finland."

"Hopefully not," said Crystal. "It still is her home in a way, I see."

"Very much so." Alice thought of the many times Kaisa had called herself ET or an alien. Kaisa always smiled at her nicknames for herself, cloaking the sadness in humor.

Chapter 56

Niles watched Lisa from behind the forsythia bush. He was an indoor cat, and Lisa didn't trust him to survive the outside for longer than a few moments. He had snuck out through the front door, which Lisa had left ajar in her hurry to the mailbox. Earl, the mailman, was almost a daily visitor, his appearance an anticipated event in Lisa's life. Lisa herself smiled at her almost childlike eagerness to receive an anxiously awaited piece of mail. A few minutes ago, Earl had deposited several envelopes and pamphlets in the mailbox.

Niles watched in amazement as Lisa picked one envelope from the others, read what was in it, and all of a sudden sat down on the lawn and stared ahead of her.

The greatly anticipated envelope had a return address in the upper left corner:

Medicins Sans Frontieres

Doctors Without Borders

New York, NY

A logo of a stick figure breaking through a red wall was above the text.

Lisa opened the envelope with shaky hands. She scanned through the polite text and zeroed in on the suggested assignment: Kabul, Afghanistan. Lisa had reviewed all possibilities in her mind numerous times, knowing no place would be a tourist destination. She had pictured herself in faraway huts in African countries, the heat of the Philippines, Haiti, and South American nations. She had not considered the Middle East with any seriousness. Afghanistan… She imagined poppy fields contrasted with soldiers and guns amidst ruins. Lisa felt the only appropriate protocol was to accept the assignment. As Margaret would say, it would be gauche to object to an offer to serve in a place where the need was great.

Lisa made up her mind to learn as much as she possibly could about the distant as well as the current history of Afghanistan, along with its customs and its culture. She remembered there was an Afghani professor at the university. She would contact him to get a personal view on the country.

Niles, baffled about his mistress' sitting on the ground, came out of his hiding place and rubbed his head on Lisa's elbow.

"Good boy." Lisa grabbed Niles, carried him into the house, and told him to stay put. She then drove to the library. She could spend time searching for information online, but she always preferred the feel of an old-fashioned book in her hands, especially in bed right before falling to sleep. She also wanted to avoid screen time at that hour of the night—or any time, for that matter.

With a reusable grocery bag full of books, Lisa was on a roll. She felt relieved to have a destination, a focus to her future.

Lisa drove to Fitzpatrick Realty in hopes Tom would be in his office. She was in luck.

"I'm sorry to bother you with a personal issue during your work hours." Lisa looked at Tom, who at first had wondered if Lisa wanted to list her house. "As you know, I will soon join Doctors Without Borders. I just got my assignment, so to say. I am going to Kabul."

"Afghanistan?" Tom's utterance sounded like a question. He whistled, indicating his esteem. "You are a brave lady, but we've always known that. When will you leave?"

"Early January, it looks like. I was wondering if you wouldn't mind looking after the house while I'm gone. Check on it now and then, control the heat, clean the furnace, that sort of thing. What you did with Magnus' house before he bought it. I'll pay you, of course."

"I'd be happy to," said Tom.

"I'm asking Gavin to take care of the mowing, trimming the bushes, plowing the driveway, et cetera. I do want the house to look lived-in for the year."

"I think we can handle it."

The call to Gavin resulted in equally pleasant results. Lisa drove to the local hardware store and had two keys made: one for Tom and one for Gavin. Walking to her car with the keys in her hand, Lisa laughed at herself. *What am I doing? It's four months until January.* Either she herself or Tom and/or Gavin could lose the keys many times over before it was time. Back at home, she put the keys next to her passport in her safe.

Chapter 57

The late afternoon was cloudy. Lola didn't want to risk getting her canvas wet, and instead, "just in case," settled inside to work on a still life—Kaisa's antique wooden coffee grinder next to an old coffee cup and saucer, the cup clearly showing a crack, which only added to its charm.

Kaisa had informed Lola that on a cloudy, rainy day, the seawater felt warmer, and that jumping in from the sauna was more pleasant than ever without the shock of the water's coldness. Kaisa started down the steep path, the first part of the routine of heating the sauna.

Lola heard laughter and ran out the door to discover Kaisa sitting on the side of the path halfway down the hill. Laughter was a good sign, but Lola kept her fingers crossed. Kaisa had obviously fallen again, this time into a thicket of nettles. Lola reached out her arm and pulled her out, carefully avoiding the itchy, burning welts on Kaisa's arms and legs.

"Why don't you get rid of those damned things?" asked Lola, tilting her head toward the flattened plants.

"What do you think you've been eating for greens all this time? Nettles are a great source of vitamin C."

"Not worth it, with the welts you have."

"I know I am not supposed to roll in them. I just took a detour."

"Make sure you don't scratch yourself bloody." Lola sounded maternal.

"The sauna will take care of the itch."

"Really?" Lola was incredulous. Kaisa would say the sauna cured cancer and stop all wars, as well.

"Oh, yes. It's also great as first aid for sunburns. There is a saying here that 'if sauna, tar, or booze don't cure you, you are a goner."

Lola laughed. "You're okay otherwise, I take it?" She wanted to establish that Kaisa's bones were whole, without cracks.

"Certainly. The sauna will be ready in about an hour."

Later, having alternated between the heat of the sauna and dips into the Baltic, Kaisa and Lola threw water on the rocks one more time.

"I am so glad you like the sauna. It cleanses you inside and out. Do this," said Kaisa, rubbing the front of her leg the whole length of the tibia with her index finger. Lola obeyed and looked up at Kaisa. "Ewww," she said feeling the dead skin under her finger. "I am filthy!"

Kaisa laughed, "It's normal, but the sauna does a better job getting rid of it than a shower."

"It's interesting," noted Lola. "I don't think people in the States think of the sauna as a bath. It's more like a very warm room for relaxation."

"You said it! There are businesses near us advertising saunas with 'fabulous features'—piped in music, lights for reading a book or a newspaper, or even a TV. Don't you just love soggy, wet books? They have missed the whole idea."

Lola laughed. "I went into a sauna in a hotel once

and was thrown out for pouring water on the rocks. The management's explanation was that 'the stove operates with electricity, and mixing water and electricity would put you in great danger of being electrocuted.' "

"There are strange ideas out there," said Kaisa.

" 'Out there,' people would think your ideas are strange, like being naked. I imagine, though, that children in Finland must grow up to have a much more natural attitude toward nudity than children elsewhere."

Kaisa looked thoughtful. "I think if you played an association game with random Finns and Americans in the street—you know, like what's the first word that comes to your mind when you hear the word 'naked'— the Finns would say 'sauna' and the Americans would say 'sex.' "

"That's just it. Because the word is connected so strongly with sex, nudity has become something dirty. Here's another question: Why do some people think of sex as dirty?"

"Oh, Lola, that is a huge question. Goes back to the Bible or before. We probably don't have enough years left in our lives to figure that one out."

Afterward, they sat on the small deck outside the sauna door, listening to the waves under the deck a few seconds after a boat sailed or motored by. They were wrapped in beach towels—the summer had taken a turn into early fall.

Lola felt relaxed. She had toyed with the idea of confiding in Kaisa in order to free herself of the confusion she felt about her life. She sensed she could trust Kaisa, to pour her soul out to her. "A shared sorrow is half a sorrow." How ironic that it was a saying of Swedish origin, of all things, another

Lindqvist connection…

"I am sorry I've been rather distant at times on this trip," Lola began hesitantly. "I've had a lot on my mind."

Kaisa admitted having noticed how Lola was greatly disturbed about Margaret's death.

"Everything isn't always what it seems to be," said Lola. She readjusted her towel around her. "Did you know Margaret had an affair with John Lindqvist for many years?" She had now tapped the fragile ice with her toe.

"I'm not one bit surprised," said Kaisa. "He carried on with Faith Collins for years. You know, the tall paralegal in Richard's office."

The other foot had dropped for Lola without her expecting it. She felt like vomiting, but desperately held onto preserving her dignity. Margaret wasn't so special to John after all. It then followed that she herself wasn't so special to John, either. Reality hit her hard in the face like a boxing glove.

"Do you think Carol knew?" asked Lola, desperately hoping for an answer in the negative.

"Sure she did. The wife always knows," said Kaisa, "if she has any kind of an antenna at all."

What does that make Carol? A queen of suffering in silence? Some sort of Saint of Forgiveness? A Mother Teresa of Haudenosaunee Hills?

The sun moved slowly closer to the horizon. Lola gathered her courage. "Kaisa, I also had a long affair with John Lindqvist. John is Crystal's father."

Kaisa sat motionless. After a while, she dared look at Lola and imagined her pain. "I am sorry, I didn't mean to…" Kaisa was reeling back.

"No, no," said Lola. "I'm all right. I'm relieved I could get it off my chest." The heartache she felt was colossal.

Kaisa was quiet. Lola was quiet. Lola leaned her head back. Her terrycloth towel fell on her lap, exposing her upper body. She did not care that the three thousand passengers of the cruise ship bound for Sweden saw all she had to reveal.

After the enormous waves from the ship had crashed to the shore, Lola felt cold. She pulled up her towel. "You must think I'm despicable," she whispered.

"My husband was the judge. I am not."

Chapter 58

On Saturday, Kaisa made a no-bake cheesecake, a contribution to the party at Mauno's. The American-style calorie-bomb dessert and a bottle of bourbon would represent the United States food culture at dinner, the best Kaisa and Lola felt like mustering.

Kaisa looked forward to visiting with old friends, and Lola was curious to see a modern Finnish house. She knew that, as wonderful as Kaisa's cottage was, it in no way represented current Finnish architecture or style.

"I will drive," said Kaisa and sat behind the wheel. She was glad the road to Mauno's was not a highway but rather a narrow country road. A couple of days ago on their way to Turku on the smooth four-laner, Kaisa had noticed that when her hands rested on the steering wheel, both hands had been shaking. Now, bumps on the road camouflaged the movement of her hands. She recalled that she had an appointment with her neurologist at the end of September.

After a quiet drive through the greenery of fields and forests, they arrived at Mauno's modern hilltop house, a large wooden structure with glass walls facing the sea. The view in all directions took Lola's breath away. There was no lawn to mow. Between the boulders and the crevices in the bedrock were wild bilberries and heather, all natural, yet as if planned and planted with meticulous care.

"Do we have to go inside? I could stand here forever," said Lola staring at the sea.

"Here," said Kaisa handing her the bourbon bottle. "You take that. I will bring the cheesecake." Lola's bubble had been burst. She would have been happy outside without people around her.

Mauno greeted them at the door. Beyond the foyer was the living room with the wall of windows. Light wood and shades of white paint dominated the space. The house was roomy and airy, showcasing furniture by famous Finnish architects, simple designs with well-thought-out functionality. Either Mauno had an eye for interior design or the room was his late wife's handiwork. Oversized, abstract paintings in hues of blue and turquoise were strategically placed on the walls. Lola noticed a signature, M. Kuusinen, in the bottom right corner of the pieces. *Paintings by Mauno?*

Mauno caught Lola squatting down to see the small signature on a narrow, vertical piece. Lola felt embarrassed. Margaret would have chided her for acting so conspicuously curious in someone's home.

"I'm sorry to be so nosy, but I find these paintings fantastic. There is a feeling of the sea in every one of them. They are yours, correct?"

"Yes, I am just an amateur. Painting relaxes me. I hear that you paint, as well..." Mauno was interrupted by the doorbell.

A dozen people came in the door at the same time, all carrying dishes of food.

"We are sorry we are late," said a man in his seventies or so. "The ferry had just left the continental side when we got there, and we had to wait for the next run." Kaisa explained to Lola that the gentleman was distraught for being late, as Finns are known to be extraordinarily prompt.

When Kaisa looked more closely at the man and the others who, according to the Finnish custom, were removing their shoes in the foyer, she ran over with her arms wide open. They were all Kaisa's cousins and their children. Only a few years ago, older people had found Kaisa's obviously American habit of embracing her relatives awkward, and had handed her a stiff arm and hand for a formal handshake. Recently, hugging had become commonplace in the Finnish society, and Kaisa was happy to reinforce the custom.

"Mauno, you sweet man, you have orchestrated a family reunion for me, haven't you?"

Kaisa made the rounds and hugged her relatives. As they exchanged news with joyful laughter and quieted down to talk about Richard's passing, Mauno stole Lola away.

"I know it can be boring, when you don't know the language. Tell me about yourself."

Lola discovered that, in addition to painting, she and Mauno shared a love of travel. She envied Mauno's experiences of climbing Mount Kilimanjaro, visiting with the aborigines in the Philippines, and taking part in the reindeer separation in Lapland, the latter being a common wintertime activity in northern Finland, according to Mauno.

"Sounds exotic to me," said Lola.

Driving home, Kaisa told Lola excitedly and in detail the news of her relatives, from births of their grandchildren to confirmations and graduations, events that meant very little to Lola. She listened politely, until she was able to insert into the conversation, "Mauno's house is quite something, isn't it?"

"Truly," said Kaisa. "No extra paraphernalia anywhere. He told me last year that he had gotten rid of everything but the essential."

Lola had in fact meant the quality of the architecture and the design in the structure and furnishings, but she was willing to veer off the road in the conversation.

"I could tell," said Lola. "Could you do that?"

"I am a bit of an emotional saver. Who else would drag a hundred-year-old spinning wheel across half the world just because it belonged to your grandmother?"

"I know what you mean. I still have all of Crystal's report cards and artwork from kindergarten on."

Kaisa sighed. "It almost gives me physical pain to think our daughters might destroy what we have saved. Why do you suppose we save things?"

Lola thought for a moment. "For me, it may be that we had a huge family and there wasn't always enough to go around. I suppose I cling to things once I get them."

"In my case," said Kaisa, "it was most likely the way my parents lived. After the war, nobody had much, and we never threw away anything, because 'you might be able to use it someday.' "

"It was easy for me to throw away Margaret's old things, but my own belongings are different," said Lola, opening the car door.

"I…" Kaisa exited the car and tripped on a tree root. "Here I go again." She got up holding onto the car and then felt burning and wetness on her patella. Oh, yes, she had skinned her knee and was bleeding.

With the help of a flashlight, they walked to the cottage, holding onto each other. Once inside, Lola turned on some battery-operated candles.

"You know, Lola, we should have come in June, when the sun never sets. At least I could see where I am going."

Kaisa sat on a chair straightening her leg out in front of her. "Would you get some hydrogen peroxide from the cabinet and some paper towels, please?"

Lola read foreign labels on the bottles. "Your words are entirely too long," she said. She picked up a brown bottle and tried to sound out the name. "Vetyperoksidiliuos."

"That's it," said Kaisa. "You'll be a Finn yet."

Lola cleansed Kaisa's knee in spite of her objections. She put the peroxide back in the cabinet with the help of a candle.

"What do you do in the winter, when the sun rises only for a couple of hours?" wondered Lola. She couldn't imagine living mostly in artificial light.

"People are used to it. It has its negative side, of course. A lot of alcoholism, a great many cases of suicide and domestic violence."

"Sounds awful," said Lola.

"It's worse in winters with very little snow. All that white makes the world so much brighter. That's why we love the sun and spend as much time outside as we can."

Lola noticed Kaisa alternated between "we" and "they" when referring to her countrymen. She was going to pay attention to whether Kaisa used "we" consistently when speaking exclusively of positive features. She didn't appear to be hiding the negatives.

Chapter 59

"You're doing quite well," Alice said to Pamela, as her daughter concentrated on oncoming traffic and the white line on the right. "Just remember the speed limit goes down to forty when you get to the next light."

"I know, I know," said Pam, sounding a bit annoyed. Alice felt the tone of voice was part of the "parent teaching the child to drive" deal, and took it in stride.

"Let's turn right at the light and then immediately to the left onto Main Street. We can go to the empty Ames parking lot and practice backing up," Alice instructed her daughter. Being a teacher did not hurt in this task.

When Pamela was about to turn left, the driver in the car behind her leaned on his horn. Pamela startled.

"You're okay. You forgot to use the blinker, didn't you?" Alice calmed her down.

"I guess so. I had just blinked to the right and didn't realize..." Her voice trailed off.

Alice's phone rang. "Hi, Mom." Alice looked at the time on the phone. "What time is it there? One o'clock in the morning?"

"Something like that. I wanted to talk in private."

"Don't get so close," said Alice. "You're tailgating."

"What?" said Kaisa.

Pamela slowed down and turned into the empty Ames parking lot.

"Nothing, Mom, I was talking to Pam. I'm teaching her to drive."

"Of all things," said Kaisa. "Can you concentrate on me for a second? I have something to tell you."

Thousands of miles away, and she is giving me orders.

Pamela parked the car and lowered her seat into a reclining position, communicating her understanding that her mother would be on the phone for a while.

"I have been thinking." Kaisa cleared her throat. "The big house is way too much for me. I didn't tell you, but my shaking has become worse, and I have fallen a few times. I love my house and all the memories in it, but I need to be realistic. The cottage has made me realize that bigger isn't always better. Without Richard, I roam around the big place. I don't need all that space. It's not that I have to move next week. In fact, I have read that after a big change like a death of a spouse or a divorce, if at all possible, you should wait a year or more to make any big changes. I don't want to wait that long, and I would like to move before next year. Would you put a bug in Tom's ear to look for a small ranch or a condominium for me? All rooms on the first floor. A quiet neighborhood would be a plus, and a place near the water would be ideal."

Alice was quiet.

"Hello," said Kaisa, "are you there?"

"Mom, you don't know how relieved I am to hear you say that. I've been concerned about you ever since Dad died. It's not safe for a person with your issues to be alone in that big house. To tell you the truth, I've been on pins and needles, worried sick about you."

"I'm glad you feel okay about my decision. Are you sure you don't have any emotional attachments to the house or difficulties letting go of it?" Kaisa paused. "Maybe you and Tom could buy it," she added.

Whoa! thought Alice. *No way. Not all those rooms. Not the thousands of window corners!*

"We'll see," said Alice hesitantly. "It almost sounds like you want me to want to hold onto the house."

"No, no, I just wanted you to know I would give you and Tom first dibs."

Alice was now aware this was obviously a sensitive topic, and Kaisa had most likely thought this through before making the call. Maybe Kaisa wanted her and Tom to buy the house and create a chance for herself to keep a connection to her past, like she had done with the cottage in Finland.

"Is everything in order at the house? Have you checked?"

"Tom and I both have. Everything is fine. You can relax."

"Thank you so much. I think Lola is awake." Kaisa whispered. "Give your family a kiss for me. I'll see you soon."

"Bye, Mom."

"What's Grandma up to now? She wants to sell her house?" Pamela lifted her seat into the upright position.

"That's what she said."

"Will she be happy someplace else?"

"Time will tell, I would say. Okay, back to business. Let's do some backing up. What's the first thing you do?"

"You make sure there's nothing behind you."

"Good," said Alice.

Pam's job of backing up the car was acceptable but in need of further practice.

At home, Alice bent over and kissed Tom on the cheek. He was paying bills online, both their own and Kaisa's.

"Hey, you want to buy Mom's house?" Alice asked casually.

"Right," Tom rolled his eyes. "Why do you ask?"

"Mom has made a very good decision. She wants to downsize, and she has some marching orders for you, to find her a ranch or a condo."

"That's great, isn't it? Finding a smaller place for her should be doable. Any other specifications?"

"A waterfront property in a quiet neighborhood. Well, at least a place with a water view."

"I know," said Tom turning around his swivel office chair, snapping his fingers, "Crystal's place. She'll probably sell her condo when she and Gavin get married. At least I'm assuming she'll sell. Fairly new construction, two-bedroom unit, with a balcony overlooking the lake. She would need to use the stairs only to go down to the level of the lake."

"Why didn't I think of that?" Alice shook her head.

"Hey, I'm the professional here. Does Kaisa want to list her house now?"

"I told you, she's counting on our buying it. I wasn't kidding. No listing needed." Alice laughed. "I'm assuming she will list it after you find her a suitable place to move into and she acknowledges we are staying put."

Alice thought of possible changes needed to accommodate Kaisa's future physical needs. Christine would know all about door widths and sink heights to make Kaisa as comfortable as possible in her new home for a long time, even if she ended up in a wheelchair eventually.

This will work out. Alice crossed her fingers.

Chapter 60

Lola took a bite of her round slice of dark rye bread covered with soft cheese and cucumbers, her usual breakfast. She tried to formulate sentences in her mind for the best possible presentation of her proposal to Kaisa.

When Kaisa came to the table, Lola brought a mug of coffee to her.

"I've been thinking," Lola started. "These couple of weeks have been wonderful. I'm so thankful you let me come with you. As you know, I just love it here." She cleared her throat. "Do you think it's possible for me to stay longer after you leave? I have some things to straighten out in my mind, as you probably can imagine."

"It's fine, as far as I'm concerned. You are lucky I am Americanized. I think it's a lot easier for me to consider this situation than it would be for a true Finn. They are much more wary. This cottage was not built for year-round living, and it does get cold. There's enough firewood and water to last you until you have to return to the States. Let's see, it would be the middle of November when your ninety days are up for visitors. Sorry, we don't let you stay longer."

"Great! I want to do some more painting and sort out my miserable life."

"Here," Kaisa handed Lola her cell phone. "You

won't be able to change your flight by writing a letter to the airlines."

Lola laughed. "Thanks."

Later, Lola picked up her stationery and, sitting on the deck of the sauna by the sea, wrote a letter to Crystal. Kaisa would most likely be home in the States before Crystal received her mother's letter and could fill her in on all the happenings. Lola was writing old news for the future.

Kaisa and Lola drove to the airport in comfortable silence, a habit Lola had become accustomed to, conversing with Finns. "Not every quiet moment needs to be filled with unimportant chatter" was their motto. At Mauno's party, Lola had watched in puzzlement when, sitting in a small group on the sectional sofa, a silence fell on them. For a while, Lola followed what she thought to be a deep contemplation on a serious topic; however, the facial expressions did not support that hypothesis. Kaisa's cousin Eeva was intently checking the polish on her fingernails while her husband Jari had his lips pursed as if in a whistle with no discernable sound. Others were looking out the window into the dusk. Lola joined them, wondering what was happening.

"So, what do you think of Finland so far?" asked Jari all of a sudden, with a heavy accent, after what seemed to be an inordinately long silence.

"I like it very much," said Lola politely. She chuckled to herself. *Except for your weird conversation style.*

At the airport, Kaisa got her ticket, checked in her luggage, and also ensured her connecting flight arrangements were clear, with wheelchair transportation at the terminal in New York. They said goodbye, Kaisa emotional about leaving her homeland perhaps for the last time and slightly concerned about Lola's ability to "rough it" in the cool Finnish late fall and early winter. Lola didn't worry. She was excited about another, different experience. Little did she know Kaisa had left her detailed instructions in writing for any possible inconveniences, from running out of firewood to mice or bats in the cottage.

Sipping on her coffee by the large windows of the airport cafeteria, Lola watched as the plane soared toward the clouds. At this point, Kaisa was most likely crying. Lola felt like a fledgling whose mother had flown away. She was about to repeat the solo experiences from her past travels, ready for the next adventure around the corner.

With Kaisa's old-fashioned paper map, Lola started her trip back to the island. On the way, she stopped in small villages, visited local sights, and disappeared into small crowds in the village streets. The only thing keeping her from total assimilation was the language. She felt free. A few more weeks of paradise, and she would be as good as new.

When Lola arrived at the cottage, a small, blue plastic bucket waited for her on the step. A note attached to it read, "I thought you would enjoy these. Simply fry them in butter and add salt. Mauno." Inside the bucket were bright yellow, curly chanterelles, Lola's favorite mushrooms.

Chapter 61

Back at home, Kaisa's bedroom felt palatial to her after the cramped quarters of the small cottage. The trip had tired her, and the sense of vulnerability overwhelmed her. The decision to downsize was a sensible one, yet it was unusual for Kaisa to let go, to give in on any issue, and she felt defeated.

Kaisa stepped down from her king-sized bed. Where most people get up out of bed, she slid down to the floor until her toes touched the carpet. Climbing into bed required the help of a step stool. A thinner mattress was in order, or her place to sleep was in danger of turning into a safety risk for her.

Alice had offered to pick Kaisa up to tour Crystal's condominium. To Alice's amazement, Kaisa casually let Alice know that she would drive herself and meet her there.

Tom had wasted no time in designing Kaisa's residential future, and when Crystal heard about the idea, she jumped at the chance. Crystal agreed that her place was perfect for a single woman of any age, and with Kaisa's Parkinson's in mind, a desirable location with no accessibility issues to speak of other than the access to the lake, which required using steps.

Kaisa entered the foyer of the condominium, looked through the living room out to the shimmering lake, and said, "When can I move in?"

Crystal laughed. "If you're serious, I'll be moving out at the end of December."

Kaisa looked at Alice. "I was joking. I do want to see the rest of the place, but if Tom can sell my house within the same timeline, it's workable."

Alice winked. "Don't worry. He has it all under control. There's a professor at the college whose children are growing up and will soon need rooms of their own. It's a sad story. He lost his wife to cancer a few months ago, and was left to raise their five children alone."

"I remember that," said Crystal. The family is from Afghanistan, right?"

"I think so. Their name is Nazari."

"You mean Tom's seriously working on this already?" asked Kaisa. Waves of worry flooded her thoughts. What if she couldn't get everything in order by the end of the year? What if the professor wanted the house before Crystal's place was ready for her? The house deal would have to stipulate that Kaisa didn't end up in the street.

"From what Tom tells me, things could be worked out." Alice looked at her mom. "Of course, you will be part of the negotiations, set the price, decide on what is sold as part of the house, and so on."

"This sounds almost too easy," Kaisa shook her head slowly.

Tom worked in his most professional way with Crystal, Kaisa, and Dr. Abdul Nazari. Negotiations resulted in two of Tom's most successful real estate contracts, leaving behind a trail of happy sellers and buyers. It was agreed that Crystal would vacate the condominium the week after Christmas and that the

Nazari family would move into Kaisa's house in the middle of February. This generous timeline gave Kaisa a chance to plan thoroughly and carefully.

Kaisa began to categorize her belongings. As the first priority, she identified furniture and other items to take with her to her new home. She invited Alice to go through the rest with her family. Kaisa made a solemn vow that should Alice place in the discard pile an item she herself had thought to suit her daughter, she would accept Alice's decision as final.

A week later, when Alice lifted up an artistic wall hanging and placed it in the charity pile, Kaisa couldn't help herself. "That's the ryijy-rug my aunt wove in the nineteen forties!"

"That's nice," said Alice.

Kaisa bit her lip and swallowed hard.

Chapter 62

Magnus and Christine sat on a cliff overlook in Letchworth State Park.

Christine had decided to visit her mother before another six months had gone by, to see how Magnus was progressing on the house restoration, and to see the magnificent fall colors of the Finger Lakes, always at their most spectacular in the middle of October.

Below them were small waves like crystals in a winding creek. Having survived the powerful waterfalls up above, they would move on in anticipation of becoming part of a larger water downstream—Lake Ontario.

Christine had been happy to find her mother content and well cared for. Her worry about Carol had diminished greatly after Magnus' move into town. Carol's friend Elizabeth was still in the picture, which Christine found to be a godsend.

"I'm surprised you've gotten so far with the renovation—I mean, restoration—project," Christine said, taking chicken sandwiches out of Magnus' backpack made heavy by frozen plastic ice blocks.

"I'm slowing down a bit now. I get excited in the beginning of any project, but when it turns routine, I lose interest."

"Lose interest? That's not like you. You used to work on a science project forever, until it was just right."

"I know. In those days, I had the luxury of being able to concentrate on one thing. Now, I am distracted. You know, the co-parenting group."

"So is there something new to report? The last time we talked about it, you had met a couple of potential mothers for your child."

Magnus reached into the single-serving potato chip bag. "I've met with these women a few times individually. One of them is really interesting. She and her parents are all dentists. Her mom and dad immigrated here from Delhi, India. She herself was born in New York City a couple of years after the parents' arrival. She is smart, beautiful, and interested in all types of endurance sports, Ironman triathlon races being one of her favorites. Besides, she is a child of two people whose marriage was arranged. The co-parenting idea is not strange to her at all."

"What about the other woman?"

"She's a hoot. I wish I had her sense of humor. She works as a social worker in Canandaigua. You can tell she has faced serious issues in her job. There's a lot of empathy there. I haven't gotten to the root of it, but I have a feeling there's a reason she doesn't want a man around in her life full time."

"What do you mean?"

"I just feel she may have veered toward social work as a career choice on the basis of some bad experiences in her childhood. I don't know. Just a hunch, but I intend to find out. I'm not saying that these women are the two finalists or anything. I have plenty of time, even if I'm getting old."

"Old? Since when is a person in his thirties old?"

"Well, ask Alice and Tom's kids, for instance. According to them, we are all pretty ripe, if not rotted." Magnus laughed.

Christine became serious, "Have you considered how you would handle it if your child's co-parent later brought a romantic partner into the picture?"

"Or I myself might find someone. That's probably the issue that bothers me the most, but then I think of the countless children whose parents are divorced and find new partners. I'm not saying that any of this is easy, but neither is regular marriage."

"You're telling me." Christine got up and brushed the dried leaves off the back of her jeans.

They continued to hike on the narrow path, admiring the blaze of reds, yellows, and rust colors in the landscape around them. Christine had timed her trip just right. In a couple of weeks, the leaves would drop, leaving the trees standing as brown skeletons. The world would have a different scent, a scent of humus and decay.

"Speaking of marriage," said Magnus, "How do you suppose our parents managed to stay happily married for so long?"

"A lot of compromise, communication, and a great deal of caring about the other person, I would assume. And love, of course."

"Of course. Probably the fact that Dad was gone on his lecture tours for days at a time helped the matter. Both were able to have some time for themselves that way."

"No doubt," said Christine.

Chapter 63

On Thanksgiving Day, a close group of people gathered around as Lola spread Margaret's ashes in the milkweed field on the Pure Earth farm—a gesture of forgiveness, a release of old hurts, a beginning of a new existence.

Lola had returned home enriched by countless experiences, including the change in fall colors in Finnish Lapland and toughing out the Baltic Sea daily, until the very last day, when she had plunged in after sauna, gritting her teeth. Lola had learned about "sisu," the Finnish quality of perseverance beyond grit, and she had adopted it for herself.

Lola looked around at those gathered in the field: friends of Margaret's, including Carol, dressed in black, and Kaisa, relying on a cane; Chrysalis members except for Christine, who was in China on a business trip; and Magnus, Tom, and Gavin. All of them had had their unique relationships with Margaret, some closer than others. All but Magnus. Lola wondered if he even knew Margaret other than as his mother's friend. He was most likely present as his mother's ride to the event. Lola looked at him. Magnus no longer made her uncomfortable or restless, yet his handsome face brought back memories.

Crystal observed Lola's almost mesmerized stare. She pulled her aside. "You're not thinking of talking to

Magnus about his father and you, are you?"

"Don't worry, my dear. That would only cause hurt and anguish, serving no purpose."

Crystal was visibly relieved.

The milkweed field appeared to have grown larger during the summer. Crystal had meticulously pruned the dead flowers, encouraging new blooms on the plants, plants that generously shared their poison with the monarchs and kept them safe from predators. After the wind took the ashes and settled them on the dry, empty milkweed pods and the ground, everyone observed a moment of silence.

While the rest of the group went into the house, Alice was drawn to the shed and the apple tree, the spot where she had admired the chrysalises in June. She gestured for Crystal and Lisa to join her.

"Check this out." Alice pointed to a used, empty cocoon shivering in the gentle breeze. "There we are, a collective chrysalis. Gavin really knows his monarchs. He told me a fascinating fact about their development earlier this summer. Did you know that the new butterfly emerges with three pairs of legs, although it has more of them during the metamorphosis?"

Crystal and Lisa looked at each other and at Alice. "Once a teacher, always a teacher," said Crystal. "It's true for both you and Gavin."

"I guess," said Alice. "Which one of us four is the fourth pair left behind, the unnecessary one?"

Crystal and Lisa felt uncomfortable. Lisa spoke up. "I think Christine flew away a long time ago. She has a very strong pair of wings. I, on the other hand, feel I am an unfinished job. I'm still looking for something, still in the chrysalis stage."

"No, I think it's me," said Crystal. "I feel I am incomplete until I become a mother."

"I have always thought the three of you are terrific, strong women," Alice chimed in. "I am the insecure one, somehow left in the dust by the three of you."

"Don't be silly," said Crystal. "There is no one more caring, more considerate and thoughtful than you. Those are not qualities of a weak woman. Quite the opposite."

Lisa reached out and hugged Alice. "We are all very different from each other—and, let's face it, overly critical of ourselves. Could it be that we will remain unfinished jobs, in the chrysalis forever?"

"Most likely!" Crystal laughed. "Look at the searching, exploring, and changing our mothers are still going through."

"You know what Christine would say?" suggested Lisa. "She would say that instead of one chrysalis, we are four separate monarchs, each unique and each with three pairs of legs of our own."

"I like that," said Alice. "But think of the bill we would have for shoes!"

They walked, laughing, side by side to join the others in the farmhouse for tea and crumpets in Margaret's memory.

Chapter 63

After Lola's return in early November, Crystal and her mother had spent time sorting out Margaret's belongings in Gavin's barn. In addition to furniture, there were large boxes of dishes and books, lamps, and paintings. In a tall movers' box for clothing on hangers, most likely kept by Margaret after her move from the townhouse to Long House, Crystal discovered an assortment of evening gowns and capes. Most of them were costumes from Margaret's operatic roles. Colorful gowns with long trains, kimono or Juliet sleeves, all adorned with beads and sequins. Costumes in bright colors easily visible from the last seat in the back of the opera house. They were masterful. Crystal wondered what to do with them. *Bob Mackey would be jealous.*

In full agreement, Lola and Crystal decided to donate the lot to the Theater Arts Department of the university. Closing the box, Crystal noticed an empty hanger and picked up a fallen dress on the bottom of the deep box. She lifted up a white garment, a simple three-quarter-length dress with a handkerchief hemline. Its soft material had settled in flattened pleats between the heavy gowns before falling to the bottom of the box. Flattened and wrinkled, it was nevertheless perfect in Crystal's mind.

"Mom, look at this."

"That's lovely," said Lola.

"What do you think about this for a wedding gown for me? I know it belonged to Margaret. Do you think you could forget that for one day?"

For one day, yes, and each time I look at your wedding pictures till I die. Lola said, "The dress is you. It's your wedding, your decision."

Crystal hugged her mother and gingerly put the dress back on a hanger and walked it to the house to try it on. With high heels, the dress would be impeccably right for her.

Putting aside all Christmas-related hoopla and fuss, Crystal concentrated on the preparations for her Christmas Eve wedding. She bought white stilettos to go with the dress, an effort that did little to make her look tall beside Gavin.

Crystal worked hand in hand with Mary, who was thrilled to cater the wedding at her place. To finish the healthy main meal, Crystal chose a decadent coconut cake with white frosting. Mary promised to try her best to create marzipan calla lilies for the top of the cake to match the flowers in Crystal's small bouquet.

Christmas Eve arrived. Crystal looked at the sky. No promise of snow yet. As she ate her breakfast, the doorbell rang. Arthur, a neighbor of Gavin's, stood in the hallway in dirty overalls. Crystal was startled. Was something wrong? A farm accident? Gavin wouldn't be working on his wedding day. Arthur handed her a small package wrapped in brown paper.

"This is from Gavin," said Arthur, tipping his baseball cap. "Congratulations on your wedding," he said and walked out.

Crystal removed the wrapping. On the small card were the words, "To my very nearly wife. May we always let each other develop, grow and fly." In the box was a necklace with a cloisonné monarch butterfly with shiny orange-and-black wings. Tears came to Crystal's eyes.

Crystal and Gavin wanted the wedding to be a simple, small occasion with a limited number of guests and a casual atmosphere. They wanted to stay away from the routine traditions. No "Here Comes the Bride" music, no garter, no bouquet throwing.

After the vows written by Crystal and Gavin themselves, Crystal stepped from Gavin's side to join her Chrysalis sisters to sing "Love Is Like a Butterfly."

As the new couple and their guests enjoyed dinner, a thick carpet of heavy snow covered the already slightly white ground. Crystal had gotten her wish of a white wedding in every sense.

No one discussed later how some older wedding guests had reconsidered driving down the steep, snow-covered hill and instead booked themselves for the night at the bed-and-breakfast.

In the bridal suite, Crystal and Gavin giggled in their efforts not to disturb the other guests on their wedding night.

Chapter 64

Kaisa had sorted and studied, categorized and evaluated her belongings, alternately laughing and crying at memories brought about with the opening of every stored box. She was ready for a future with less baggage.

To say goodbye to 2019 and to her past, Kaisa planned one last party at the house where she and Richard had lived for over forty years. She cooked her favorite foods, using whatever pots, pans, and utensils were yet to be packed for her move.

Carol, accompanied by Christine and Magnus, was the last to arrive. She greeted everyone by shaking their hand. When she saw Lola, she went to her and hugged her. Staring deep into her eyes, she said, "Hello, I believe you and I have a lot in common."

Lola wanted to escape. All she could manage was, "Yes. Hello." *What does Carol mean by that? Was Kaisa right? "The wife always knows," she had said. Or, did she simply mean that they had Margaret in common?*

For the moment, Lola chose to believe Carol's statement referred to Margaret's friendship with both of them.

Kaisa thanked everyone for coming.

After dinner, she asked Tom to assist her in the old Finnish New Year's custom—pouring of lead.

Tom set up a "station" outside on the patio with a small gas camp stove and a bucket filled with ice water. He explained to those complaining about the cold that lead can have poisonous fumes and Kaisa was particular about everyone's safety. Magnus nodded as Tom spoke.

"Besides, this is a tradition, and as such, we have always done it as an outside activity," added Tom.

"Who wants to go first?" he called.

"I will," said Crystal, putting a small horseshoe-shaped piece of lead in the nest of the ladle and placing the ladle on the flame. The horseshoe softened slowly until it was a puddle of liquid metal.

"Now," said Kaisa, "you will pour the lead into the ice water. The trick is to do it quickly with a sharp snap of your wrist. Be careful."

Crystal followed Kaisa's directions and plunked the lead into the water. The lead made a hissing sound and sank onto the bottom of the bucket in one piece.

"Now what?" asked Crystal.

"Pick it up and hold onto it. I'll tell you later," said Kaisa.

Everyone else took their turn, some pouring the lead with self-assurance, some hesitantly. Back inside, Kaisa set up a desk lamp in such a way it allowed for shadow-casting on the wall of the living room.

"You take your lead and place it in front of the light. The silhouette on the wall will depict something important about the coming year for you. Crystal, you went first, so let's see what is in your future."

Crystal twisted the glob of lead in front of the light. Everyone's gaze was directed at the white wall.

"I don't know," said Crystal.

"Wait," Lisa joined Crystal. "Let me see." She positioned the chunk of lead just so, placing the elongated piece, thicker in one end, in horizontal position. "There it is," she said.

Crystal looked at the wall and then at Lisa. "A baby!" she exclaimed.

"I haven't looked at thousands of uterine ultrasounds for nothing all these years." Lisa smiled.

"I'll take that." Crystal looked at Gavin over her shoulder.

Lisa placed her piece in the light. Clearly a plane. Clearly predictable. Similar findings were evident for Magnus and Tom, a hammer and a car, respectively. Alice saw a butterfly on the wall, and Lisa and Crystal rushed to agree with her wholeheartedly. Christine could not decipher her future from the uneven figure on the wall, but she felt that, with its very ragged edges, it looked rather like a seahorse. Lisa thought that appropriate. "The seahorse is a symbol of strength and power," she told Christine.

Like Lisa's, Lola's silhouette was clearly a plane. Lola informed everyone that she would, indeed, be flying again, when she returned to Finland in February to travel above the Arctic Circle for Northern Lights and skiing. Kaisa looked at Lola and smiled knowingly. *I'll be!* she thought. *That Mauno!*

Carol's long, thin lead piece looked like a narrow sword to most, but she thought it to be a knitting needle.

"I wonder if I could pick up knitting again?" She looked at Kaisa, the apparent authority on the subject, and recited,

"You know how to knit

By using your wit
Creating great sweaters and socks?
They can't be a hit
When you're totally lit
And your foolish head's full of rocks."

Opening his fist, full of small pieces, Gavin informed them he had not been quick enough in pouring the lead and ended up with peas, jelly beans, or deer droppings.

"This is always fun," said Alice. "The greatest part is that we can make ourselves see whatever we want to see. Mom, what about you?" Alice turned to Kaisa.

Kaisa thought for a moment and said, "I've decided that whatever comes, comes, and I will be happy about it." Alice gave her mother a warm hug.

It was nearing midnight. Kaisa and Alice brought out glasses and local pink sparkling wine. Tom popped the cork almost without a sound, like a professional, and filled the flutes.

The clock struck twelve. Everyone kissed and hugged each other. "2019," said Kaisa, "a memorable year of losses and joys. I want to thank all of you for the past year and wish you well for the next. 2020 will be a perfect year!" Everyone raised their glasses.

Chrysalis sang the first verse of "Auld Lang Syne" in perfect four-part harmony, and others joined in the refrain. Carol was the only one who remembered the lyrics to the second verse, which she sang with joy and abandon:

"And surely you'll buy your pint cup
And surely I'll buy mine.
We'll take a cup of kindness yet
For Auld Lang Syne."

Would you like more about the Chrysalis mothers and daughters? The author is planning a sequel—here's a sample:

Chapter 1

It's scary when you forget your own name. I had to verify it on the bracelet they wrapped around my wrist prior to surgery: 4/2/2021 Kaisa Weston 6/6/1949. God, I'm older than dirt! Reaching for my phone to check the time, I hit the guard rail of the bed with the hard, plastic venous port on my hand, making a hollow, metallic sound. No phone. No expected bedside table.

"How are we doing, sweetie?" The nurse appeared to be addressing me. "We are fine, honeybun," I said, annoyed at yet another patronizing person in a helping profession. "I may have lived longer than you, girlie, but I am not your sweetie."

The blood pressure cuff squeezed my arm. I realized I was still in the recovery room. Oh, crap, Alice will kill me! She swore me to a solemn promise never to use the stairs to the lakeside. Why does she always have to manage my life? I moved into a small condominium from my beloved house because Alice said it was a good idea. I started driving again because Alice thought I should try to hold onto all skills and abilities as long as possible.

I listen when Alice speaks. She can't help but offer me solutions to my problems. She even has answers to issues that are not problematic—at least, not to me. Once a teacher, always a teacher. She bosses her kids around, too. The only one she leaves alone is Tom, but he is almost non-human with his sweet disposition and a way with people, all people. He knows exactly how to handle Alice.

Who is Alice to control her mother's life anyway? So I have Parkinson's. That doesn't make me an invalid. In valid. Void of relevance. Without importance.

Besides, I do need to get to the bottom of the mystery of who moved next door. You can only get a glimpse of the condominium next to mine from the dock. The balcony may give some hints. It bothers me that the woman stays to herself. Who moves in and pays no attention to her neighbors?

I'll work on that when I get out of here.

My eternal curiosity! It probably wasn't worth the broken hip this time around.

****

Watch for *Weaver* by Maija DeRoche.

A word about the author...

Supported by a year's scholarship to the State University of New York, great enthusiasm, and rose-colored glasses, Maija DeRoche came to the United States from Finland in 1967. The year has stretched to over fifty, so far.

After obtaining degrees in German Literature and Speech/Language Pathology and a more than thirty-year career in the field of developmental disabilities, she retired, and rediscovered her first love—writing.

Maija's writings have been published in *Kuntta 2019*, an anthology about Finnishness, written in Finnish. Her essays in English can be found in the Canandaigua Writers Group blog.

Parents of two and grandparents of three, Maija and her husband enjoy kayaking and walking in New York's beautiful Finger Lakes region.